CW01664277

A Lester McFarl

SHORTCUT

CHAP HARPER

Smoking Gun Publishing, LLC
St. Louis, Missouri

Cover and Interior Design by Smoking Gun Publishing, LLC

ISBN: 9781940586526

Library of Congress Control Number: 2018948253

SMOKING GUN
Publishing

Visit us on the web at www.smokinggunpublishing.com

Published by Smoking Gun Publishing, LLC
Printed in the United States of America

Dedication

This book is dedicated to the agencies who work behind the scenes to keep our nation safe and to our military who tirelessly man posts all over the world so that we can go about our lives without fear. This novel fictitiously describes heroic feats from those agencies and our military, but the real stories are even more profound. You know who you are. Thank you for your service.

Chapter One

Kingston, Jamaica—A Few Years Ago

The Jamaican instructor, Glenmore Higgins, greeted one of the sixteen Middle Eastern men who had paid in cash for a year's instruction at Kingston's Caribbean Marine Academy.

"Mon, see if I gots ya name right. It be Zukaullah Kazim. Dat right, mon?" Glenmore asked as the small young man stood facing the taller black man.

The Islamic man nodded his head and said, "Hadha Sahih—uh—correct."

"You may call me Glen," the instructor said, motioning him to be seated.

Zukaullah sat down at his desk and watched as the Jamaican teacher struggled through fifteen more names. The native islander was patient, quick to smile, and soon found the group from the Middle East to be excellent students in spite of minor language barriers. All the students had acceptable English skills.

They claimed their home countries were desperate for diesel mechanics and marine engineers. Undoubtedly, local wars, refugee movements, and constant turmoil had led to the decimation and displacement of qualified skilled seamen. It didn't matter to the school that the homelands of eight of the new students were in the landlocked nations of Afghanistan and Kyrgyzstan. The appeal of signing on for work on an ocean-going vessel could easily be understood by those who suffered the monotony of living on a sand dune.

With the exception of Iran, which was engaged in replacing some domestic ships and adding to their small naval force, the other countries represented at the school, Syria and Yemen, were both small players in the ship business. The Russians, however, had invested heavily in the construction of the large Tartus Naval Base in Syria, reportedly capable of servicing nuclear powered vessels. However, the Russians were not sharing their vessels with Syria.

The Jamaican school wasn't concerned about their students' final dispositions, or their home countries' capacity to float boats in local harbors. There was a great need for paying customers of any endeavor. Jamaica's economy was in shambles caused by the country investing too much in tourism and not enough in agriculture. So, when tourism faltered, expensive imported food contributed to the imbalance. The people of Jamaica needed money now from any source possible. In Kingston, sixteen men had paid $4,000 each for one year of room, board, and tuition, and likely would pay ahead every year for four years. The strange arrival of these Muslim men at Glenmore's class was overlooked by the cash being placed in his hands. All had preregistered by mail, so the school had adequate time to decide if they would accept them.

Most would test for advanced certifications after four years with a few studying for only two years to earn associate degrees. In a few years, these graduates would find themselves competing for engineering officer jobs on cargo ships, cruise lines, and other civilian vessels. It is safe to say that this group would make their mark on the shipping industry for many years to come.

*****

Walnut Creek, California—Present Day

Lester McFarlin was quietly excited about the ocean voyage that lay before him. It had been three years since he had assisted large forces of law enforcement personnel in taking down a massive crime syndicate in Arkansas and Louisiana. He was wounded in a gun battle, and his then-girlfriend Debi briefly found herself kidnapped by Spider Gambini, the pretty crime boss of the entire operation.

For a long while, Lester had suffered with dyslexia so severe that he couldn't read or write. After a brain operation to remove scar tissue on his brain, Lester had recovered and now possessed an uncanny ability to memorize most everything he read. Now, his life-long dream of going to law school was fulfilled, and he was taking advantage of the semester break to take a cruise given to the couple as a wedding present from Debi's parents. He didn't expect anything too exciting would occur on the journey, but it had to be better than mock trials and case studies. A cruise seemed so self-indulgent, but just maybe he would learn to relax and enjoy the ride.

"Are you guys sure you can get by without the jeep for a few weeks?" Debi McFarlin asked.

"Debi, we have three cars. One is the old jeep, which we rarely drive. You lucky kids will get to ride animal style—no air conditioning, stick shift, mud tires, no cd player, and a canvas top with plastic windows," Debi's brother, Ray Green, said. "It will be a big step down from Lester's GMC Yukon."

"We're damn proud to have it. Thanks so much," Lester said as he patted the spare tire mounted on the rear of the Jeep Wrangler.

The Yukon was in a body shop getting major repairs after Lester got rear-ended on the Bay Bridge. Debi had an older two-seater BMW, but it was having some well-deserved and lengthy engine work completed. They couldn't believe that both of their cars could be disabled at the same time. Their apartment only had one garage parking space, so the last person in had to find a parking spot on the street. Horror stories abounded about cars left on the street in the city and accumulating two- and three-thousand-dollar fines. It was not unusual to have them towed and sold at auction to pay the penalties. Both would need cars when they got back from the cruise. Hopefully, one of the disabled vehicles would be ready and the other could use the Jeep. Neither would have time to fight the traffic to pick up the Jeep twenty-five miles away in Walnut Creek.

Ray was a successful mortgage banker with an office in San Francisco. He had explained his job to Debi several times, but he could see her eyes glaze over during every explanation.

A couple weeks back, Debi had married Lester McFarlin. He was a former officer with the Hot Springs Sheriff's Office and now was in his final year at Hastings Law School in San Francisco. He was a local cult hero back in Arkansas, where he had solved some major crimes. Debi was a speech therapist and had set up shop in San Francisco while Lester finished law school. Tomorrow was to be the start of their delayed honeymoon. Their plan was to park the jeep at their apartment and catch an Uber to the cruise terminal. Ray had agreed to take them but had to back out because of an important customer in town who needed some hand holding and entertaining. Ray's wife, Shasha, couldn't do it since their two kids had ball games, music practice, and teacher conferences. Ray and Shasha had helped Debi and Lester so much in the last two years. They even let them stay in their home for a few weeks until they got settled. Now they were lending them a car. Lester and Debi had repaid them by babysitting their two kids on many occasions. However, tomorrow the day would be saved by an Uber driver. For some reason, Lester felt the need to give Debi the blow-by-blow description of the history of Uber.

"You may not know the Uber company started here in San Francisco, and they do it right. It's fun to order a car and watch them move toward your location using an app on your phone. The company has tried Ubercopters and Uberboats, but they have had limited success so far. They're open to just about any new idea," Lester said as they drove across the new Bay Bridge towards their exit which would take them to their apartment a few blocks off Van Ness Street.

"I'd love this city if there was more room. You fight for every inch of space here. Too damn crowded, too hilly, and too damn cold in the summertime," Debi said, as she tried to secure a plastic window on the Jeep that was letting in cold air from the Bay. "Why didn't my brother get normal roll-up windows?"

"It's an old jeep and the plastic windows match the plastic sun roof—all after-market stuff, I would guess. It's still pretty cool," Lester said with a broad smile, and then changed the subject.

"Where do you want to live when I get out of law school?"

"Somewhere within driving distance of my parents. I want kids—soon. I will need my mother's help. The kids will have two grandfathers in Hot Springs and one grandmother—unless your dad marries one of the girls he picks up at Boot Scooters Night Club."

"Oh—he has promised me he will marry one from the Electric Cowboy in Little Rock. Much classier there," Lester said, laughing.

When they arrived at their apartment, someone was in the process of parking in front of their garage driveway. Lester honked and motioned the guy to move.

"Another reason I don't want to live here," Debi said and punched Lester's arm for emphasis.

He looked at her and smiled. "I can't see our child playing in traffic all day either."

"Oh, yeah. That too," she said. "By the way, where is that kid?"

"I'll work on it, if you will," Lester said.

"I'm going to wear you out on this cruise. You up for it?"

"Have mercy on me, my dear." They both laughed as the car moved away, letting them enter their garage.

*****

Lester laughed as the blue dot on his phone app appeared just as a black Uber car approached in front of him. It stopped near where he and Debi were standing by the curb.

"It doesn't take much to entertain you, does it, Lester?"

"Nope."

The driver helped Lester load their bags and inquired about their cruise and what it was like on the ship as he pulled out into heavy traffic. "I'm afraid I can't tell you. The closest boat to a cruise liner I've experienced was the Hamilton Princess on a lake back in Arkansas. But Debi has been on a cruise before," Lester said, recalling that her boyfriend, Brad, had taken her to the Caribbean on a Princess Cruise. Debi, who was well-aware that Lester wasn't pleased with her live-in arrangement with her former lover, frowned.

"As I recall, they're always trying to sell you something. The rooms are tiny, but there's always something to do and plenty to eat," Debi said, sticking her tongue out at Lester, who had made a circle with his fingers and was thrusting his finger from his other hand through it in a symbolic screwing motion. He stopped when the driver took his eyes off the traffic and looked in Lester's direction.

They tipped the driver and found their way to the long line that snaked around the inside of the huge terminal. Surprisingly, they moved quickly since the experienced cruise line wasted no time. They had given the couple color-coded tags to attach to their bags, so all they had to do was drop them off. Someone snapped a quick departing picture to sell back to them later, issued an onboard credit card, and ushered them onto the ship. They would find their luggage outside their room later in the day.

Once aboard, they located a bar near the center of the ship and settled down to finalize their excursions and spa visits. For the first time in their almost three-year relationship, they had signed up for a couple's massage. Lester had promised to not talk and to enjoy the event. The cost was over $300, and he was not about to mess up the experience for Debi. Even so, he thought it was a little kinky.

After about an hour, they went to their rooms. Their luggage was placed as promised. As they unpacked, the muster point for the lifeboat drill was announced through their in-room speakers for a 3:00 p.m. drill. Both showed up on time, carrying their life vests.

"Debi, I was on the Hamilton Princess when they held a lifeboat drill. The lady in charge held up a life preserver and said, 'I'm sorry all the life preservers are wet, but we had to use them on the last cruise.'"

Debi laughed and said, "Knowing that old tub, they might very well have used them."

"It was an old joke, but new to me. Do we have reservations for early or late dinner seatings?" Lester asked as they walked back to their room after the short life boat education.

"Early—Sea Dog specialty restaurant—we paid twenty bucks extra."

"Each?"

"Lester, we've saved up for this cruise and along with the money my parents gave us for a wedding present, everything is paid for. Just relax and enjoy it."

"I may write some articles for the law review while we're here. Should I not ask about internet rates on board?"

"You should not, but don't go over the two-hundred-fifty-minute package I bought," Debi said.

"How much if I go over?" Lester asked.

"Seventy-five cents a minute," she said bluntly.

"Holy batshit—no way will I pay that!"

"Lester, you're on vacation—write your article, just hold off on a lot of research."

"I'll spend more time here in bed with you, then, my dear."

"I'm sure you will."

"So, Debi, when does that multi-million-dollar massage take place?"

"Tomorrow at eleven a.m. on Deck Fourteen," Debi answered.

"What if I get a boner?"

"Try not to."

"What if I have one now?"

"Ask for assistance from your friendly roommate."

"Help, I'm in agony! I have moderate-to-severe horniness," Lester said, clearly starting to enjoy his vacation.

"I'll be right there."

"I like being on a cruise," Lester said as he began to undress.

"Tomorrow night is a formal night, by the way."

"You're trying to destroy my erection, aren't you?"

"Nope, I want you in fine form. Just trying to prepare you for putting on a tux. Now come here and punish me for being such a bad, bad girl who makes you dress up," Debi said, laughing.

"Sweetheart, you are toast!" Lester moved toward the bed, leaving a trail of discarded clothes.

*****

The Royal Spa aboard the Tropic Queen, currently docked in San Francisco, was beautiful and offered the latest treatments for even grizzled veterans of health resorts. This huge vessel was part of ten ships in the Queen of the Seas fleet. Simone Visser had taken the position of manager, signed a contract for nine months, and said goodbye to Cape Town, South Africa. She had managed and owned one of the largest salons in the city but now needed to get away. During her interview with the cruise line, the HR person had said, "Most people take jobs on cruise lines to run away from something. Some are in it for the adventure with the hope of meeting a new love, but most, sure as hell, don't do it for the cash rewards."

Maybe the servers and room maids needed the money since they were mainly from poor countries like the Philippines or India, where good jobs were nonexistent. Simone would be making about one-third of her income in South Africa, but that wasn't important right now.

She was recently divorced after catching her husband performing in doggie style with one of her massage therapists. After she investigated, she found that he had helped himself to at least three of them.

Simone couldn't face her employees, so she sold the operation, stuck the money in the bank, and listed her house. It sold quickly, not for what she wanted, but she felt the need to get rid of anything that tied her there. She knew about health salons on cruise ships since some of her massage therapists had worked on them. With a little research, she learned that the *Queen of the Seas* had one of the best spas. It should have been a clue to her, though, when she found out that the last manager had left six months before her contract was over. But it didn't matter. She had to get away.

Dating, flirting, making out, and hooking up with someone other than her now ex-husband seemed like another world to Simone. She knew she was attractive, and the opportunity to have numerous affairs had presented themselves while she was married to Peter. Her co-workers had gone a step further and told her she was "hot." She remained faithful, however, throughout the four-year marriage.

Simone's body was shapely and well-proportioned. She was extremely tall at 5'10" with legs that went on forever. Tanning was a weakness for her. She knew she shouldn't do it but didn't want to be white and pasty if the right guy did come along. Her face was classically beautiful and set off by large and inviting lips. She had long, cascading, natural-blonde hair, which she had recently shortened to shoulder length. Green eyes only appear in two percent of the people on earth, and hers were a shade that matched the tropical waters in the path of the ship. Many men had hit on her since the divorce, but she was determined to be patient and selective.

Simone looked over her personnel roster, which had been given to her earlier in the day. Currently, she was the only person in the spa since it was closed, and she knew for the next two weeks there would be no moments of solitude like the one she was enjoying now. Tomorrow, the ship would begin to fill again with passengers seeking entertainment and fun. There wasn't much time to get ready for all the bookings for massages, pedicures, and other spa treatments. It was her first day on the ship, but she felt the need to meet her crew and lay down the law. Simone had called a meeting for 6:00 p.m. with all her employees. Glancing down again at her roster, she found the word "trouble" written next to one employee.

Oh shit. I see the problem. Been there before, she said to herself.

Her name was Ziya Moussa. Simone had Muslim women working in her spa in Cape Town and knew most of the procedures performed at the salon ran afoul of Islamic principles. She would meet Ziya tonight and decide if it was worth the trouble to keep her.

For now, she sat by herself in the beautiful facility, sipping a glass of white wine and wondering what this job would be like. She felt confident and excited. This was a new life. A new start. When she set her empty wine glass down on her desk, she looked up and saw a handsome blue-eyed ship's officer standing in front of her. He was smiling.

Chapter Two

Interpol Headquarters
Lyon, France

Jordan Michaels had been on assignment at Interpol Headquarters for a full month now. He wasn't sure exactly which regulation he broke that pissed off his superiors back in London, but given his reputation, it could have been numerous infractions. Detective Chief Inspector Michaels drank too much, was known to start brawls and to take married men's wives to bed. He should have been promoted to Superintendent a couple of years back but was caught in a compromising position with the wife of a member of the parliament. The parliament member was an older man married to a lovely girl twenty-five years younger. Jordan said he was just trying to help the old man out. Anyone else would have been fired, but Jordan was the best detective in all of London, maybe all of England. In order to save him, he was being exiled to Paris and attached to Interpol to learn something from them. Paris would allow him to screw himself silly and maybe get his wild side satisfied for a while.

When he had to explain his bad behavior to his superiors, his typical excuse was, "If their husbands would pay a little more attention to them, they might not jump in bed with me."

Jordan was tall, muscular, and handsome. In his late thirties, he had startling blue eyes, a chiseled jaw, and thick, dark brown hair that was much too long to be within regulation guidelines. It was possible some of the ladies might have come to his bedside on their own accord. He didn't have a problem getting women—his problem was getting rid of them later.

As he sat looking at his TAG watch, waiting for quitting time, the phone on his desk came to life. It was an old, strange-looking hard-plastic French phone. He hated anything made in France, except the women.

"Yes, Inspector Michaels here."

"What's your full name and rank?" the gruff American voice barked.

"Detective Chief Inspector Jordan Michaels—London Office. Here in France on assignment. What's your full name and rank?" He used his tough guy voice—reserved for people who acted like assholes.

"Bill Samuelsson, Assistant Executive Director of Homeland Security. Is the General Secretariat there?" Bill said in an increasingly aggravated tone.

"Nope! I'm going to be the highest muckety-muck you get to talk to today. Rest of 'em are at a soccer game. What can I help you with?" Michaels asked.

"Have you guys been picking up chatter from sat phones with people talking in Arabic?"

"Everyday. What's unusual about hearing voices?"

"These are coming from strange places," the American said.

"Such as. . .?" Jordan asked.

"Middle of the ocean, around docks, and all over the fucking world—but always near the water. It might not mean anything, but we wanted you to be aware of it. Please pass this information on to the General Secretariat, but be careful who you tell about this."

"I will tell him you called. And if we find anything, should I call your office?"

"Yes, and request to speak to me," Samuelsson replied and gave him his direct number.

"Thanks for the information," Jordan said.

Jordan started asking around the huge office complex for the individuals that monitor terrorist activities. After questioning no fewer than ten people, he found his man, or rather his woman. According to a plaque on her desk, her name was Maria Moreau. She was hiding a pretty face behind large glasses and frazzled blond-streaked hair. It was one of the hairstyles that he liked because it was wild looking but just tame enough to be fashionable. Her hair was actually two shades of blond, and on one side it hung down just above her left eye. Jordan felt sure she had a nice body to go along with the gorgeous face, but she was wearing baggy pants. They weren't fashionable pants —just baggy pants.

"Miss Moreau, I am Jordan Michaels. Over from London for a few days or months. Maybe the rest of my life, if I can't stay out of trouble."

"You look like trouble," she laughed.

"Listen, have you been picking up Arabic noise coming from the middle of the ocean and around docks and such?"

"Yes. I pointed it out to my supervisor, and they said it was normal chatter."

"If I wanted you to pinpoint those signals, could you do it?" Jordan asked with real excitement in his voice.

"Close, but not precisely on the spot, since some were moving as they talked on their satellite phones. Their trail is captured in our scanners. Would you like me to start on the project?"

"Yes, and if anyone wants to know what you're doing, tell them it's for Homeland Security in the States."

"Is it?" she asked.

"I'm not at liberty to speak about it," Jordan said, with a crooked smile.

"Are you at liberty to buy me a drink after work tonight?" Maria asked, locking eyes with the man who had just given her a work assignment. She liked him instantly.

"Uh . . . of course. You name the place. I'll be back by at 5:30," Jordan stuttered.

Jordan tried to picture her naked. It was always the first thing that came to his mind when he went out with a new woman. Next, he would plan how to get her to bed. It was a game he usually won. In this case, the baggy pants didn't help his normal fantasies, but her face wasn't just pretty, but gorgeous. Her lips were full, especially her top lip—and he couldn't wait to kiss her. She was very forward, and he found that sexy. Jordan was under the assumption that Maria was someone's secretary or maybe a file clerk, and he could use the power of his position to his advantage. What he had failed to notice below her name plate was her title—Senior Intel Director.

*****

"I had to come meet the new manager of the spa. A spy friend of mine in human resources said you had a great background with managing salons and health resorts. This same clandestine person said you were single and very attractive," the officer said.

"I would think personnel could root out these spies, so they wouldn't be breaking confidentiality laws. Someone appears to be in the matchmaking game. And you are . . .?" asked Simone.

"Second Engineer Officer Monte Hendrix, and you, of course, are . . .?"

"Simone Visser from South Africa and you are from . . .?" She took his outstretched hand and shook it.

"Fort Lauderdale, Florida, but went to school here in California. Would it be possible for us to have a drink together later tonight?" Monte said with a persistent smile.

"I guess so. I have a meeting with my staff in a few minutes. What bar and where?" she asked.

"The officer's bar, since I know it's open. I will be back to escort you after your meeting. How long will it take?" Monte asked. He kept his eyes trained directly on hers.

"Not sure. One of the staff is supposed to be trouble. I may need to do either counseling or something worse."

As Simone looked closer at Monte, she realized that she was actually taller than him—not much, but when she put heels on he would be looking up at her. Nevertheless, he was very handsome. She thought, *Tom Cruise is very short, and Monte is taller than Cruise.*

"Is it that one wearing the hijab?" Monte asked, snatching her back from her movie star fantasy.

She nodded. *He is really good-looking,* she mused. *Deep blue eyes.*

"Her husband works with me as an electrical engineer. He's very good at his job, but kind of quiet. I've tried to talk to him, and he's courteous, but not much of a talker. Some of the staff say they're a little frightened by him and his prayer rug."

"Jesus! I have worked with them in South Africa, and they never scared me. They seemed harmless enough. The big problem in spas is that they can't do any jobs except clean up and keep the fresh towels and linens in stock. They're not allowed to use perfume. They can't help with hair extensions. They're not allowed to see anyone naked. No way can they see people getting bikini waxing. Pretty much just towels, linens, and sweeping up," Simone said.

"Good luck with your problem child. I'll be back in an hour," Monte said.

"Thanks. I believe I will need a drink afterwards," Simone laughed and watched as Monte left through an automatic glass door.

Most of the spa crew showed up for the meeting. A few had gone ashore and some of the new personnel were still being processed; Simone would have to call these employees tonight and touch base with them. She laid out her rules and regulations, as well as the policies from the cruise line, and reviewed the massages and hair salon appointments for the next day. Simone repeated the rules about cruise workers having sexual relationships with passengers.

"Locked in your room until the next port. You will be taken ashore and then it's up to you to find a way home."

After the meeting was over, she asked to see Ziya Moussa in her office. Once there, Simone asked her to be seated.

"I would rather stand," Ziya said in a shaky, accented voice.

"Suit yourself, Ziya." Simone said sternly. "Tell me about your relationship with the former manager."

"She was always after me. Very unfair!" Ziya answered.

"I would like to know more about that," Simone said.

"Suzanne would make me clean up after bikini waxing. I cannot see those hairs, and I cannot touch them."

"I had Muslim women working in my South African salon. We had a high cleric rule that they could not look at pubic hair on a person, either male or female, but after it is taken from the body, it is okay to see it then. Also, you may wear plastic gloves to remove it to the trash. Would you like to see a copy of the cleric's ruling? I will see if I still have it." Simone hadn't seen the document for years, but at least she would make an effort.

"Yes, thank you," Ziya said, pleased to know Simone had worked with members of her faith before.

"What else is bothering you?"

"I cannot take towels into the sauna since nude women are in there."

"Again, it is only against Islamic principles if you look at their pubic area. Just look down and take the towel in and pick up the used ones. There is no need to stare at their crotches. Anything else?"

"My prayers. I have to have time to say my prayers."

"Use your breaks for that. I'll not allow extra time, or I would have to allot everyone prayer time. If you have problems with anything we discussed here, let me know now, and we can part company."

"I am fine. Thank you." Ziya turned and walked out of the spa.

Monte said hello to Ziya as he walked past her on his way into the facility.

"Need that drink?" Monte asked Simone as he neared the front reception desk.

"Yes. Several, please."

Simone followed him to the elevator and talked all the way from the fourteenth deck to the fifth deck, and then all the way to the officer's bar. She liked him immediately. He was easy to talk to, funny, and treated her like a lady. He introduced her to several officers, both men and women. Afterwards, he escorted her to her room. He asked if he could see her again. She really did want to see him, at least for a second time. Maybe more.

"How about dinner tomorrow after your first full day?" Monte asked.

"I may not have time for dinner, but I'll take drinks again, if you want. Just call me tomorrow evening to see how things are going."

She then leaned forward and gently kissed him on his lips. He smiled as he walked away.

Simone thought about Peter, her ex, as Monte walked away. He had been a stock broker, handsome, tall and intelligent. Initially, they both wanted kids. After failing to get pregnant, they sought medical advice and found Peter was sterile. They discussed adoption, in vitro fertilization, and other methods of having a child.

Peter had said, "I want a child who is my offspring—not from some test tube or some kid thrown away from a crackhead family!"

Peter became depressed over his sterility and used his new spermless condition to freely spread his barren seed everywhere he could. Effectively, the beginning of the end of their marriage started when he was told he couldn't father a child. Simone rightfully saw his behavior as immaturity.

Even though it was early in their relationship, Monte seemed so much more mature.

*****

Jordan and Maria drove to a bar called Rock 'n' Eat that was in the middle of the rock-and-metal-scene in Lyon. After obtaining a table away from the loud group playing near the bar, they placed orders for hamburgers and fries. They then began to go over Maria's notes. She laid out a condensed map of the world marked with highlighters where there had been recent chatter in Arabic—San Francisco, LA, several ports along the Mexican Riviera, then all along Central America, on both oceans. Great ports in China and Japan, along with many in Europe, had multiple hits. Several spots were around the eastern coast line of Australia.

"It seems that most of the chatter is around Central America on both sides. Yet, it's all over the world," Jordan remarked, scratching his head.

"If we could pinpoint and identify one ship, then maybe we could find what they have in common," Maria said. She was drawing circles around hits near France as drinks were placed on their table.

"It would be great if you could," Jordan mused.

"Marseille! Marseille! I have two hits and it appears one ship is still there—just got the hit yesterday," Maria said, almost knocking over her beer reaching to show Jordan the spot.

"How long is the drive from here?" Jordan asked.

"About three and a half hours on A7. I would need to get our portable scanner at the office and pick up a few things from my flat. What do you need, and can you get permission to go?

"I'm a Chief Inspector, so I plan my own investigations. We can take my car, and I'll take you by your flat, but are you sure as a clerk you'll be able to just take off on a case?"

"Clerk! I probably outrank you. I am a Senior Intel Director," she said with a great deal of indignity in her voice.

"Sorry, Maria—I sort of assumed—sorry about that. But, correct me if I'm wrong—Interpol doesn't have a police force. It contacts the police that are members of Interpol, and they go out and get the bad guys you have found. Is that right?"

"Yes, you're right. I didn't mean to snap at you, but women—that is, as a woman, it seems we are taken lightly unless we assert ourselves," Maria said in a much calmer tone.

"So, when you asked me out for a drink, I should have known you ranked way up there next to chief inspector?" Jordan asked.

"You could have inquired about my position. Let's just forget it. No harm, no foul. Are you married?" It appeared that this question came out of nowhere.

"Uhhh, was . . . not since two years ago. You?" Jordan wondered why she asked, but he wasn't going to pry for fear of his life.

"Also 'was.' It's been a year. I have a teenage daughter in boarding school in Paris. I was just curious whether I should bother to like you. You will find I'm rather direct. Not much of a bullshitter. I'm thirty-five and really haven't had many dates since the divorce. My ex-husband has already remarried. Same girl he was seeing before the divorce. I was putting in a lot of hours, and he had too much time on his hands. He's good to our daughter, though. He wasn't as handsome as you. Not too many men are. You must be incredibly successful with women."

"I have two boys, seven and nine, who live with their mum. They spend most of the summer with me. Take my vacation then. I don't really formally date much, Maria—don't waste much time either, which places me in a lot of one-night stands, which I'm not proud of.

I'm thirty-eight next month. I already like you, and I've never met a woman in law enforcement as pretty as you—or any place else either. Let's be ourselves and see what happens."

Maria smiled and reached across the table and gently squeezed his hand. They were obviously attracted to each other, but some egos might have to be pushed aside for them to take this much farther. She had purposely worn clothes that made her less attractive and less approachable. Since her divorce, the pain was still fresh, and those horrible feelings of rejection were still close to the surface. Maria desperately wanted to have the good parts of a relationship back. Maybe this guy was the one to make it happen.

They quickly finished their meals and filed the necessary reports to their superiors. Not included in the reports were the feelings developing between the two officers.

Jordan couldn't wait until Maria changed out of those baggy pants. He didn't trust his ability to keep a relationship going after the sexual intensity cooled down. Maria was the best-looking woman he had ever known. He knew he had to change for many reasons. If he continued to lead a wild and promiscuous lifestyle, there was a chance he would lose his job and compromise his relationship with his kids. He mumbled to himself, *You asshole. Get your shit together and quit acting like a teenager.*

As they finalized their overnight trip to Marseille, it was likely they both shared a common thought: would they share the same room?

Chapter Three

Lester had an early breakfast served in his room and consumed on his small balcony. He sipped coffee and watched the ocean roll by. It was peaceful. Debi went for a jog around the fourteenth deck and said she would either bring breakfast with her or order when she returned. Everything on the ship was so flexible and laid back. Lester and Debi took showers in preparation for their massages, dressed in sweats, and headed to the spa. For the first few months they were together, they always took showers together, but now the privacy and solitude rose above unbridled passion.

They were greeted by Simone and given robes with an explanation of how to use the lockers. After undressing and getting into the robes, they sat in the waiting area reading magazines and sipping water from plastic cups. An attractive young woman wearing a pretty, lavender hijab and white spa smock over it worked feverishly at stacking large, thick towels on racks at one end of the lounge. Her pretty, brown eyes darted around the room as though she wasn't comfortable in her surroundings. She was the only woman Lester had seen on the cruise wearing the traditional Muslim scarf. She was exotic and beautiful, so she held his interest.

As a sheriff's officer in Hot Springs, Arkansas, he had assisted a Muslim family that was the object of a hate crime. The husband had been shot as he left his men's clothing store. He survived and was able to give Lester enough information to bring the shooter to justice. He wondered if this woman was treated fairly by the other employees of the cruise ship.

She crossed the waiting area, still carrying a load of towels at an awkward angle. As she walked directly in front of Lester and Debi, the towels slid from her hands and landed in a clump by Lester's chair. He immediately bent over and helped her pick them up. As she leaned forward to reach a towel that had fallen the farthest away, her phone slipped out of the inside pocket of her smock onto the carpet without her noticing it. Lester was quick to grab it, glance at the front of the phone, and hand it to her. She thanked him and apologized for dropping the towels.

"No problem, ma'am," Lester said.

As she walked off, he turned to Debi. "Why would a spa worker who is obviously not in a supervisory position need an expensive satellite phone?"

"Lester, what in the hell are you talking about?"

"That woman dropped her phone, and I handed it back to her. I know that phone because I almost bought one like it. It is an Iridium Extreme below-deck satellite model. Somewhere on this ship is a GPS repeater that allows for the signal to get out even from the boiler room. The phone itself costs over twelve-hundred dollars, and then two-hundred minutes of airtime is about five-hundred dollars. I say to you, it isn't an item issued to a towel sorter," Lester said. His tone signaled to Debi he was in full investigation mode.

"Damn it, Lester, how many times do I have to remind you about the 'on vacation dealie'?" Debi said, glaring at her husband, who obviously wasn't going to relax.

"I'll be quiet for now but may ask a few questions," he said.

"Are you afraid she'll beat us to death with a frigging cell phone?" Debi said.

Before they could discuss it further, two massage therapists appeared and escorted the couple to a room with two massage tables about five feet apart. Before leaving them alone, the therapists instructed the couple to disrobe and lie face down on the table and cover themselves with a sheet.

They did so, then heard a knock on the door and told the therapists to come in.

Debi spoke softly to her therapist during the massage. Lester was unusually quiet. He was turning things over in his mind. As soon as the massage was over, he thanked his therapist and gave both a tip (he would find out later that the tip had already been added to his bill, which didn't make him happy); then he disappeared to the men's changing room. Before Debi could speak to him, Lester had changed and stood across from Simone at the reception desk.

"Sir, I hope you enjoyed your massage. Is there anything else I can help you with?" She sensed he had something to tell her.

"It was great. You have a beautiful facility here on the ship. Are you the manager?" Lester asked, even though he read her name tag, which gave her away.

"Yes, I am Simone Visser." She thrust out her hand.

"Lester McFarlin." He quickly shook her hand, probably harder than he meant to.

"I used to be a sheriff's officer back in Arkansas, and I kinda miss it. Now I'm in law school, which isn't nearly as exciting. So, when I see something out of place, it bothers me. Somewhere on this ship I saw a crew member with a very expensive phone. It looked out of place, but I might be wrong. Does the ship furnish expensive phones to deck hands or servers—jobs like that?"

"No. But some of us have two-way communicators for use on the ship. Only myself and two assistants have them. The officers have all kind of phones. You might ask them." Simone was a little irritated by the questioning.

Lester had avoided mentioning the words "satellite phone" and made no reference to Simone's employees.

"Look, you've been very helpful. I'm sure it's just my inability to leave well enough alone. Thanks for the great massage and the information."

"What's Arkansas like? I'm from Cape Town, South Africa, and I know nothing about it, except I know we don't sail there." She laughed and smiled at Lester. His handsome movie star looks had not gone unnoticed.

"It would be mighty rough on your ship if you did," Lester said. "I've seen pictures of the forests north of Cape Town, and Arkansas looks much like your Orange Kloof Forest. Pretty streams, trees, and rocky hills," he continued, remembering his studies of Africa, which had always fascinated him.

"How would you know about that forest? Many people in South Africa aren't aware of it."

Debi walked up, and it appeared to her that Lester had been flirting with a pretty salon manager. He excused himself and told Debi he would meet her at his bar. She knew that was code for a special place on the ship.

"I'll meet you there after making my hair and nail appointment."

"Was that your husband?" Simone asked. "He asked me some questions. Said he used to be a cop in Arkansas. He's smart. Good looking guy. You better look out or some girl will snatch him away from you."

"Yes, he's my husband, and this boat isn't so big that I couldn't find them. He was one of the best investigators in the American south. If he sees anything out of place, he goes nuts until he can put it straight. Can't get him to just relax. I hope he didn't bother you too much."

"No. He wasn't a problem," Simone said. Now she began thinking about Monte and their possible date later in the day.

On the other side of the buffet line, Debi spotted Lester. He stood at the ice cream bar with a proud look on his face, as though he had just bagged a lion in Africa. He held up a large chocolate malt, which Debi knew had to be prepared exactly to his demanding standards.

"Did they fix it properly?" she asked.

"Per my instructions—four scoops of hard vanilla ice cream, three tablespoons of powdered malt, one third cup of chocolate syrup, a pinch of salt, and one full minute in the blender. She even lined the glass with chocolate syrup for effect. I feel much better," Lester said, truly trying to calm down.

"Sorry, Debi, I don't know why I can't leave things alone. I'm going to try relaxing." He could read the anger and frustration on her face.

"I can't believe you bothered the spa manager about that frigging phone."

"Was she mad at me?"

"No, she thinks you're a hunk."

"The phone doesn't belong to the boat. She makes minimum cruise wages—whatever that may be. I'll let it lie for now because I don't want to ruin our vacation. Will you forgive me?"

"Yes. If you should think we're in some kind of danger, come talk to me first," Debi said. She leaned in and made eye contact. "Promise?"

"Promise," Lester said defeatedly, as he fished the cherry from the bottom of his glass.

"Why don't you call Jim Webb and run it by him?" Debi asked. "He's with Interpol now in D.C. and can maybe ease your worries. No one has to know you talked to him. Keep the call to ten minutes. Our phone package is designed to call home quickly when the ship starts sinking." She knew Lester would agree to call his old friend, formerly with the FBI.

"Ok, I'll leave time for that for sure. What's next on the agenda? Nap, and then sex, or sex, and then a nap?"

"Now you're beginning to sound like a guy on a cruise ship with a pretty girl."

"Not just pretty--scorching hot!"

*****

A light January snow was falling as Jordan drove his Range Rover slightly above the speed limit on the French highway. He and Maria were on their way to Marseille to help solve an Interpol mystery. Neither of them was thinking about that right now.

It was night, and the interior of the car's cabin was relatively quiet. A powerful heater toasted the air while the supercharged V6 purred like a big jungle cat. An American country music CD was playing "Girl Crush" at a low volume. Maria had picked the Little Big Town album from Jordan's collection. She found several Johnny Cash and Willie Nelson CDs but passed on them. It was widely believed in France that Brits were big country fans. It must be true.

Both stared at the snow swirling in different directions, illuminated by the bluish halogen headlights. It was beautiful and mesmerizing. It rarely snowed in Marseille since it was on the Mediterranean coast, but they wouldn't be there for a couple of hours. The sexual tension in the car was unbearable. Jordan decided to slice right through it.

"When we have sex tonight, you're welcome to be on top." His car sped up as he made the statement.

First, he heard a laugh from Maria, followed by a long span of time when she was unusually quiet. He felt it was calculated to make him uncomfortable. Finally, she broke the silence.

"You are lazy. Do you think I'm going do all the work while you lay there, and I pump good feelings into you? You'll be on top. You'll work hard to ensure I reach an outstanding climax. Once that's achieved, if you still have the strength, then you are welcome to get your cookies," she said, smiling and placing her hand seductively on Jordan's thigh.

Jordan laughed and squeezed her hand which was still molesting his leg.

When they reached the port at Marseille, Maria turned on her portable scanner as Jordan drove through the docks. After about thirty minutes, they realized that the ship had left. Jordan suggested they see the harbor master.

The man they found was one of the assistants who took over at night. He said a large cargo ship bound for Oakland, California had left earlier in the day, and one of the Chinese cargo vessels had left about an hour ago, headed back to China. He had ships due in later tonight and at several times the next day. When he asked about their inquiry, Maria told him they couldn't tell him. She asked what information was given to the harbor master by the ships. He said mainly inventories of container ships, but cruise ships did give the number of passengers and how many were leaving for tours. Smaller ships gave a list of crew members, and if anyone went ashore, they would have to go through customs and immigration.

They thanked him and told him they needed to find a hotel. The assistant harbor master recommended a sea-view hotel called *Escale Oceania.*

Disappointed at the results of the scanner, they checked into the hotel and picked a room with a king-sized bed with a great view of the harbor. Once they checked in, they decided to have drinks in the bar. It was for sure that they were going to sleep together, but at this point they hadn't even kissed each other. Maybe several drinks would smooth out the awkwardness of making love to a total stranger. If liquor had been designed as a courage booster, its usefulness would be appreciated this evening.

The bar had a dance floor and Jordan asked Maria to dance. The music was slow, perfect for an intimate, embracing dance. He pulled her close, wrapped his arm around her slim waist, and pressed his cheek next to hers. Jordan felt her hot breath on his cheek. After a few minutes, he moved his face directly in front of hers, locked his eyes on hers, and kissed her very gently. The passionate kisses would come later. It would be an interesting and exciting night.

Chapter Four

Sex seemed better on a cruise ship. At least that's what Lester told Debi after their afternoon nap. No worries about work or school later on. Just more naps and more sex.

"Debi, I'm going to call Jim," Lester said as he moved to the balcony. He looked around to see if anyone was on the adjoining balconies. They were clear. So, he began dialing.

"Ten minutes, Lester!" Debi said, as she stuck her head out of the glass sliding door.

Lester gave her the finger and smiled. She returned the favor.

Finally, after being passed around to a couple departments, he successfully connected with his old friend.

"Jim, it's Lester. How are you, good buddy?"

"Lester, you're on your honeymoon—don't you have things to do?"

"Just did! Thanks for coming to the wedding and for the case of wine. I'm working my way through it."

"I'm going to guess, Lester, you have something on your mind or you wouldn't take time out from your duties—ha—to call me at work."

"This may not be anything, but I just wanted to run it by you. Went to the spa on our ship—that's a place where you get your butt rubbed. This pretty Muslim girl dropped some towels on the floor and her phone slid out of her pocket when she went to pick them up."

"Gee whiz, Lester, this is really exciting," Jim said sarcastically.

"Do you remember when I wanted the expensive Iridium Extreme satellite phone? It requires a GPS relay to broadcast and receive from buildings or ships. This phone is state of the art. Have their own network of satellites. Expensive. Probably the best one sold anywhere. Clearly not required for her position but, by god, she sure as hell has one. If an iPhone is a firecracker, this baby is a cruise missile.

"Now, I have told you about it and have done my duty. I have nothing against Muslims and, believe me, this girl is beautiful. Islamic terrorists with specialized equipment could fuck up my honeymoon. I haven't said anything to anyone except you and Debi. She thinks I'm nuts, as usual."

"He is nuts, Jim!" Debi said, as she stuck her head out the balcony door again. She had been listening to the conversation.

"Lester, I agree you're nuts, but for the safety of all those people on the ship, I'll make some calls to NSA, Homeland, and the CIA. I think you guys are on the Tropic Queen, aren't you? Where are you going?" Jim asked.

"I think the Mexican Riviera, Costa Rica, Colombia, then over to Aruba and end up in Miami. You want to come along?" Lester said.

"Hell, they might assign me to stay in your room and watch over you," Jim laughed.

"I believe we'll pass on that. So, what happens next?" Lester asked.

"We will report this to our main office in Lyon, France. They may think it's no big deal, and that's the last you will hear about it. If not, we'll contact you on what to do next. Have your phone set to receive calls."

"Wow! Will I be on the payroll? Maybe you'll ask me to sleep with the pretty Muslim girl."

"It's not a James Bond movie, Lester."

"Shit! I never have any fun."

"Look, I've got real work to do. Give my love to Debi."

"Love you, Jim!" Debi emerged through the doorway one last time.

*****

"Jordan, are you drunk enough to go to our room?" Maria asked.

"Are you?"

"Calmed down a little. I'm actually looking forward to it. If we were working permanently in the same office, we wouldn't be allowed to be romantically involved," Maria said, smiling. As they got up from the table, she put her arm in his. "Since we don't have our own police force, law enforcement personnel are loaned to us all the time. It's usually local police or cops wanting to learn how to collect intel to gain rank. You came because you had been a bad boy."

"Thank God for loopholes," Jordan said as he leaned into her and gave her a long, soft kiss.

Their room featured a large bathroom with a glassed-in shower big enough for two. They undressed and explored each other's bodies as they took a hot shower. Jordan noticed that Maria had beautiful legs.

"Why do you wear those baggy pants? You have great legs and should show them off."

"If someone asks me out, maybe I can assume it's because they like me and not just my body," Maria said.

Both avoided getting their hair wet, so they could immediately get into bed. After helping each other dry off, they laid on top of the covers and made love. All the sex positions they had both done without for the last few months came back into play. Jordan introduced Maria to a new technique for her. He placed her legs together and entered her from on top. He placed his feet on the outside of her legs to help him penetrate deeper inside her. She enjoyed it, and they climaxed quickly.

"Wow! Where have you been for the last few months?" Maria said.

"Waiting to meet you I guess. Damn, that was fun!"

"You ready to go again?" Maria asked.

"Give me a minute to recharge my batteries," Jordan said as he kissed her gently and traced her lips with his finger.

"I like looking at your face when we make love," Maria said, as she held his face in both hands. She was smiling and obviously very happy.

Jordan moved his hands over her breasts and held her nipples between his fingers. Next, he ran his hand over her flat stomach and on down through her pubic hair, which was thick and unmolested.

"You haven't gotten into the fad of trimming landing strips and cute designs?"

"Oh, I have before. I just haven't had anyone checking it out lately.

Do you have a design you prefer?"

"The kind covering the source of pleasure and entertainment for me," Jordan said with a laugh.

After a few minutes of caressing each other's bodies, they made love again.

They slept well, or maybe they were just great bed partners. Their nude bodies pulled each other closer, and legs and arms draped and intertwined in an attempt to absorb maximum sensations.

At some time during the night, Maria became aware of Jordan engaging in oral sex with her. She awoke and returned the favor. Both needed to connect so badly; it was like an illness. It had been so long—too long—too little intimate touching.

Once the soft light from another cloudy day filtered into their room, they had exhausted themselves again with sex so passionate, it bordered on violence. Neither knew if their feelings would last, so subconsciously, they wanted to make the best of their short time together.

Both were out of breath. They wanted to speak to each other but couldn't. Finally, Jordan kissed Maria lightly and said, "Jesus H. Christ, do you know how wonderful that was?"

"I do—I was there."

They held each other tightly and spoke in lowered voices for a long time.

"Maria, do you realize that you are still pretty without your makeup?"

"Well, you look handsome without your lipstick as well." Maria laughed and got up to go to the bathroom. As she passed by the portable scanner lying on the dresser, she flipped the switch on. She was behind the closed door of the bathroom when the instrument began to beep.

"How does this damn thing work?" Jordan asked Maria as he stood in front of her while she sat on the toilet, peeing at midstream.

"Is there no privacy in this household? Here, let me see."

She placed the phone in her naked lap, adjusted some knobs and focused the screen. "My God! We have a hit!" she screamed.

*****

"It's Australia on the sat phone," Ziya said. "What should I say to him?"

"Tell him exactly what happened. He will yell at you, I'm sure, for having your phone at work," Salama Moussa said to his wife, unsympathetically.

"You told me to check with the man, so I took it to get good reception. I will tell him you asked me to report our progress," Ziya said, sobbing.

"It will not matter what you say. If he was here—you would be beaten."

Ziya moved near the window on their Deck Four cabin. Above the window were two strategically-located booster relays installed by her husband, Marine Electrician Salama Moussa, one on Deck 10 and one mixed in with a mass of other electrical instruments on the main mast above the fifteenth deck. Their phone was part of the Iridium network, which included over sixty satellites and boasted worldwide coverage. Even though it was the primary choice for Islamic groups, there was a problem. Most intelligence agencies around the world had endorsed the new GMR-2 encryption algorithm, so no satellite phone could hide behind their best cryptanalysed versions. Messages were short, coded Arabic phrases. This system might keep Ziya from a serious ass chewing. She wrote a note so that she would not be on the line long. With much trepidation she dialed the +881-6-number assigned to the Iridium network.

Nazeem Dastyari answered on the second ring. "How is my paradise girl?" He knew it would be her since her husband never reported in.

"Well, Father. Are my goats giving milk?" Her voiced shook, and he sensed a problem.

"Poorly, as they miss you. Tell me you are fine," Nazeem said.

"The big toy fell from my robe at work and a nice man retrieved it for me," she said.

"Did this man hold it long, my dear?" Nazeem probed.

"Handed to me very quickly," she said much calmer now.

"Find out about this man as we should send a note of thanks. No toy at work. I must go. Allah is great!"

"Allah be with you, Father!" she said and watched as the green light faded out on the phone.

Chapter Five

Monte called Simone at the spa desk as he was directed, and it was a go for drinks.

"Monte, can we run through the buffet? I need to grab a bite to eat before we hit the bar," Simone asked.

"Of course. If you're up to it, there's a theater show at nine forty-five. Supposed to be good," Monte said with enthusiasm. "I'll come by at eight-thirty—we'll get some food, have a couple drinks, and see the song and dance number."

"Sounds great. Thanks for calling. Here's my cell phone number in case you get held up," Simone said and gave him the number.

She hung up the ship's phone and walked through her kingdom to see how things were going. There were appointments for massage, hair, and nails through 9:30, but both of her assistants were scheduled to close on this night. She smiled as she passed Ziya, who was entering a massage room to change the linens. Simone went into the hair salon to talk to customers and hairdressers.

Ziya closed the door behind her as she entered the massage room. Before she began to strip the sheets from the massage tables, she had another task. All the therapists kept notebooks with their appointments listed by name and cabin number. She sighed with relief when she spotted it. The second page of the appointment book lying on a credenza held the names of those who had received couples' massages. Only one couple was listed in the book, and Ziya remembered the room they occupied. She carried her own notebook and pen in her pocket. Nazeem didn't want her using her phone to take pictures at work. Quickly, she copied down Lester and Debi's information. It wasn't much to go on, but it was a start. She finished cleaning the room, satisfied she had a start for her search.

Monte sat and watched Simone eat a small salad decorated with a few boiled shrimp on top. He found a piece of cheesecake to enjoy while she told him about her day. Monte then described the events of his day. He and Salama had replaced an air conditioner thermostat in one of the large luxury suites.

"The man and his younger girlfriend stayed in their hot tub the entire time while the repair was being made. The man got out and wrapped a towel around himself to open the door for us, then dropped his towel, and jumped back in. He and his girlfriend were totally nude. Salama freaked and turned his head away. The woman was a bit overweight from what I could see, and I tried not to stare," Monte said with a chuckle.

"I bet you didn't," Simone said, laughing.

"How is Salama's wife doing since you had your little talk?"

"Much better. I've even seen her smile a couple of times," Simone said.

"Why don't we have a drink at the piano bar on Deck Seven while we wait on the show to start?" Monte was trying hard to entertain Simone, but she would've been happy just talking and getting to know her new boyfriend. She would get that opportunity after leaving the theater that evening.

"I have a bottle of wine in my room. Would you like to visit for a while?" Simone asked

"Yes, of course. I'd love to. But don't you have a roommate?"

"No. When I negotiated my contract I asked for my own balcony room—well, I asked for a suite but didn't get it, so I settled for a little less."

"What a slick-tongued rascal you are," Monte laughed.

Once in Simone's room, Monte opened the wine and poured the South African cabernet sauvignon into a couple of water glasses.

"To our friendship—may it grow," Monte said and clinked his glass against hers.

They sat on the balcony and talked until one in the morning. Simone recounted all the reasons for her divorce. As she talked to

Monte, she noticed how he listened and was genuinely interested in what she said. Occasionally, he would lean in to her and kiss her softly. If the kissing was more passionate, she took the lead. She steered the conversation over to his past. She wanted to know about him and couldn't believe she had found someone so nice and handsome on the first day at work. Simone loved looking at his face and was drawn to his blue eyes as he told her the story of his wife's untimely death from a rare form of brain cancer. It had occurred two years before, and he was just now getting back into circulation.

He had gone to college at the University of California San Diego, obtained a degree in Mechanical Engineering, and had married a pretty, blond California girl who was a political science major. They married when they were juniors in college and remained married until her death two years later. After graduation, he took a job with a firm in La Jolla that manufactured diesel engine parts for ships. One day after work, he came home and found his wife passed out in her car, which was parked in their driveway. He called an ambulance. They revived her, but while in the hospital they found the brain tumor. She only survived three months after the diagnosis. He felt he had to get away and start over. Even though he was overqualified for the officer's position he held, it was more or less an escape for him rather than a job.

As they parted early in the morning, the last kiss was very passionate. Monte didn't cross any boundaries too soon. He wanted Simone to give the signal when she wanted more from him. They were on for the captain's formal dinner in the evening. Before he left the room, Simone showed him her choices for evening dresses. He helped her pick a simple black dress with spaghetti straps. She didn't need to hide behind her dress; she needed to let her body explode through a slinky piece of cloth.

The ship would be at sea for a couple of days before it reached the first planned port of call in Puerto Vallarta. Until then, the people on board would have to find ways to entertain themselves.

*****

Jordan and Maria dressed quickly and practically ran to Jordan's car. He drove at idle speed, beginning at one end of the docks until they located the source of the signal. After about twenty minutes of creeping along the long harbor area, they finally adjusted the scanner signal history to a medium-sized cargo vessel named *Hercule II.* It was loaded with containers and a few Smart cars, fresh from the factory in Hambach, France. The ship was headed to Los Angeles, they would soon learn. After flashing Interpol IDs in the duty officer's face, they were reluctantly given permission to board. He didn't have much of a choice and quickly pointed to the bridge where the captain ruled over his crew. They took the gangway to the wheelhouse and found the man in charge pouring them both a cup of coffee. He was genuinely nice and helpful at first. His name was Herman Kruger, and although he was German, he worked for a French shipping company. They told him about the Arabic chatter coming from his ship on satellite phones. He didn't volunteer any information on his crew.

"As far as I know, we only have three sat phones and they are all in a rack over here by the communication desk." He walked a few feet to a long table where two-way radios, cell phones, and three sat phones sat upright in metal sleeves.

"Can any of the crew check out these phones for their personal use?" Maria asked as she examined one of the units.

"No way. First, they are assigned special numbers for our network which the crew wouldn't know, and second, it costs a lot to use them. We have them in case all other communication fails," the captain said as he gently took the phone from Maria and placed it back in its housing.

Maria frowned and faced the ship's leader.

"Captain Kruger, we would like to see your list of personnel and your cargo manifest."

Maria saw he was hesitating. "If you want to sail on time, you might hurry up with that list. Interpol can stop or delay any ship if we suspect illegal activity," she said, resting her hand on her 9mm Berretta, a personal weapon that few people in France can own, let alone carry. She had a special Category 2 permit allocated to her after the November 2015 terrorist attack in Paris.

Herman Kruger sent one of his officers to retrieve his crew list. They both spoke German. His instructions to his officer was, "Get the crew list and manifest for these assholes."

Maria smiled at him and said to both of them in perfect German, "Us assholes are in a hurry, so step on it!"

The two Germans grimaced but didn't reply.

In a few minutes, the Captain handed over his cargo manifest and crew roster. The main part of the cargo was to be off-loaded in Los Angeles. Maria and Jordan quickly ran their fingers down the list. The total crew for this ship was only 24 people, so it didn't take long to go through it. The *Hercule II* was 500 feet long, which was about half the size of a big container ship, but crew size depended on the sophistication of the equipment on board. Attached to the roster was a *Minimum Safe Manning Certificate* requiring a minimum of 18 people to man the *Hercule II*.

The captain explained, "We have more than the required eighteen seamen, so the men in critical jobs can work in shifts and get plenty of rest."

The certificate listed a Master, which was the captain, and other officers, including deck and engineering officers. Job titles were listed by the names on the roster. About ten names down was listed 2nd Engineering Officer. Both Interpol agents froze when they saw it.

"Captain, tell us about Abu Ali Al-Najdi," Jordan said.

"He came to work here in 2016 after graduating from a marine diesel school in France. Top of his class and does excellent work. Keeps to himself and passes on dinner when we have pork," Herman said, laughing. "He uses his prayer rug at the very bow of the ship. A compass lets him know the western location of Mecca."

"May we talk to him?" Maria asked.

"Sounds like you're profiling one of my employees," the captain said, yet he was walking towards the gangway.

He led them through a metal door and down a long hallway. Some of the doors to the cabins were open, and small bunks could be seen on both sides. Suddenly he stopped and knocked on a door. A dark-skinned man with a mustache answered in English and came to the door.

"We are looking for Abu," Jordan said.

"Yes. I am Abu Ali Al-Najdi. How can I help you?"

"We have some questions for you. We are from Interpol. Do you own or have access to a satellite phone?" Maria asked.

Abu turned to Jordan to give the answer since he obviously didn't like being questioned by a woman—particularly by a Western woman.

"No, but I do have a cell phone." He reached in his uniform jacket and pulled out an ancient flip phone with a large crack on the glass face.

Both Interpol agents asked him numerous questions about his military background and affiliation to various groups. He came across as a saint and was very put out that he was being harassed because of his Muslim religion. Maria took his picture and attempted to take a couple of thumb prints with a portable kit she carried with her, even though she probably didn't have the authority. Abu pulled his hand back and asked Jordan to take the print. He said he couldn't touch a woman.

Jordan and Maria also searched his room and found nothing. Getting nowhere with him, the duo left the ship and returned to Jordan's car. Interpol now knew all the ports that the *Hercule II* would enter, along with prints and a picture of the suspect.

"They're up to something, but we have no idea what. Let's pack up and go back to the office, unless you want to stay at this hotel for a few weeks and check all the ships that come in," Jordan said. He noticed Maria was smiling.

"Please, please, let's stay. Wouldn't it be fun?"

At that moment, Jordan's phone buzzed.

"Hello. Is this Chief Inspector Agent Michaels—Jordan Michaels?"

"Yes, who am I speaking to?"

I'm Jim Webb with Interpol in DC. Anyone with you?"

"Senior Intel Officer Maria Moreau of Interpol," Jordan said.

"Okay. I don't know if this will interest you or not, but an old sheriff's officer friend is on a cruise ship named *Tropic Queen*. He said a young Muslim woman was stacking towels in the spa and an Iridium Extreme sat phone fell out of her smock. He found out they aren't issued these phones. Anything there you want to look into?"

"Yes, Jim, there is. Currently we are in Marseille checking into a similar issue. We are headed back to the office in Lyon. Takes about three hours, so we'll call you with the information we have later today. Is the number you called me on a good one, and can you relay the information to Samuelsson at Homeland Security?"

"Good as any," Jim said. "It's my cell, and I have Lester McFarlin's cell number if you want to talk to him later. Samuelsson has already been informed that I'm talking to you guys. Hey, I didn't think Interpol officers went in the field."

"I'm a new breed who hates paperwork," Maria said, grabbing the phone away from Jordan.

"Oh, thanks for calling," Jordan said as he took the phone back, then clicked it off. He looked at Maria. Both sets of eyes were huge.

"Holy shit!" they said at the same time.

Chapter Six

"Why do we have to dress up while we're on vacation?" Lester asked, while Debi worked on tying his black bowtie. She bit her bottom lip while working to get it perfect.

"It reminds everyone that we're educated humans and not just naked beasts who lie around the pool all day," she said.

"The real reason is the women on board like to play dress up. The men would never dream of wearing a suit or tux while on vacation in the tropics."

"Maybe gay guys started it?" she said laughing, knowing Lester would go along with that explanation.

"That's it! A bunch of interior decorators and hair dressers started the whole damn thing, and now, I'm caught up in the backwash," Lester said, laughing. "Not that I have anything against gays."

Debi knew he clearly didn't feel comfortable around homosexual men. "Right, Lester. Is that why you have no friends of that persuasion?"

Lester changed the subject. "What time is our seating tonight?"

"Same as every night, 5:30 p.m."

"We had a table by ourselves last night. Think we'll luck out tonight?" Lester asked.

"I'm going to guess the couple didn't show up because they aren't feeling well, or maybe they decided to try the buffet. But be prepared to share a table and be nice to them."

"When am I not nice to people?"

"Zip me up in the back, please." He zipped her dress and grabbed her butt cheeks as his reward for taking care of the zipper.

"You always have to mess with me."

"It's my job."

"You're proficient," Debi said, as she kissed him lightly on the lips and wiped the lipstick away. They left the cabin and walked to the elevator. Debi slipped her lipstick and some tissues in Lester's pocket, as she did at most formal functions.

As they entered the restaurant, the maître d' asked for their table number. "One thirty-nine," Lester told him, and he led them to a table for four. Two young men with carefully-cropped hair and pastel-colored sport coats sat at the table. In unison, they stood and introduced themselves.

One was Lance Gordon. With him was Holton Matthews. Lester introduced Debi and himself, adding that they were from San Francisco. They realized they had tapped into common ground when they learned the couple across from them was from the same city. The other couple further explained they had just married and were on their honeymoon. Again, their circumstances were identical to Lester and Debi.

Lester and Debi lived in San Francisco and were familiar with the culture, even though Lester felt it was too liberal and was populated with a disproportionate number of same-sex couples. He was careful with what he said and always tried to treat them with respect. He, however, had been raised in a very different world.

"Where do you guys work in the city?" Lester asked.

"We're both computer nerds and work for the government," Lance said, looking a little nervous.

"CIA, NSA, DEA, or the FBI?" Lester laughed a little when he asked.

"We've been working on a special project for the NSA, but most of what we work on is classified," Holton said.

"You don't have to tell me if what I say is true, but I've read a lot about the giant Bluffdale project in Utah. I study all the time because I'm in law school, but this stuff I research for the fun of it. As I understand, the computers there will be able to store a yottabyte of data, which is a septillion bytes. The number is so large there isn't yet a name for the next largest amount. It truly will be the 'Spy Center' for the US," Lester said, beaming with pride at the amount of research he had done.

"Lester, your research is amazing, but we can't say it exists, or if it does, what the color of the curtains are or even the type of flowers planted in front of it. We certainly couldn't comment on it having the biggest supercomputer in the world," Lance said as he put both hands over his mouth in an effeminate manner.

Lester and Debi joined the laughter of the two men. As they looked up from their levity, a server arrived to discuss the menu. Everyone ordered, and then began discussing the upcoming shore excursions.

"We're doing the pirate ship in Puerto Vallarta," Debi said.

"No, there's no way we will be stuck on a leaky old ship with a bunch of smelly pirates," Lance said.

"We're getting a massage at a local place that has strong Mexican attendants," Holton said, covering his face in obvious excitement.

Debi smiled. "Whoa! I smell trouble for the new marriage."

"He thinks he'll make me jealous, but I don't care if he has a good time," Lance said. "And remember, I'll be getting my butt rubbed too."

Lester and Debi laughed through the entire meal and truly enjoyed the conversation of the same-sex couple. However, Lester knew these men had a great deal of knowledge about a world of secrecy that interested him immensely. He excused himself to go to the bathroom and when he left the table, Holton began to fan himself with his hands.

"Damn, is he hot!" Holton said, looking at Lance who was fanning himself as well.

"Boys, boys. Calm down! He's taken, you know, "Debi chuckled.

Things had gotten back to normal by the time Lester returned. After he sat down again, he wanted them to know he knew a little about computers.

"Okay, guys, here are some terms that I heard might be used for data over a yottabyte. A brontobyte. It would represent a thousand yottabytes. Then there would be a geopbyte, and it would be a thousand brontobytes. Some others they are playing with are hellabytes, ninabytes, and tenabytes. It's kinda like the rocket scientists who ran out of equations for space travel because it didn't exist, so they invented a new math to deal with it," Lester said, more seriously.

"You said you're going to law school, Lester. Are you only going to represent mathematicians, rocket scientists, and computer nerds like us?" Holton asked.

"No—well, maybe, if they pay well. I get interested in things where there is no broad knowledge—such as the dark web. The NSA hangs out there a lot. The place is like the seventh circle of hell. You can't trace people because they have no IP address, and everything is encrypted," Lester said as he stared at the vanilla ice cream with chocolate syrup in front of him.

Debi looked at Lester. "What's wrong?" she asked.

"Nothing. This dessert is so simple and perfect. But if you think about it very long, each molecule and atom in this bowl of ice cream has been around on this planet for billions of years. It may consist of an atom that was in a caveman or a dinosaur or a primeval forest. Now I'm taking all the fun out of my dessert. Sorry."

"Damn, Lester, you 're too smart for your own good. Relax and have a good time. You might jump ship from those pirates and get your ass rubbed by a wild Mexican," Holton said, starting a round of laughter that lasted a while.

After dinner, the two parties said they would see each other the next night. Lester and Debi decided to see the show later that evening after a few drinks at the piano bar. After the singing and dancing on the stage, and Lester's favorite bar afterwards, it seemed like a perfect day.

While Lester was nursing his malted milkshake, Ziya and her husband Salama walked past him on the way to the buffet line where most of the crew ate their meals. It was his first clue that Ziya had a partner on board. She looked even more beautiful with a pink hijab and a long dress that clung to her shapely torso. Debi noticed him staring and kicked him from under the table.

"Ouch! Why did you do that?"

"Quit looking at her like you could eat her alive."

"Me?" Lester said, smiling. It truly was a flaw with Lester. He most assuredly loved Debi and had no plans to be unfaithful, but nothing could stop him from being attracted to beautiful women. He told himself to be more subtle.

"Are you ready to go to our room so you can pay some attention to me? I believe I may be ovulating and we better take advantage of it."

Debi was trying to time getting pregnant and starting a family at about the time Lester finished law school. It was the main purpose of the cruise, and so far, they had taken advantage of being at sea for a few days.

Sex had become a different experience. It had a clinical purpose rather than just for fun and pleasure. And for Lester, it wasn't spontaneous when his wife took her temperature and then yelled, "Okay, it's time to do it again."

Lester did his duty but thought about the exotic Middle-Eastern girl the whole time. Dark smooth skin. She was tall with long legs and a flat stomach. Her face was gorgeous, and her lips were very large. His fantasy helped him make love to Debi with new found enthusiasm. She was very pleased and told him he should make love to her like that all the time. Now he felt guilty, but only for a moment.

"Sweetie, let's watch TV for a while and do it again before we go to sleep," Debi said. She had become a desperate woman who wanted all guns fired at her eggs as they dropped. It wasn't sexy. It was scientific, raw, and a gynecological activity to Lester.

"Why don't we do the 'in vitro' thing and then go back to the spontaneous sex after that," Lester said. Debi realized that her husband wasn't enjoying this new experience.

"Lester, don't you want a baby?" she sniffed, and acted as if she was going to cry.

"You know I do, and the cruise was my idea. This screwing on demand is a little weird, though. I'll get used to it. Be patient with me. I feel like a stud race horse that has to be observed by the owner, so it can be registered."

"You're my stud, baby," Debi said as she pushed her hand into his groin.

"Just call me Trigger!" Lester said as he went back to work. He tried again to focus back on the Muslim girl. Maybe he would buy some Viagra in Mexico tomorrow.

*****

Mr. Nazeen Dastyari ruled an area of Sydney near the Lakemba Mosque and the community of Bankstown where the local police hated to answer calls. Sharia law overruled Australian Law, and only when someone escaped the area did they find proper justice from the country where they lived. So many Australian civil and criminal codes were broken by thousands of these radical Islamists, it would take the Sydney police's full forces patrolling 24 hours a day to make a small dent in it. If the local law enforcement knew the extent of Dastyari's evil rule, they certainly would have made more of an effort.

On this day, the same day that Dastyari had heard from Ziya on the Tropic Queen and his Muslim engineer Abu Ali Al-Najdi on the *Hercule II*, he had a public task to perform. Frustrated that many of his followers were not taking him, a Muslim cleric, or Sharia law seriously, he decided to make an example. It would not be the first time. Or the last.

"Bring them to the square and read their charges!" Dastyari said as he carried a huge Jowhar sword at his side. Two men and one woman had been blindfolded and led to the concrete parking area near a group of small shops and Nazeen Dastyari's office. Charges were read that ranged from apostasy to adultery. There was no trial, only the word of the accusers who were Dastyari's toadies. The three were placed on their knees and instructed to lean forward. Dastyari wore a Muslim-styled white robe and a red-and-white-checkered Afghan-style turban, made of fabric that was possibly influenced by a Purina Dog Chow sack. The Muslim leader stood to the side of the first accused.

It is important to know that Dastyari was a world-class sword collector. He had a Phil sword which had a curved blade constructed with a great deal of heavy metal. The Scimitar was probably the most beautiful one in his collection, but the Jowhar was the sword of choice for the professional executioner. Saudi Arabia uses them exclusively.

He deftly severed the heads of all three, using one stroke each. No one could possibly recover from the sound of a severed head bouncing off an asphalt parking lot, or the image of streams of squirting blood from the big arteries in their necks. There is sometimes discussion afterwards concerning the question of whether the head briefly knew it was no longer attached to the main body before everything went black.

In any case, the bodies were carried off quickly and disposed of while a couple of water hoses were brought out to clean the blood from the parking lot. He had performed enough of these beheadings that the area in front of his office was now referred to as Chop-Chop Square South because of Saudi Arabia's famous execution location with the same name. The crowd knew better than to film the execution in fear of their own death. Everyone had to leave their cell phones and cameras in a box in the square before the head removals took place. The Australian police had heard about the events but could never get proof it was happening. There was always a short speech after the main attraction.

"Sharia law is the law. Obey the Quran. Be pure in thought and deed. Allah is great. Allah is the only God! Allah be with you!" Dastyari turned and disappeared into the crowd in the direction of his office.

Later, Dastyari sat with four of his leaders and gave instructions. "We have problems. Here are the names of people we know are investigating our sat phone use on our ships. Intercept them—kill them. Only two of you go—less likely to arouse suspicion. You decide who goes. Do not fail me."

He left the group and took refuge in his private office. The four men knew the fellow Muslims who went could never return unless they were successful—otherwise it would be their blood on the parking lot.

Chapter Seven

Maria took notes and discussed with Jordan what steps they should take in the investigation. He drove towards Lyon on roads that were now clear from the dusting of snow that had fallen the night before. They decided to look at the sat phone chatter to find the highest concentrations and try to pick up a pattern. While she had a good signal on her cell phone, she called the office and had someone run down the phone number and address of the French marine mechanic school that the man on the *Hercule II* had attended.

"Jordan, when we get to the office, let's make a crime board like this was a murder. We'll post all the information about the ships and even put up pictures of the suspects with them. Whaddya think?" Maria said, nearly breathless with excitement.

"I don't think we got enough sex on this trip. See if we can go to another town, snoop around, and spend a few nights, while we really work hard." Jordan tried to bring her down from her detective work high.

Maria's phone rang before she could respond to Jordan's banter. It was one of her assistants from the Lyon office.

"I have information on the marine school in France for you," the woman said.

"Okay, give it to me, please," Maria said with a pen in hand to take notes.

"The Le Havre Marine Academy is where your person of interest completed his studies." She gave the address and phone number plus the supervisor's name. Neither of the investigators had ever been to Le Havre, but if things worked out it wouldn't be necessary. In size, the port of Le Havre was large and came in second to the port of Marseille-Fos. Maria dialed the number and asked for the supervisor.

"Hello, Pierre Dishongh speaking."

"I am Captain Maria Moreau of Interpol in Lyon, and I think my people informed you that I would be calling. Please tell me about your student, Mr. Al-Najdi." She was not prepared for what she would hear next.

"He was the best student or at least one of the best of all those Middle Eastern students I had for four years. Studied hard. Never gave me any trouble. None of that large group did. One or two of them took an associate degree in two years, and three dropped out. Most of the rest got degrees," Dishongh said, confident they would be pleased with his answer.

"Uh . . . a group of them? How many Middle Easterners did you have and from what countries?" Jordan could read the shock on her face.

"Started in 2012 with twenty-seven, and twenty-two got four-year degrees in 2016. I have heard from all of them about the jobs they got. Mostly marine engineering and electrical jobs. All of them on ships that paid them pretty well. Oh, the countries they came from were Syria, Iraq, Afghanistan, Yemen, Iran, and Somalia," he said with pride.

"Thanks. We will be in touch. Oh, how many Middle Eastern students do you have in class this year?"

"One. But he's a French citizen from Paris. His parents were from Saudi Arabia, and I'm pretty sure he was born in this country. Anything else you need?"

"No. Thanks for the information," Maria said and quickly dialed Jim Webb with the information on everything they had discovered so far.

Jim said, "Wow! Wow! Thanks. I've got work to do. I'll get on it and get back to you."

Except for a few intermittent curse words, Maria and Jordan were silent all the way to Interpol headquarters.

*****

Monte called Simone and nailed down the time they were to meet in the evening. They also met for lunch at the buffet. They were very comfortable together. Simone had to work on this night until closing time, so Monte knew he would be picking her up at around 10:00 p.m. Most contracts for work on cruise ships stated each person works eleven-hour days seven days a week. Most workers still found time to fool around. Monte and Simone certainly were not an exception.

At 3:00 p.m., one of the powerful diesel generators began making a strange noise. Monte, Salama, and four other crew members swarmed around the giant apparatus. It ran the air conditioning for the entire ship. Most of the passengers were ashore in Puerto Vallarta buying cheap trinkets and enjoying excursions. The chief engineer made the decision to shut it down and take it apart for repairs. This was not a small feat and would require quick work by the team. An air conditioner shutdown would be noticed quickly in the tropics, even though the temperature that day was a mild 82 degrees. The heat in the huge engine room would quickly reach 120 degrees without the big generator's power.

"Salama, let's remove the heads and examine the valves and pistons. Do you agree?" Monte said.

"Yes, sir. It sounds like a bent valve. If it is, we can replace it quickly, if we have a spare."

Using every available person in the engine room, the two head covers were removed from the huge, multi-cylindered diesel engine. Once they were off, Monte and Salama started inspecting the valves and found the bent valve within minutes. A search for spare parts was successful, and the repair began in earnest. In exactly thirty minutes, it was running again, smoother and quieter.

"Thanks, Salama. You guessed right on the repair," Monte said, as he helped Salama put away some tools.

"I have heard that sound before when we repaired one in Jamaica while I was in school."

Monte didn't carry on conversations with Salama very often, as the Muslim man kept to himself and rarely spoke much.

"Where did you meet your wife? She is very beautiful." Monte thought he would attempt to get to know him.

"It was arranged by my parents and hers. Things were bad in Syria, so she was sent to Jamaica to marry me a short time before my degree was awarded. My parents made a wise choice. I am blessed by Allah."

"Indeed you are, Salama," Monte said as he left to go to his cabin to clean off the grease. His thoughts were on Simone, and he imagined that if his parents had sent Simone to him to marry, it also would have been a good choice. A great choice.

*****

The pirate ship may have had some good qualities, but they weren't all that obvious to Lester and Debi. The wooden benches were hard and seemed harder as the day went on. The sword fighters were fun for the first few minutes, but it lasted way too long. Then there was a shore excursion and snorkeling. The water was dingy, cold, and void of fish life, and once it was done, the shore excursion was followed by some snacks and drinks. The pirate crew had a few chairs but not enough for the snorkelers when they arrived. Back onboard, lunch was served, more swords clattered together, and they spent more time on wooden benches. Finally, it was over, and Lester and Debi shopped through the many vendors on their way back to the ship.

"Well, Deb, do you like the life aboard a pirate ship?" Lester asked. He was laughing since he already knew the answer.

"Real pirates couldn't have been that uncomfortable or they would have killed everyone aboard. Truthfully, I was so miserable, I wanted the guys with the swords to use them on each other for real!" Debi said in her semi-serious voice.

"Now, dear, tell me how you really feel." Lester continued laughing as Debi shook her head in disgust.

"I suggest a shower and a nap. Any takers?" she asked.

"I kinda wanted to go back on the pirate ship," Lester joked.

Debi ignored him and opened a brochure she had brought with her about Granada, Nicaragua, which was their next tour on the following day. As they walked toward the ship, she read out loud the details of the horse carriage and bus ride awaiting them then.

*****

Jim Webb sat down with his section chief, Mike Browning, and reviewed the information given to him by the officers in France. He was a veteran of fighting jihadist movements.

"Jim, this stinks to high heaven. I'm going to guess you're already checking marine academies or schools—whatever in the fuck they're called. You're looking all over the world, I hope?"

"We have a whole team working on enrollments in 2012. We have two hits so far: Jamaica and Norway. I'm sure we'll find more."

"How many in each class?" Mike asked

"Sixteen in Jamaica—twenty-eight in Norway," Jim said as he looked at the list of schools still not checked.

"I'm going to throw this out there, crazy as it seems. Osama bin Laden was killed on May 2, 2011. He always said he was planning something really big—something that would prove that his organization was still viable. If he had this funded—four years of school for who the fuck knows how many jihadist Islamic dickheads—then maybe this is it," Mike said, burying his head in his hands on the table. "For God's sake, he had millions from his family inheritance to buy anything he wanted."

"How are we going to find these people, and how much time do we have?" Jim asked.

"Don't have a clue, but we better put everyone on it. I will inform NSA, Homeland, and the CIA. You know, Samuelsson started this mess along with your sheriff friend, but now we're doing all the heavy lifting. As soon as we can get these other agencies helping us, we can solve this quicker," Mike said. He was suddenly very tired.

"I'm going to ask our people in France to visit the school and see if they can find the ships where these people are hired on," said Jim.

"You know, Jim, somebody has to be in charge of this operation, and we have to find him," Mike said. His determination and anger were reflected in his voice.

*****

Jordan and Maria had been back in the Lyon office about an hour when they got Jim's call. During that hour, it was difficult for them not to touch either other. The attraction had grown to the boiling point.

"We need for you two to go to Le Havre and get the best list you can of the ships where these yahoos went to work. Fly, take a train, but get there as fast as you can. Call me as soon as you get the information," Jim said. "Something big is going down, and we have to stop it."

"You know, if we had a computer freak who could track all these sat phone conversations and make something out of them, we might find the person in charge," Maria said.

"I'll keep that in mind. Gotta go." He hung up and again Maria and Jordan looked at each other for a few seconds without speaking. Jordan took her hand and squeezed it, and she quivered.

Maria broke the silence. "Jordan, we'll need to catch a flight to Le Havre since it's over 600 kilometers. Do you have enough clean clothes to make the trip?"

"Yeah, let's go. If I run out of underwear, I'll go commando."

"Damn, we'll have to stay overnight again. Can you stand it?"

"Oh, yeah! I'm good with that news," Jordan said, as he started towards the door behind Maria.

As they approached Jordan's car, Maria's cell phone rang.

"Hey, Jim here. Just wanted to warn you all that your guy on the boat in Marseille may have called his boss, and like all good little Islamic terrorists everywhere, he may have someone looking to erase you before you find out anything more. Just a heads up. Have fun in Le Havre."

"Well, doesn't that put a damper on our little parade?" Maria said as she relayed the conversation to Jordan.

"Just makes the trip more exciting. Let's get to the airport. We'll look to see if anyone follows us," Jordan said as he checked his Kimber

1911 .45 automatic. "My ammo is getting old—needs to be used for a good cause." Jordan had obtained a ten-round clip to extend the capacity of his weapon.

Maria laughed but turned in her seat to see if they were being followed.

*****

Lester had taken a shower and was about to take a nap when his cell phone buzzed.

"Lester McFarlin."

"Jim Webb. How you doing with the cruise? Good, I hope. Hey, I think you'd better keep a watch out while you're on these excursions on shore."

"What? Why would I need to watch out?"

"I shouldn't be telling you all this, but you are involved somewhat. We have found out that dozens of Middle Eastern men signed up for marine academies all over the world at the same time your towel girl's husband did. We think they may know you informed on them. Anyway, we have sat phone chatter out the butt but can't pinpoint who the leader is or much of anything else. I just have an uneasy feeling it's all going to come to a head soon. Watch yourself. Where're y'all going tomorrow?"

"Nicaragua. Town called Granada. On buses, donkey carts, and boats. Do I have a chance of staying alive?"

"Sounds dangerous enough without Islamic terrorists hunting you down. Have fun and I'll keep you informed."

Debi stepped out of the shower, "Was that Jim? What's the update?"

"Apparently, a bunch of these Middle Eastern wackos went to schools all over at the same time. Seems weird."

"Forget it for now. It's nap time and both of us are naked. I'll watch out to make sure that pretty Muslim girl doesn't sneak in and beat us on the head with her sat phone," Debi laughed.

"I feel so much safer now. Come under the covers and hug me so I don't get scared," Lester said as he gently gathered her into his arms.

Chapter Eight

Yazid Waheed landed at Augusto C. Sandino airport in Managua, Nicaragua at almost midnight. The flight from Sydney had a stop in Chile and included at least twenty hours of flying and waiting in airports. He was young, however, and fanatically devoted to Nazeem. He would complete his mission or die trying.

He had checked in with Salama on the sat phone and had been given the description of Lester McFarlin. Salama had forwarded a picture of him pulled from the internet on his cell phone, which worked well now that they were nearing a port. One of Salama's friends let him read the shore excursion list on the pretense he was looking for one of the passengers who wanted work done on their room. Knowing the time that Lester's bus would arrive in Granada, Yazid decided to rent a car, drive there, and find a hotel for a few hours' nap. He also had some shopping to do at a local store. He would be ready when they arrived.

*****

Lance and Holton were in fine form at dinner. They had Lester and Debi laughing continuously throughout the meal. It was hard to believe two people could have such a hilarious adventure in a Mexican spa.

Towards the end of the meal, Lester had a rather serious question for the two computer nerds.

"Listen, if you guys were presented with a series of sat phone conversations—all coded and encrypted, which took place on various times all over the world—could you find the common source for most of the calls? Can the computer find the conversation that is taking place within a millisecond of the person answering on the other line?"

"If we could feed it into this place that doesn't exist in Utah. Yeah, if there was a supercomputer which doesn't exist at the place that doesn't exist, I could do it. I don't know yet how to enter the information, but my guess is the computer that isn't there could read the scanners on its own and tell you what you need to know. It would also break codes and decipher, if it existed, of course," Holton said, laughing.

Lester checked to see if he had a signal on his iPhone as they were getting closer to shore, and he did. He dialed up Jim; even though it was late, Lester felt sure he would be working.

"Jim, you awake?"

"I am now, Lester. What's up?"

"Did I really wake you? I remember that you rarely slept when a big case was working."

"The TV is on and I'm fully clothed—fell asleep during 'Dancing with the Stars.'"

"How could you, with all those skimpy, sexy outfits, and hot girls?"

"What's up, Lester?" Jim asked, ignoring his remarks.

"Look, I have an idea regarding the scanner information the people have in France. I read some place that the NSA has this big, hairy supercomputer at this place that doesn't exist called Bluffdale, Utah. I may or may not know some people who work as programmers for them. They may or may not have said that this Godzilla of a computer might be able to read the information on the scanners and tell us who might be the main recipient of all the sat phone calls. Can you talk to your buddies at NSA for me? Ask them if they want to be heroes. And have them call me right back, as I might be or might not be with their employees."

"I might or might not call you back," Jim said, chuckling, as he hung up.

"Are we going to get in trouble? Oh, my God, we're going to be shot at sunrise!" Lance said, holding his hands over his mouth in mock horror.

The group had dessert and waited for the phone to ring. After about ten minutes, Lester's phone sounded, using the same ringtone that the factory assigned to it.

"Lester, I'm going to have a man talk directly to Holton, only I'm told that may or may not be his name. Afterwards, Holton will not be able to tell you much or if he even talked to anyone at the company he works for. Got that?" Jim said.

Lester handed the phone over to Holton, who got up and walked outside the restaurant to talk. He was gone several minutes and then returned and handed Lester his phone.

"I can't tell you that I talked to someone. Maybe it was me talking to myself," Holton giggled. "These guys are worse than the ones you see in the movies and a hell of a lot less intelligent. Okay, here's the deal. They want the Interpol people in France to put the scanner on a US Air Force plane in Le Havre, and it will be flown to someplace in the US."

At this point Holton said, "Wink—wink" and then winked for effect. "Once it's at this place," he winked again, "they may ask that two people on this boat get on a secured internet connection and help run a big bad-ass computer remotely to retrieve the information. The captain has that equipment, and they will clear it with him. All I can say, Lester, is that it better not interfere with my spa session tomorrow. If it does, you might have to come rub my butt," Holton said, laughing and fanning his face with his hand, as though it had suddenly gotten hot in the room.

"Ain't gonna happen, Holton. Just tell the folks at your three-lettered agency that they have to work around your schedule, and that you're a busy man," Lester said as he got up to escort Debi out of the room.

"Also, have Lance call me when you are contacted, no matter what time. I have to know what steps to take to protect this ship if it's a part of some master plan, and before you say it, I know I'm not supposed to be there. I will be as quiet as a mouse in the background."

Everyone left the restaurant and went to other parts of the ship. Debi and Lester went to Lester's favorite bar on the fourteenth deck and then to a show. Holton and Lance had heard there was an LGBT get together at one of the bars. If they told their Mexican massage story, they would be the hit of the gathering.

Simone and Monte also went to the theater and landed at the same bar with Lester and Debi. After a few minutes, they discovered each other and introduced themselves to Monte. The conversation finally got around to the pretty Muslim girl. At that point, Lester learned that Monte worked with Salama, the Muslim girl's husband. Lester stored that information and shifted the conversation to anything not remotely attached to the investigation. They all had a good time and drank a lot before returning to their rooms.

Lance never called that evening. Lester would see him the next night at dinner, after his excursion to Granada.

*****

Jordan and Maria got the message to bring the scanner and any tapes or external drives while they were about halfway to the airport. They still had time to go back to retrieve it and catch the flight. A US Air Force officer would meet them as they deplaned. But they didn't have a clue about what would happen after that. Perhaps the scanner would be put on a U2 plane or one of the stealth B-1 bombers and rushed to some secret base.

They arrived there at about 8:00 p.m. and were stepping off the plane when four officers met them and took the scanner. They were armed and serious-looking. Two of the men followed them to the car rental area where Maria and Jordan completed the paperwork on a small red Fiat. The two serious men walked them to their car. Jordan always walked around the cars he rented, looking for damage. Maria looked down at a small dent on the passenger side door; she bent over and rubbed it with her finger. Jordan clicked the remote lock, complaining that the two men were treating them like children. While Maria was still examining the spot on the car, Jordan looked up and noticed a dark figure who had stepped out from behind a pillar. He had a beard and was dressed in loose, white, baggy pants and a pullover white shirt with designs along the V-neck of the garment. He reached behind him and grabbed what Jordan assumed would be a gun, so his reflexes told him to protect Maria. Without thinking about his own safety, he fell on Maria and pushed her to the ground.

"What the fu—!" Maria was able to say, as a bullet flew right above Jordan's back and struck the Fiat at the bottom of the door.

The man was shot several times by the military officers. He turned his weapon and got off a couple of shots in the direction of the servicemen. One took a bullet in the shoulder. An ambulance was there in minutes, but Jordan and the other officer had already stopped the bleeding, using his belt. The other two air force officers showed up quickly, along with the police and two men in suits who appeared to be Americans. They instructed the police not to touch the body of the shooter until they had searched him. Jordan guessed they were CIA, but there was no way an identity would be announced. The two Interpol agents were dismissed without any discussions about what had just happened.

Jordan and Maria found a small hotel near the port and then found a bar a few doors down. After they checked in, they practically ran to the bar. Maria looked Jordan in the eyes as soon as she got her favorite drink, a rum and coke, and said, "This shit is real!"

"It's something huge, and we have to figure it out," Jordan said as he gulped a Guinness stout. He leaned over and gently kissed her on the lips. He raked back her hair that had fallen in her face.

"You are so beautiful," Jordan said.

"We could have easily died tonight! Neither of us were able to draw our guns. Didn't have time to think about it. Those two men saved our lives, and we don't even know their names," Maria said. She noticed her hands were shaking as she held her drink. "My daughter—what would she do? Shit—you saved my life first—pushed me down and the bullet went right over us into the door. God—how can I ever thank you? Don't say it! Don't cheapen the fact you really saved my life," Maria said, her voice trembling.

"I can't think about dying. My kids need me for money for one thing. Maybe that's the only thing, but we do have great summers," Jordan said with a chuckle.

"I did save some printouts of those calls, but they're hard to read since only so many will fit on a page. When we both get drunk enough to get over being shot at, we'll go to the room and look at them."

"I wonder what almost-dying sex is like. Maybe a mix between makeup sex and breaking up sex?" Jordan said.

"Maybe it's 'make-me-feel-good-that-I-almost-died' sex," Maria said as she squeezed Jordan's hand. She was still shaking.

After they went to their room, they did make love. Later, it was described as comfort sex, much like comfort food—mashed-potatoes-and-gravy-and-fried-chicken kind of sex.

They had breakfast at a small café near the marine academy, then showed up at Pierre's office as he was walking in. Their staff had called ahead, so he knew what they wanted and actually had it ready for them. He had listed all the ships he recalled where his students had taken jobs. He had to send transcripts and proof of graduation to them, so he also had the ship names, addresses, personnel names, and ship phone numbers. Jordan asked Pierre if the students seemed odd, radical, or belligerent. He asked about weapons.

"They studied hard, got along with most everyone, and showed very little of radical ideological views. There was one woman in the class, and they did seem offended by having a Western woman without a hijab sitting next to them in class. I did have to tell them the rules for the academy, and that they either treated the lady with respect or they couldn't stay in class. I had no more trouble with them."

Jordan and Maria dropped off the rental car and apologized for the bullet hole in the door. Interpol had a group rental agreement that included the insurance on rental cars, and there was a good chance the premium might be adjusted if too many bullet holes showed up as claims.

Since the flight back to Lyon arrived about 2:00 p.m., they had time to go back to the office and look at the printouts and the list of ships. Maria made her murder board and began to print out pictures of all the ships, placing them on the board. Most had pictures available on Google; others had to come directly from the ships. She and Jordan began to call them and get their itineraries, even though they varied at times. Many of the cruise ships transitioned or had repositioning cruises in the winter and summer. Most had long-reaching itineraries covering both oceans. None of it made any sense.

Maria went to the printouts and tacked them on a separate board. Jordan noticed something.

"Why do there seem to be more hits in the South Pacific? Especially Australia. Do you see it?"

"Yes, I guess so. I think it might just be the population is larger there."

"Maria, Sydney is a hot spot! Can you pinpoint an area where a lot of calls are going in and out?" asked Jordan. He felt as if he were on to something.

"Not really. Maybe the guys who feed the information into a supercomputer could find something. Tell you what. Since we're poking around in the dark, why don't we research Islamic radicals in Australia?"

"Don't you have a staff here that can help?"

"I am giving that order as we speak."

"You make a sexy boss."

"Do we plan to work late tonight?" she asked.

"Your place or mine?" Jordan asked, not expecting an answer. He did get the smile he was looking for.

Chapter Nine

The cabin steward, Ralph, had parked his cart outside Lester's cabin and was in the next room up the hall when Lester left to meet Debi on the fifth deck. As Lester walked along the narrow space between cruise ship cabins, he looked in through the glass on the top of a door leading into the food prep station. He had passed it several times each day and noticed that between meals, it wasn't very busy. It was empty, so he rushed in and gathered what he wanted and stored it in his windbreaker. Debi would ask him later why he brought a coat when it was 90 degrees outside. His lie to her was that he thought someone said it might rain later that day.

The gangway leaving the ship required that you had the attendants scan your ship identification as you left and reentered the ship. Armed with this information, the crew of the cruise line knew exactly how many passengers wouldn't be there for lunch. Maybe it meant more food for the crew. Buses, very nice Mercedes buses, awaited those that had signed up for all sorts of adventures. Debi didn't want Lester to know they had spent almost as much on tours, beverages, and photos as the original cost of the cruise. He was financially conservative, or as Debi defined it—a penny pincher.

A chubby tour guide with stringy frosted hair was aboard the bus with a microphone. She explained all about Nicaragua's volcanos, and how they were still active and might blow at any minute. By the time the ride had hit one and a half hours, the people on the bus were walking Wikipedia experts on everything that had ever happened in this small country.

Once in Granada, the people were divided into fours and led to small brightly painted horse-drawn carriages and given tours by non-English-speaking drivers. Next came a boat ride that buzzed around in a lake and around a bunch of small islands; many were for sale, and many had large beautiful homes sitting on them.

After this ride, the couple had lunch and then took more walking tours. Lester took a picture of Debi by a carved stone figure. The guests at this location were outside the main building and spread out somewhat as they were looking at different exhibits. Lester was vigilant and spotted the person he had been waiting on. He ordered Debi to step inside of the main museum while he waited outside. Debi saw the intense look on his face and made no protest. The man who was the focus of Lester's attention was dark with a mustache and a well-cropped beard. His hair and features seemed Middle Eastern to Lester. Overall, he was a small man, probably agile, but much too confident.

Lester moved to the side of one of the large stone figures and took the 10-inch kitchen knife he had borrowed from the food prep room out of his jacket, gripping it tightly in his right hand. The windbreaker was now wrapped around his left wrist and forearm. The man was approaching fast—almost running, but he slowed somewhat when he saw Lester's six-foot, three-inch frame and his long-bladed knife. He hadn't considered that the man he had come to kill would be huge and armed as well. He had thought it would be easy.

From his backside, he pulled out a machete, a new one purchased earlier in the day. It was a slashing weapon—not a stabbing-type blade. He was now near Lester and was about to find he was outclassed in so many ways. The terrorist swung his machete with both hands over his head. Lester quickly stepped aside, faster than the man ever believed a person that large could move and sliced upward with tremendous force through both of the man's wrists, as the energy of the attacker on his downward swing met Lester's razor-sharp kitchen knife going up. Lester lunged inward and sunk his kitchen prep knife up the hilt between his ribs and into his heart. He died with a shocked and puzzled look on his face.

The hands of the attacker lay on the ground next to his body, still holding the machete but no longer attached to their owner. The police might ask why Lester didn't stop when his attacker's hands were cut off. Lester would explain the countermoves were a learned sequence of strokes taught in his hand-to-hand combat classes, intended to finish an attacker. There was no time to judge if the first few blows were enough to stop the assailant. His black belt in karate, had he wanted to risk it, would have allowed him to take him without a knife. However, there was always a danger of an error in judgement.

The crowd had been screaming when the attack was going on but was now quiet. Debi ran out and hugged him.

"Who in the fuck was that? Lester, what happened? Did you know this was going to happen?"

"One of the bad guys Jim told me about. He just said they might be after me because of the sat phone I reported. I borrowed a knife just in case. Glad I did."

Shortly afterwards, police arrived in droves; by then Jim had called all his contacts for the area after he received a message from Lester. They questioned him briefly but received most of their intel straight from Washington and in Spanish. Jim told him the team in France had also been attacked, but survived as well. The Nicaraguan local authorities, which also consisted of some men in suits, later reported to Jim that his attacker had a passport issued by Syria and listed an address on the car rental from Sydney, Australia. Using this information, his profile was sent through Interpol's network. He popped up with a record of terrorist and criminal activities going back several years. How Australia let him in their country was a puzzle, but most believed he was smuggled in during the dark of night. Australian authorities knew of his existence since he was being watched as a close associate of Nazeem. They were waiting to take all these Islamic jihadists out in one fatal blow.

"You are free to go now, Mr. McFarlin. I have been informed about the work you are doing trying to find out what these terrorists are up to. Good luck. The knife you borrowed from the ship will be returned to the ship before you sail tonight. Other than you being attacked, I hope you have good feelings about our beautiful country," one of the men in a suit said.

"Your country is incredibly beautiful, and I will tell my friends about it with pleasure," Lester said, shaking the hand of the police officer.

The ride back to the ship was quiet, and many of the passengers avoided making eye contact with Lester out of fear they would be butchered as well. When Debi and Lester boarded the ship, the captain was waiting and escorted them into an interview room on Deck Five. Three men in suits were already there positioned around a large oblong table. They offered Lester and Debi bottled water. Debi was given the choice to leave if she so wished, but she elected to stay and find out her husband's fate.

The captain introduced himself as Nickolas Polycron. He explained he was Greek and still maintained a home there on the island of Mykonos. The other three people at the table introduced themselves but only said they worked for the US government. The captain addressed the three men and demanded to know what was going on aboard his ship.

A tall, rugged man with a military-style haircut and a long scar, which extended his smile line about an inch upwards, spoke first.

"I'm Franklin Grissom, and I'm going to ask Mr. McFarlin to speak first with the information he knows." He pointed to Lester and nodded his head.

"Well, I don't know much, but I suspect a lot is going to happen. You have two employees on this ship that could very well be Islamic terrorists. I first noticed that a spa worker named Ziya had in her possession a very expensive Iridium Extreme sat phone, which has no connection to her duties on this ship. Her chief engineer husband, named Salama, must have called in the hit on me that was attempted today. I believe the Tropic Seas is in imminent danger of being damaged or sunk by these two jihadists.

"There is a bigger picture. In 2012, I believe as a last-ditch effort from the ghost of a once powerful Al Qaeda, a coordinated plot was designed to place Middle Eastern soldiers in marine academies in several countries, with the final objective of placing about one-hundred eight new graduates all over the world on a hundred and four different ships. We can only guess the goal was blowing all of them up at a given time. We have lost track of four of the graduates. They all told their school that they were getting extra training but would not share what or where the facility was located.

"Here's what we don't know. Who is their leader? The team in France suspects someone in Australia, but we've got nothing concrete. When are they going to set off their bombs? We don't know but believe soon, since the chatter has been high. Where are the explosives, and are they on a timer or booby trapped? What do all the hundred and four ships have in common? Why do some have wives along? Are the women taking part? At this point we are recommending the jurisdictions for each ship that has these individuals implanted to send out arrest warrants for the entire 2016 class, wherever they are. It will not be easy, since these ships are all over the world, and a few of them are lost to us. They must be taken quickly, so there is no chance of setting off explosives. It's clear that if we are not careful, they will talk to their leader who will warn all of them, forcing them to detonate early.

"The two Muslims on this ship need to be arrested and interrogated immediately; however, the other side of the issue would mean they would be off the grid, and immediately alarms would be sent out to all their people. If we arrest them, they cannot be allowed the freedom to return to their cabins or even reach in their pockets, as they may have trigger devices on them. As we all know, cell phones can be used to detonate, as can sat phones. These are not dumb Islamic radicals, they are smart, educated, and motivated militants determined to declare a death sentence fatwa all over our asses.

"I hope this gives everyone an overview of what we are dealing with. I have a background in investigating large criminal organizations and hope I can be of help here. If we could time a hundred and eight arrests at the same time and stop the 'Big Bang Event,' we would pull off one of the greatest law enforcement feats in history. I'm motivated since I don't care to be blown up on my honeymoon," Lester said emphatically.

"Thank you, Lester. I see that Jim Webb keeps you very informed. The other gentlemen at this table have the capacity to place personnel on cruise ships, and they will blend in with the other passengers. Probably two couples placed as close as possible to the suspected terrorists. The container ships would receive personnel or assets who would pose as friends or relatives of the captain or other senior officers who were catching a ride to their favorite vacation spot. Many freighters carry a few travelers, but these will be loaded by helicopter unless they are stopping someplace for supplies. Meetings like this are taking place around the world. Bomb experts will be mixed in with the phony passengers. The ones for this ship are already aboard. We think we only have a few days to do all this, and we are still identifying the ships where the graduates went to work. All agencies are working twenty-four/seven to get people in place to play their parts, but Interpol is the central collector of information. A supercomputer is looking at all the intercepted sat phone conversations. We should know most everything we need to know in a day or two. Any questions?" Franklin asked.

"You mean we're going to let these maniac Islamic terrorists run free on my ship?" Captain Polycron shouted.

"If we arrest them now, a hundred and three other ships could be blown out of the water. We will keep an eye on them. The entire team is armed, plus we have a scanner that intercepts all encrypted sat phone calls. We have two explosive-sniffing dogs hidden in the lower levels of the ship. When it's time to move on the suspects, we will be ready," Franklin said. He hoped he sounded reassuring.

When the meeting ended, Lester and Debi took the elevator to their room and wondered if the guys with suits were going to stay on board. They looked very much like the spooks they actually were. Lester knew most of them had never taken down a suspect and wouldn't have a clue about how to do it right. Debi was upset, but as usual she was mad. When anyone threatened her, shot at her, or wanted to harm her in any way, her temper overruled her fear. Once, she and Lester pulled up to a robbery in progress. Lester gave her a gun to protect herself, and she helped shoot at one of the suspects until Lester could finish him off.

"Lester, I agree with the captain. We should shoot the fuckers and then piss on their heads."

"You have a real dark side, Debi. It comes out when you're angry."

"Look, some Muslim jihadist, head-chopping Hodgie wants to blow my ass all the way back to California, I got no love for them." Debi was ranting, and it puzzled Lester where she learned all this street talk. Her mother was a respected real estate agent, college graduate, and sorority sister. Her dad was a doctor. Unless she hung around street gangs as a kid or just watched a lot of war movies, Lester didn't get it. And "Hodgie?" How did she learn the soldier's racist slang for the native people of Iraq and Afghanistan? It was like using the name gook in Vietnam. He would ask her later when her blood cooled.

"Someday, you will tell me how you really feel. How about we make a baby before dinner? I need to get out of these bloody clothes." He was just realizing how much blood had splashed on him during the fight. He didn't like taking someone's life, but the man didn't leave him much choice.

"This may be the one that counts," Lester said.

"If not, I'll give you a coupon for a do-over," Debi smiled.

Chapter Ten

Jordan and Maria had now heard about the attack on Lester McFarlin and admired the way he defended himself.

"I googled some information about Lester. While he was working for the Sheriff's Office in Hot Springs, Arkansas, he was awarded a fourth-degree black belt in karate. I understand he still trains in San Francisco. He shoots pistols and shotguns in competition and is an expert with automatic weapons. He also boxes in his spare time for exercise. He completed the Little Rock Marathon five years in a row," Maria said, as she skimmed through the information on his attacker. "This Muslim clown never stood a chance—even had Lester been barehanded. He is like a superhero and now is completing law school. I want to marry this guy," Maria said.

"He has a pretty wife. And now I'm jealous. I have competition out there," Jordan said, lowering his head in a mock pout. "He probably likes country music since he's from Arkansas."

Maria laughed. "Honey, you got me as long as you want me. I wouldn't be alive without you." She kissed him and quickly pulled away realizing they were in the office, even though it was so early it was still dark out, and only a couple of people were there. "I could get used to country music, I think," she laughed.

They had spent an enjoyable night together, and being eight hours ahead of North American Central Time Zone, they were back at the office working in front of a giant murder board with almost 100 ship pictures on the wall. Using specs they had collected from several sources, they first tried to see what they had in common.

It appeared there wasn't anything similar. Almost all of them had different itineraries, different cargo, different cruise amenities, and different sizes. They decided to look for ships that were not infiltrated with Muslim jihadists and compare those to the infected ones to see if there was a difference. Nothing made any sense, and they began to believe that finding something in common wasn't even necessary. At a given time, they would just blow up 104 ships. It would be horrific, brutal, and would undoubtedly usurp the 9/11 tragedy. Both were hoping that today they would get the supercomputer results. They had their eyes on a certain radical cleric in Sydney, Australia, as did the authorities there. They decided to go to breakfast and tackle it on a full stomach later.

*****

Lester was anxious to be seated at dinner, so he could find out what Holton and Lance had discovered from the Bluffdale. As he and Debi were seated next to the two men, Lester noticed they were looking at him with unusual expressions. Lance spoke first.

"Please don't kill us with your butter knife because we didn't call you last night."

"We didn't hear from Bluffdale until 5:30 this morning," Holton said. "We went back to bed, and you had already left—to go on your killing-spree—when we woke up. What in the hell happened out there?"

Lester explained, "I got a warning from DC that someone was probably after me. I was prepared to be attacked and took care of the situation. That's done, so tell me what happened when all the information was fed into Godzilla."

"Godzilla found the source rather easily. It timed the calls from all the ships to a common destination in Sydney, Australia. Some goofball radical cleric named Nazeem Dastyari, has been on their radar for some time. Can't do anything to him that would bring down a hundred ships, so we're marching in place until somebody says go," Holton said, wiping imaginary sweat from his brow.

"Can you guys add all the ships that have terrorists on board into the computer with their itineraries to see if we have something in common or something that might tell us when the optimum time would be to blow them all up? Boys, we've got to get on this," Lester said. He knew they didn't have much time.

"Lester, they were adding that information today, so I expect they will be calling you soon with an answer. You realize that if we find that out, we still would have to find the explosives and defuse them before they triggered the event. We are truly sitting on a powder keg," Lance said, wiggling his bottom on his chair causing an eruption of laughter from the entire group.

*****

Monte and Simone decided this night to eat at one of the fancy restaurants that had a cover charge. Monte insisted on paying for both since it was a date. He also felt that tonight would be the time Simone would ask him to spend the night in her room. Both were starving for steak since it rarely shows up on the regular menus.

Monte had worn his best dress uniform, and Simone looked beautiful in her black dress with thin straps. When she walked, her breasts fought against the thin material and threatened to jump completely out of her dress. Monte was mesmerized by how beautiful she was on this night. How could he have gotten so lucky as to be starting a relationship with a walking, talking goddess? He found himself staring at her at times but worked to avoid it.

"Should I get a filet or a ribeye, Monte?"

"Let's see. The filet is a full eight ounces and the ribeye is twelve ounces. The filet will be tenderer and have zero waste. The ribeye will have more flavor because of the heavy marbling of fat. You choose—flavor or tenderness."

"What are you getting?" Simone asked.

"The sixteen-ounce porterhouse—king of steaks, but rather large," Monte said, holding his hands apart like he was demonstrating the size of a fish he caught.

"I want to taste steak—it's going to be ribeye for me. Had them quite often in South Africa. Big cattle ranchers there."

"Think you'll go back there to live someday?" Monte asked, wondering if he would he go to live there if things progressed.

"Probably. My parents are there and a sister and brother. A bunch of other relatives. I'm not sure all of them will stay there. Parts of South Africa are dangerous. Johannesburg has riots, murders, rapes, and robberies it seems every day," Simone said with a faraway look in her eyes.

Both ordered the main course and a chocolate brownie with ice cream for dessert. Monte had the staff dig around for a South African wine and they came up with a Graham Beck pinot noir. Simone was thrilled and read to Monte the back label which described the conservation efforts done by that particular winery for native species of animals.

"The winery is in the small town of Robertson, not too far from where we lived in Cape Town. Mostly farming and wineries. Lovely area. Thanks for getting that for me. You're very sweet."

"Hey, I'm drinking it too," Monte said, "but you're welcome."

"I was able to get a second bottle sent to my room. I don't have a roommate either, and I believe it's my turn to be a host," Monte said nervously and smiling a little too much.

"Ha! All this wine and more in your room. Monte, dear, are you trying to get me drunk, so I'll be a little easier to get in bed with you?" Simone said with a smile.

"It's been a while for both of us, I'm guessing."

"Way too long," Simone said and reached over and squeezed his hand.

"Did you hear about the knife fight that that Arkansas sheriff got into today?" Monte asked.

"Yes, I heard some Middle Eastern man attacked him in Nicaragua with a machete. Somebody said that this Lester guy had brought along a big kitchen knife, cut the guy's hands off at the wrist, then drove the big knife into his heart in about two seconds flat."

"We just met them last night. He and his wife seemed nice enough," Monte said.

"I had met him a couple days back when he got a massage. He

started asking me about expensive cell phones and if they were issued to workers. I had a feeling then he was trying to investigate something," Simone said.

"My guess is he was asking about sat phones. Those would really stand out, and people can use them to call all over the world. If someone thought he was getting a little nosey, they may have sent a hit man after him. A lot of people googled his name. So did I. He is something else. Expert at hand-to-hand combat. Black belt, gun expert, knife fighter, and has a strange religion. He goes to a café in a small town in Arkansas and just listens to conversations. Somehow gets a lot out of it. He's about to finish law school in San Francisco. The weird thing is that he couldn't read or write until he had an operation about three years ago. Had to learn most everything over again. His mother was killed in a car wreck when he was five. She was classified as a genius and they think he is, too. Bunches of write-ups on him on the internet," Monte said as he looked at his iPhone for the time. He had a watch but rarely wore it.

"Are we ready to go to your room?"

"Believe so."

Monte led Simone to his room and was pleased to see that room service had delivered the South African wine, glasses, and a cheese tray and crackers. They sat on his balcony and consumed a great pinot noir. They both talked about their families and their hometowns and whether they would like to raise a family there.

After the wine was gone, Monte took her hand and led her to the bed. He slid the loose dress off her and hung it in his closet. Then he stood eye to eye and kissed her for a long time. She removed the rest of her clothes and so did Monte. He wasn't a large man but had rippled muscles on his stomach and chiseled chest muscles. Simone ran her hands over his chest and felt how hard and toned he was. She let him explore her body which was also very defined, sculpted, and beautiful. They lay on the bed and started with basic positions that felt wonderful to both since they had done without sex for a long time. The night was pure ecstasy.

Monte walked her to her room early the next morning. They would see each other for lunch and drinks the next night in her room. If there was a source of conflict or incompatibility, neither of them could sense it. They had found what they were looking for.

Chapter Eleven

Lester decided to call France. He had done his morning duty towards re-populating the earth, and now it was time for coffee and a fruit plate on his balcony. Debi had gone upstairs for her jogging session, a Pilates class, and a stone massage. He called Jordan Michaels, using an international number Jim Webb supplied.

"Mr. Jordan Michaels? Lester McFarlin here."

"Hello, Lester. I understand we're working the same case," Jordan said.

"Jordan, I feel like I'm half-ass working on it, and we appreciate the dedication you've put into the case. Of course, I understand from Jim Webb you have a pretty partner to work with."

"Uh . . . I guess he saw her picture while he was snooping around in our files. She is pretty and a damn good officer. Listen, Lester, we have a board here in our office with all the ships and beneath them are the names of the corresponding Islamic terrorist. We don't know what they are up to, or when they plan to blow it all up. Where does your cruise ship go next?" Jordan asked.

"Today we'll be in Costa Rica. Tomorrow we spend the whole day going through the canal. After that is Colombia, Aruba and then Miami. Where are all your ships going and are you tracking them?"

"They're all in the big gorilla computer, along with most of the ships in the world, including the one you're on. We have been given remote access to the computer and can key in things from here now, since all the basic info has been fed in," Jordan said.

"Really? Jordan, do this for me. I'm guessing you have ship itineraries of boats that are not compromised? Tell you what, ask the computer to compare the differences between our ship, the *Tropic Queen*, and some other bomb-infested cruise ships. See if you can ask for dissimilar qualities," Lester said excitedly.

"Maria is doing that now. We have specs on several container ships and cruises where we tried to find differences. We haven't asked the computer to do it, however. Just a second while Maria gets the printout," Jordan said.

Lester could hear him in the background talking with Maria.

"Is it a large list?" Lester asked

"Different ports, different sailing dates, different days at sea—so many listings," Jordan said.

"Read them to me, if you don't mind."

"Lester, it's Maria. I think I'm in love with you and want to marry you after reading about you online," she said, laughing.

"I hear you are very pretty, Maria, so I would take you up on the marrying part. Small bump in the road though—already married, and we're working on having a baby."

"I remember that—is she taking her temperature and telling you to be ready for love all the time?" Maria asked.

"Yes! How'd you know?"

"Been there. Got a teenaged daughter that way. Husband didn't work out."

"Sorry. Be nice to Jordan. Maybe he's single."

"He is, and I am—uh—will be nice to him. Okay, let me read these differences."

Maria read some forty variances between the two vessels.

"Read that one again, Maria," Lester said.

"The ship is Panamax-qualified but has no schedules requiring the crossing through the Panama Canal," Maria read in a shaky voice.

"Okay, put another cruise ship in and a cargo ship that doesn't have wackos aboard," Lester said and could heard Maria typing and Jordan reading files to her.

"None go through the canal," she said and was pounding on keys again.

There was silence for a while and then a scream from Maria.

"Holy fuck! I just asked how many of our one-hundred and four ships go through the canal. Care to guess how many, Lester?"

"A hundred and four is my guess, and that's my final answer, Maria," Lester said.

"I'm going to ask the computer which ships go through at the same time as yours," Maria said, followed by more key-pounding. "Wow! Wow! Almost all the ships going through are bomb-laden ones. Maybe thirty or forty ships from both sides—some ten going through the old canal—about that same amount sailing through the new bigger canal. Others will be in the two man-made lakes between the canal gates. Others lined up to start through the locks and both sides of the canal. This is horrible."

"Call your people, and I'll call Jim. We don't have much time. I wonder what the ships with jihadists will do that aren't going through the canal? I can guess, but don't want to think about them sinking in deep water."

"Lester, call us later and let me know what's planned," Jordan said.

Lester had some orange juice for breakfast. Quickly, he dug into his suitcase and pulled out a couple of small bottles of vodka. He loaded his breakfast juice with the booze and gulped it down.

The tried-and-true screwdrivers created a warmth in his temples and a numbing effect of the alcohol throughout his body. Now he would call Jim. He dialed his cell phone number. Immediately he got a message from Jim that he was in a meeting with the president. Lester messaged him back.

"Tell the president I know where the Big Bang is going to take place and when."

Lester's phone rang within seconds.

"Lester, it's Jim, and I have you on speaker with the president, the head of the FBI, CIA, NSA, and military liaisons. Go ahead."

"Mr. President and other gentlemen, you all have been following the unfortunate news that a hundred and four ships at sea have Islamic terrorists planted on them. Just a few minutes ago, working in partnership with Interpol agents in Lyon, France, we plugged into the large supercomputer in Bluffdale and found the unifying component that gave us the time and location of the detonation of several of the infected vessels. Tomorrow, about twenty to thirty of these vessels on each side of the canal, all of which house Muslim terrorists, will move to transit the Atlantic and the Pacific sides of the Isthmus of Panama at about midday. We believe the explosions will occur when the maximum numbers of ships are in the locks, both in the old and the new canals. We still don't know about the other ships not going to the canal. Most will be at the canal. We don't know how they are going to set them off, but a good guess is that the bombs will be placed below the waterline to block the canal. All the cruise ships have a husband and wife situation. We don't know their role, but if they are fanatical enough, suicide vests on a crowded deck are certainly possible. They have all had over a year to smuggle C4 and Emulex® onto the ships and hide it. We are all deeply disturbed about this plot, but we have to stop it, or thousands of people will die," Lester said, wondering about the group's reaction to his news.

"Lester, we will be in touch. Thanks so much for your work on this. You may not be aware of this, but ships only go one way at a time because of a narrow cut in the canal. They take turns every six hours. A large collection of small boats will open up two-way traffic, but it doesn't happen often. Tell Maria and Jordan thanks as well. Goodbye," Jim said solemnly.

Lester rarely got scared, but this situation caused him to shiver. His beautiful wife, who might already be pregnant with his first child, was running around the deck. He was on his balcony with his feet propped up against the bottom rail, drinking vodka. He had to prepare for war. How do you do that on a cruise ship? He had to call the captain. *Or should I wait and get instruction from Jim?* He had always received his orders on big crime busts from Jim, so he would wait. He wasn't good at waiting— he never did that well. He would call Jordan.

"Jordan, Lester again. The president knows. I'm waiting to hear back from Jim. What's happening on your side of the pond?'

"Same here. Frankly, I don't know how we're going to proceed. If we send fire teams or commando types, they may go ahead and detonate. Same with the radicals in Australia. What countries send teams? I assume we'll concentrate on the ships in the vicinity of the canal. I will wait on orders as well. All of this is above our pay grades. Lester, call if you get any direction," Jordan said.

Something just occurred to Lester. *I'm not on anyone's payroll to receive orders.*

He wanted to help but was keenly aware—*one little screw-up and the entire ship blows up.* He would go back to waiting.

*****

Nazeem Dastyari took the news of the failure of two of his disciples to kill investigators of his grand plot with anger. He was determined to complete the operation. Dastyari had met with Osama bin Laden first in 2003, a couple of years after the 9/11 attack. Discussions took place on a grand scale attack that would be even more impressive than bringing down the twin towers. Sites all over the world were discussed, including the Eiffel Tower, the United Nations building, the White House, the Sydney Opera House, and the Statue of Liberty.

The bombing must affect the whole world. It had to be horrific with a huge body count and show every nation on earth how much strength was left in the Islamic movement. It would need to be years in the planning to show the patience and determination of an organization much more complex than ever thought before.

The Panama Canal was the perfect choice to accomplish all their goals. Several meetings were held, and in 2010 recruiting started for bright, radical jihadists willing to go to marine academies for four years, and then take jobs on ships that regularly passed through the Panama Canal. They were trained in explosives, combat, and communications at various host countries on their school vacation times. The death of Osama bin Laden in 2011 only served to solidify the plans that were already in force and fully funded. Al Qaeda did lose a lot of the headlines because of ISIS and their terror tactics and public beheadings on TV. Now, the hopes of splintered factions of staunch Al Qaeda members depended on the success of this bold and complex operation. Dastyari had a capable second-in-command at the canal, so if he was taken out, the master plan would proceed unfettered.

Nazeem sat at a table with a dozen Muslim men in his office outside of Sydney. He hoped the next day would shock the whole world and bring Al Qaeda into the prominent position he believed it should enjoy. The men consisted of experts from Iraq and Syria who knew more about remote improvised explosive devices than anyone else on earth. Some were weapons dealers, pilots, ship architects, designers of suicide vests, experienced military men. And strangely enough, there was one welder.

Nazeem asked one man to speak. He was Aafrin Shareef, an expert on ship design and construction.

"Tomorrow, we will bask in the glory of all our work for the past many years. Praise the name of our great teacher, Mohammad. Praise Allah. I wish to tell you how we will bring the ships down to block the canal from both sides. All cruise ships and most cargo ships are required to have a double hull. At first, we didn't know how we were going to blow holes in two hulls to bring down the ships. If we set off explosives at the waterline, the water-tight integrity of several water doors will seal off and it will not sink. Our goal is just to sink the ship a few feet to where the clearance from the bottom of the ship and the floor of the canal meet. In most cases, it's only a few feet.

"We finally looked at what caused most ships to sink. Usually, a breach of the hull that causes free-flowing water does the trick. Between the outer hull and the inner hull, behind the bulkhead in the engine room, a great deal of the fuel is stored. In a few places, there are access panels to the sealed fuel tanks, since they have to be replaced at times. Areas next to these sealed fuel tanks have a small space between them where the outer hull is exposed. At one of the access ports, we have placed sealed Plexiglas C4 explosives. They're designed to magnetically attach to the inner and outer metal hulls, along with communication antennas. These thin wires have been run back through the edges of the outside before being welded and soldered in place. They are then painted and made almost invisible. Signal boosters are placed around the ship. If there is a search for explosives, they will never find them since the access panels have been welded back in place. Our people may be arrested on the ships. It won't matter. They will soon learn that our people on board will not be triggering the blast that will sink the ship. We'll do that from our positions on shore and from other areas. The ships will sink where they do the most damage, either in the locks or blocking the harbors on both sides. Praise Allah!"

Food was brought to the table and the men ate together and mused about the amount of shipping and loss of life that would take place the next day.

Chapter Twelve

Lester sat on his balcony watching the water rush by. How could he be in this tropical paradise setting while somewhere on the ship a bomb waited to be detonated? Possibly more than one. He closed his eyes and tried to sleep, but his mind wouldn't clear. There was a knock on his door.

A few minutes later, Lester was sitting at the captain's conference table surrounded by the two government guys who had ushered him from his room, along with several other people. Strangely enough, Monte and Simone were in attendance. Also sitting around the table were the two government officers masquerading as vacationing couples and some unidentified men who appeared to be commando-types dressed in ill-fitting, cheap suits. They would soon dump the suits and bedeck themselves in tourist garb. There were eight other men and women whom Lester didn't know at the table, but he assumed they were from various government agencies.

A conference phone was placed in the center of the table and all doors were locked, with staff posted at both doors. Captain Polycron pushed the conference button and adjusted the volume so everyone could hear. It was Jim's voice on the line.

"Gentlemen, ladies, my name's Jim Webb with Interpol. Captain Polycron has given me a list of all of you that are present. Some of you have had prior briefing, but for Ms. Simone Visser and Mr. Monte Hendrix, the information you are about to hear is classified. The reason you're at this meeting concerns two people that you directly supervise, Ziya and Salama Moussa. We've information that they may have placed a bomb on your vessel. We have been investigating this for the last few days with the assistance of Mr. Lester McFarlin, a former law enforcement officer in the states, who is at the table with you.

"After a great deal of thought from most all of our security agencies, we have decided to place these people in custody so that a thorough search can be made, and the bomb or bombs defused. All our information says that the planned detonation will be during the voyage through the locks in the Panama Canal or in the shallow harbors to block traffic. There is the risk—a very heavy risk—that they will detonate as soon as they are discovered. Each of you will be given a pocket communicator, so this group knows where they are at all times. Simone, do you know if Ziya is at work?"

"No, sir. Her shift begins at eleven this morning."

"Monte, the status of Salama?"

"Mr. Webb, I believe he and Ziya are at the buffet line having breakfast. He reports to work at ten o'clock this morning," Monte said, perplexed. "I have worked with him for a year. This is bizarre!"

"Do not—repeat—do not approach them, should they be at work when you return. Just wanted you in the loop. We believe there may be as many as one hundred ships with bombs aboard. This will be the first one where we try to take them down. The captain has ordered all personnel out of the engine room, which is the most likely place to sink it. I'm going to ask our arrest team to approach the couple from both sides of the buffet line and then converge on them. If they display any weapons—shoot to kill, but spare any of the passengers in the area. The same goes if they reach for any detonators. Good luck to you. As soon as they are subdued, take the dogs and the bomb specialist guys to the engine room. You are all dismissed," Jim said.

As everyone stood up from the meeting, Lester noticed the two fake vacationing couples had guns in their rear waist bands. The other men in suits had pistols in shoulder holsters. They decided to divide up, enter the buffet area from opposite sides, and converge on the unsuspecting couple. Lester went along to observe from a distance.

The two teams of four did not attempt to conceal themselves. Each group spotted the couple eating breakfast near a door which led to the outside deck. Lester could see from his vantage point that Salama and Ziya had spotted them at some distance. Ziya bolted for the door leading to the outside and disappeared down a gangway leading to decks below. There was no one from the two takedown teams who could go after her and soon they would have their hands full with Salama, who had now pulled a pistol from his front waistband under his shirt. Grabbing an elderly lady as a shield, Salama fired two shots at the team approaching from his right and fired three times at the other four-man team. He was a good shot. All the rounds hit flesh, and two men were down with serious wounds.

Lester ducked behind a serving counter and then slid through a door to the prep area. The door had viewing glass on the top half and large swinging hinges, so they would close on their own. He pulled it open, held it with one hand, and grabbed a large metal serving spatula with the other. Glancing through the glass window, he could see that Salama was dragging the elderly woman he had taken captive a few minutes before—who now was motionless and had apparently had fainted—towards the same doorway. Salama pulled the unconscious woman through the doorway, holding her with his left arm and carrying the pistol in his other hand.

Immediately as he cleared the door, Lester stepped out and slammed the metal spatula edgeways down on the top of his gun hand with all his strength, knocking the gun loose on the floor and cutting a large gash on the top of his adversary's hand. Salama dove for the gun. Lester beat him to it but was only able to slide it further under a big prep table.

Salama had released the woman and was still scrambling to get to the gun. Lester, who outweighed the small man by fifty pounds, crashed down on his back and wrapped his arm around his neck cutting off his oxygen. The smaller man, slick and sweaty, slipped through Lester's arms and rolled under the table and again inched toward the gun.

Lester grabbed a large metal bowl from a table, and with all his strength, hurled it at Salama's head. It knocked him unconscious just long enough for Lester to roll under the table and grab the gun. As Lester put his hand over the butt of the gun, Salama came to, grabbed the gun, and tried to turn the barrel towards Lester. The gun went off twice and missed Lester by inches. Then Lester applied his strength against the smaller man. He gradually edged the barrel next to Salama's temple and pulled the trigger once. The small Muslim man went limp, showering Lester with blood and brain matter.

Two of the government men rushed in the doorway and helped Lester to his feet and searched Salama's body for electronics triggers, detonators, and communication devices. They didn't find anything except another clip for his gun, which Lester confiscated.

Lester put the gun in his waistband, wiped blood from his face and head with a dish towel, ran to the elevators, and took it down to Deck Seven. He assumed that Ziya would go where there would be a large crowd. The elevator opened and immediately he spotted Ziya with her back towards him. She was wearing a wrap-around explosive vest which appeared to be cut-up C4 bricks. He walked slowly behind her and out of her vision. The passengers in front of her were screaming and running for cover. Anyone within fifty feet of her would most likely not survive the concussion that would slam their brains against their skulls, causing instant death. Many people die from the shock wave of an explosion, which is so strong it can break every bone in one's body without leaving a single mark.

Ziya was transfixed—looking straight ahead—almost in a trance. Death would come quickly. She probably thought her reward for martyrdom was merely an instant away. Her right thumb was held above the triggering mechanism—not touching it—but ready.

In one swift motion, Lester grabbed her thumb and broke it with a quick jerk, and then held her hand in check, as his left leg wrapped around the front of her body and trapped her other arm. No more than a millisecond later, he pushed his pistol into the back of her skull with his left hand and fired. The round tore through her skull and sprayed little, pink cauliflower-like pieces of brain towards the huge crowd of terrified passengers. He caught her limp body and held her upright so none of her appendages might set off the bomb. The huge crowd of stunned passengers stopped screaming and stood silent, unable to process what had just happened. He convinced a couple of young men to help with the corpse.

Not knowing if the vest was booby trapped or had a back-up time-delayed fuse, he felt the safest alternative was to cast her overboard. That's what they did. The body didn't immediately explode but a few seconds after it went under and out of sight, the vest detonated. The blast rocked the entire ship and threw up a column of water as tall as the top deck. Other than bathing several passengers on the lower decks, no one was seriously hurt. No one knew what mechanism triggered the blast, but Lester shook a little when he realized that it could have gone off at any minute while he fought with Ziya. He would never understand how a girl that beautiful would want to blow-up hundreds of others and herself. Lester realized she was the first woman he had killed, but probably the most deserving of all the people he had taken down.

One of the government men had died as a result of Salama's gunshots. Three others were being treated by the ship's doctor. The method they used in their attempt to capture Salama was a hurried response to the information that he and his wife were having breakfast in the buffet area. Later, it was determined they should have waited to confront them with no crowd around.

"Lester, you okay?" Jim asked as he finally reached Lester on the phone.

"Yes, but I need a drink."

"If I were there, I'd buy you one."

"You'd probably be asked to buy the ship's drink package first," Lester said lightly. "Have they started the search downstairs yet?"

"Yeah, the bomb guys and the dogs are on their way down to the engine room. You calm down and have that drink before you start down there. You did an amazing job with the two terrorists. Thank you, from me and all the other agencies," Jim said.

"Jim, I think you can see what can go wrong on these takedowns. I pity the guys that will be doing them for the rest of the day and probably tonight," Lester said. There was a certain tiredness in his voice.

His phone rang as soon as he hung up with Jim. It was Debi.

"What the fuck? Did you take down the whole jihadist movement by yourself? Tell me you're okay, baby," Debi said, crying into the phone.

"I'm fine, Debi. Having a drink at the piano bar. Come join me?"

In a matter of minutes, Debi came running to the bar wearing her spa bathrobe. When she flew into Lester and hugged and kissed him, her robe came open and swung to the side, exposing a very lovely bottom for the entire crowd to view. They both bowed when either the kiss or the bare ass got a standing applause from all the people in the area. Debi was still crying and hugging Lester when the captain came by to thank him.

The news of Lester killing two terrorists spread through the ship and eventually to the teams landing on the decks of both cruise ships and cargo ships on both sides of the Panama Canal. As reports came in, no one could find a single ounce of attached explosives in any engine room on any ship.

Chapter Thirteen

Jordan and Maria received the news about the death of the two terrorists aboard the Tropic Seas. Reports were coming in concerning gun battles and explosions from the ships where fire teams went in to remove the Islamic militants. It seemed the cruise ships were the most dangerous because there were husband and wife teams who had been warned by Nazeem that they would be boarded, and in most cases immediately executed because of their part in in the plot. The wives in several circumstances set off their vest prematurely, causing a great deal of ship damage and injury to the commando teams, but very few passengers were injured. Intensive searches still could not uncover a single explosive device.

"Something is missing here, Maria. We believe, beyond a shadow of a doubt, these ships are going to blow up when they go through the canal. We have found no detonators, either electronic or mechanical. We need to go back to Le Havre and question Pierre again. You game?" Jordan asked.

"We're flying, of course? There's a flight tonight. We take it, spend a lovely night there, and question him first thing in the morning. I'll call him and tell him to expect us tomorrow."

Maria dialed Pierre's number and set up the interview. She told him to have all files on all students out for them to examine.

"Do you think we'll find anything?" Jordan asked as he rounded up his paperwork and stuffed them in his briefcase.

"All we can do is try," she said.

After the flight, the couple checked into a hotel close to the waterfront, had dinner, and went back to their room. They showered together, then made love slowly and passionately. They were beginning to get used to the whole routine of being together and being a couple. At some point, the word would be out to both their supervisors, and they would have to be separated, dismissed, or married. They didn't like to think that far into the future. Their romance was fun and exciting, and they were not going to walk away from each other. Sleep came easily, and the next morning, after a quick breakfast, they were sitting across from Pierre Dishongh.

"You asked for all the personnel files on all the students for the last seven years and here they are," Pierre said as he pushed two large stacks of color-coded hanging files toward the two police officers.

"I have to teach a class but will have a break in fifty minutes. As I said before, I heard from all my graduates. One went on for more advanced training and he never got around to telling me where. Have your questions for me during my break." He left his office and walked down the hall to a classroom.

"Let's divide the stacks, take notes on what we find, and try to learn something we didn't already know," Jordan said.

"We could take these back to the hotel and work on them in bed," Maria said with a grin.

"Right. That's when the investigation gets bogged down," Jordan said, smiling and opening the first file.

The files were in chronological order, starting in 2011, when there were no Muslim students. The first ones started in the fall semester of 2012, and they were the most numerous then. Pierre and his staff had made personal notes in their files, chronicling their progress or lack of it in each subject. Besides the curriculum of electronics, diesel engine repair, and general mechanics, the students were taught soldering, welding, metal cutting, ship architecture, and marine plumbing. The marine academy was professional and required proficiency in all subjects to earn a degree and certification. The students were all asked to critique the classes in a common language, and they used English to rate the courses. Generally, they praised the instruction, but several had said they wanted more training in subjects such as welding and ship architecture.

“What are you taking notes on?” Jordan asked Maria.

She showed him the list. “Mainly it is their assessment of subjects where they wanted more instruction. Did you get welding and ship design a lot?” she asked.

“Almost everyone listed those. Do you think they planned to do a lot of welding?” Jordan said.

“Appears it was important. Wonder why?” Maria said. She now had three stacks of files in front of her.

“Why three piles, sweetie?” Jordan asked.

“One for those I haven’t worked yet, one for worked files, and one for dropouts and two-year students.”

“I have a pile for those, too. Do you think Pierre kept track of those? I’m thinking not,” Jordan mused.

“Maybe the two-year associates. See if he made notes of job placement,” Maria said as she pored over the last couple of pages in the associate degree pile. She saw something that made her freeze and stare at the page.

“Jordan—Jordan! Look at this.” She pointed to a note under job placement. This person, Amad bin Sodgi, landed a job with the Panama Canal Authority. It doesn’t say in what capacity, but Pierre wrote ‘ground crew’ at the bottom of the page.”

“Whoa—holy shit! Let’s see if anyone else got a job there.”

“Here’s another one that Pierre marked ‘electric train engineer—Panama Canal Authority,’” Maria said and noticed Jordan dialing his phone.

“Jim, I’m sorry. I know there’s a big time difference there, but we have discovered something of importance.”

“Forget the time deal, what do you have?” Jim asked in a voice that suggested sleep deprivation.

“We started looking at the two-year associates from one academy in France. They accepted jobs working for the Panama Canal Authority in Panama on ground crews. We have found—” Jordan glanced over at Maria who was holding up four fingers—“four, so far, but I’m guessing there are more at other schools. Can you have your teams check them, so we can know how many radicals we will meet on the ground when we get there?" Jordan said. "Put your people on the Canal Authority to pinpoint where these yoyos will be working."

"I didn't know we would be meeting any. My God, what else do these goons have in store for us?" Jim said, more to himself than to Jordan.

"One more thing Jim," Jordan said quickly, so Jim wouldn't hang up before he finished.

"What now?"

"All of the students wanted more welding time. The other non-Muslims didn't request it."

"Why do you think they wanted more welding time?" Jim asked.

"Well, I ain't too smart, but I'm guessing they wanted to weld stuff on the ship. I would look for places where they have welded crap," said Jordan, a bit sarcastically.

"Thanks, I will check all this out."

"One more thing, Jim. One of the graduates went for more advanced training and didn't give Pierre any information on the school, even when he specifically wrote and emailed him. No answer," Lester said. "We'll get his name, but I'm not sure it's important."

Jordan knew that no matter how disturbed Jim was about the new information, he would investigate every piece of new material or give it to someone else to handle.

"I'm going to call Lester. He's the best cop I've ever known, and he wants to be a stupid lawyer. He needs to go back into law enforcement. However, he isn't the prettiest cop in the world—that would be you, Maria," Jordan said, as he leaned over Pierre's desk and kissed her.

"Lester, it's Jordan here."

"I hope you have something. Nothing seems to be making sense."

"Lester, most all of the two-year associates and some of the drop outs went to work for the Panama Canal Authority as members of the grounds crew. Plus, all the Muslim students requested more instruction for welding and ship design," Jordan said, feeling relieved that Lester now had new ammunition. "Additionally, at least one of the graduates went for more training but wouldn't tell the instructor where."

"We would never solve this thing if it wasn't for you and Maria,

Jordan. You have opened two new levels for the investigation. I love you guys. Does Jim know this?"

"Yes! We're in the process of sending him the files on the ones that went to Panama and the one that went for more training. Off the top of your head, Lester, what do you think about this new information?"

"First, they wouldn't put them on ground crews unless they planned to use them. If they have explosives, which I'm sure they do, they can place them on the gates to the canal, put explosives on the bottom of the canal and float them up and attach them with magnets on the vulnerable underneath hulls, or pick up RPGs and blast away at ships trapped between gates in a lock. The welding could be why we can't find explosives in the engine rooms. And my guess on the one that went for more training is that he is building a hydrogen bomb. I wish you guys were here to help us at the canal. I don't think any of us expected to be met with force going through the canal because of so many security forces on the ground."

"They have a giant security force there, but I bet they aren't even on alert yet," Jordan said. "I'm not sure how far away the military base is from the actual canal."

"They will be alert as hell when Jim calls them. Guys, I'm headed to the engine room, and then I'm going to Panama tomorrow, if Jim will sneak me in. I don't know what I can do, but if I wore an island shirt and talked like I was a tourist from Arkansas, at least I'd be on the ground and able to help if needed.

"Lots of sightseers go through there every day. If you guys can, hop on a red-eye so you can be on tour with me. Dress like tourists—you know, shorts, big shirt with flowers and palm trees, and room to hide your guns in your ass crack. Call Jim after I work it out and see if you can join us. I would guess Interpol can go anywhere there is a crime about to interrupt a peaceful country. Good chance we'll all get killed, but hell, that's what makes it exciting. Gotta go." Lester clicked off his phone and was already on Deck Three and asking directions to the engine room. Monte had told him a few minutes before that he would be there looking for something.

*****

Nazeem Dastyari may have been fixated on his sword collection, but his love of guns came in a close second, particularly, if they were automatics. He leaned towards Mac-10s, Mac-11s, or Uzis, but was known to use old American "Tommy guns." All these were illegal in Australia when he bought them, and even more so when the country banned many types of semi-automatic shotguns and hunting rifles. In order to own certain guns in Australia, a license is required. Licenses for machine guns are non-existent, and it would be unlikely Nazeem would qualify for a paint-gun permit.

Dastyari had been following the results of raids and felt good about the suicide vests that were exploding and taking down targets. The entire plan was on automatic now. The people on board were no longer needed. He sent Aafrin Shareef to Panama to observe the final part of the plan. As the ships entered the canal, another plan would go into motion—actually, more than one plan. Many of his followers were with him in the office in front of Chop-Chop Square, all armed and expecting a large force to be there soon. Nazeem saw three American M1A1 Abrams tanks roll up to the front of the parking lot, swivel towards his office, and adjust their big guns towards his office complex. The government had traded their old German Leopard 1s in for a few of these American tanks a few years back. The first rounds fired were Dastyari's anti-tank shells, which he fired at the tanks through the glass of his front windows. Two struck tanks and exploded but did little damage.

All the Muslim militants at the Dastyari compound held automatic weapons at the ready, but none would have the chance to use them. Suddenly, the big 120mm cannons sent depleted uranium rounds into the compound, and then again, and again, until it was a pile of rubble. A team of military men were sent in to see if any reports, computers, hard drives, scraps of paper with writing on them, or any intel that would be helpful could be found. The Muslim followers in the area were rounded up by the hundreds and interviewed. Not much useful information was found since the leaders that knew the plans were buried in the rubble. At least this group would never plot an attack again. The strikes they did design would soon shock the world unless they could be stopped. The Australian government joined the military and began to sort through the small amount of information that was found at the site.

Chapter Fourteen

The engine room looked as though a cocktail party had broken out and too many uninvited guests had arrived. Standing around were ship officers, bomb experts, CIA people in flower-and-palm-tree shirts, and people wearing suits whose place of origin or function were unknown. There was a universal look of confusion.

Lester spotted Monte through the crowd. He was kneeling by a large diesel engine, running his hand around the lower edges near the floor.

"Find anything that looks out of place, Monte?" Lester asked.

"If I knew what I was looking for, it might help," Monte said, standing up and shaking Lester's hand. "Thanks for what you did today. You saved a lot of lives."

"I got lucky. Both of them were dedicated to their mission. Welding—that's what we need to look for. Floors, siding, ceiling—or bulkheads. These guys took extra welding classes and ship architecture. We have a double hull, right?" Lester's eyes were moving like a machine gun over everything he could see. Most of the space was filled with people who were getting in his way.

"Lester, how can you detonate a bomb that is sealed under a weld? Signal won't get through, will it?" Monte said. He was now down on his knees, again pushing people out of the way to search the edges of a massive engine. As he got up, he saw Lester talking to the captain.

"Sir, could you clear these people out for a few minutes? We have information on how to find the bomb but can't see because it's so crowded," Lester said.

"Sure, we'll give you thirty minutes. Don't touch it if you find it. Thanks again for what you did for us today," Captain Polycron said.

"One other thing, Captain. We know a lot of Muslims went to work on ground crews at the canal. I want to go to shore as a tourist, early tomorrow. I know you don't have an excursion to the canal since we were all sailing through without disembarking. Can you put together a phony excursion, and we can include the fake tourists on board as well. We'll need to clear it with Jim Webb, but we need to send undercover people there to stop any kind of attack. Those guys in suits can't go unless they dress the part," Lester said. He watched the captain clear out the personnel from the engine room.

"I'll talk to Jim Webb and let you know," the captain said as he ushered the rest of the people out.

"What now, Lester?" asked Monte.

"If you wanted to sink this ship, where would you place the explosives?" Lester asked.

"Well, you have two hulls to penetrate. The outer hull is under three meters of ship fuel, but if I had a way, I would start there. However, that blast would replace diesel fuel with water. It wouldn't sink. Blow a hole in the inner hull about the same time and then the engine room would fill up and lower the aft part of the ship. When the engine room filled up, the integrity of the ship would be okay for a while, but with that much water internally in the ship, you would inevitably get a list—then capsize—and then have a sinkable vessel," Monte explained.

"I get it, but tell me where to place my C4."

"You would need to get into the fuel tank or attach an explosive device under the hull—you know, like the frogmen did in the movies. Of course, the inner hull needs to be blown at floor level."

"How can I get into the fuel tank?"

"It's almost impossible to get to the fuel tanks on the bottom of the ship, but there are bulkhead sections that can be removed to get to the ones along the side hull. The tanks are sealed and won't leak if you remove the inner hull panels. So, you could take off a panel, attach a bomb on the outer hull, behind the panel for the inner wall. If you welded it back on without blowing yourself up, it would be difficult to tell if it was originally an access panel or a sealed one," Monte said, his voice trailing off, as though he had just had a revelation.

"What kind of fuel does the ship require?"

"We have diesel electric engines, gas turbines, and some gasoline auxiliary engines. The thruster pods are Rolls Royce electric Mermaid thrusters—to be changed over to a different brand call Azipods on the next refitting. But to answer your question about fuel, we carry twelve-hundred tons of diesel oil and six-hundred tons of gasoline. We have all the refrigeration rooms directly lined up with the engine room towards amidships, keeping the massive power for them right next to the freezers. Also, the auxiliary gasoline generators are adjacent to them, ready to save the day in case we lose power. We can't let the food spoil. Our total power for this ship is over a hundred thousand horse power, and we need every bit of it."

"Tell you what, Monte, you start on the port bulkhead, and I'll do the starboard side. Here's a liquid marker. Make an X anyplace that looks like a weird weld. I'll do the same."

Both men walked along opposite bulkheads, using their hands to find irregular patterns along the walls. Part of the surface was blocked by equipment, tubing, and pipes. The access panels all along the bulkhead had machine screws holding them in place with rubber gaskets, to act as watertight O rings. About halfway to the end of the engine room, Lester made a discovery and calmly signaled Monte to come join him. The engine room was still noisy, even though they were docked now and only using generators for electric power and not propulsion.

"What's behind these metal panels?" Lester asked.

"Fuel tanks, grey water, fresh water, and all sorts of liquids. In this area, it is mainly diesel oil. It's rough on the tanks and they do have to be replaced occasionally," Monte said.

"If I happen to find a panel that has both been welded together and has screws in it, what would you say about that?" Lester asked, feeling around the edges of a panel and locating two small wires next to a weld that had been painted over.

"It's not supposed to be welded. How could we get behind that panel?" Monte asked?

"You couldn't, unless you had a cutting torch—and that might cause an explosion of either the charges or the diesel fuel," Lester said, motioning to Monte to place his hands on the hull.

"Well, Lester, I suggest we find us a really brave dude who is good with a cutting torch. And by the way, it ain't me," Monte chuckled, as he nodded while running his hand over the weld and the two soldered wires hidden under several layers of paint.

"Me either. Let's ask for volunteers." Lester placed a huge black X on the panel with his felt-tipped marker, then drew a line pointing to the two communication wires soldered along the weld.

Lester notified the bomb squad and let them know the situation. They had been waiting in the hallway by the engine room and were amazed that Monte and Lester had found what they had searched feverishly for. However, they didn't look too excited when they were told they had to get out their cutting torches.

Lester decided it was time for a shower and a drink. Not necessarily in that order.

*****

"How quickly can the US put together a strike team?" Jim asked a CIA officer on the other end of a frustrating phone conversation.

"I'm not sure we can, without Panama's permission," the officer answered abruptly.

"You do realize that Panama gave up their military in 1990, and the US closed Fort Clayton in the Canal Zone in 1999. Hell, they listed their entire list of weapons on Wikipedia, and it wouldn't scare off a large Boy Scout troop. The entire government owns seven helicopters, none of which is armed with even a BB gun. They supposedly have some sort of national police force of eleven-thousand men, but I really don't think over a half a dozen of them have guns. We need to fly in Marines, Navy SEALs, Green Berets, some kind of force to stop these idiots when our ships enter the canal," Jim said.

"Why don't you just stop the ships from going through until these guys are dealt with?" the officer said.

"If we stay in deep water and there are still explosives aboard, they might sink us in deep water. Sinking in the canal means only the first couple of decks take on water, since the bottom of the canal is only ten to fifteen feet below them. We'll lose the ship in deep water and put the passengers in even more jeopardy. We can't move them to other ships, since they have explosives on them as well. Where can we find enough ships to offload tens of thousands of passengers? If we had a large portion of our naval ships here we could take quite a few, but they are out of the area; and although we're moving them to what might be the theater of battle, we don't think they can get here in time. Our best bet to put shore forces out there is to take out the militants. Now get me some help, or I'm calling the president," Jim said, knowing he could get the CIA in a lot of trouble for dragging their feet.

*****

Despite everything that was going on, Debi informed Lester of the shore excursion planned for the afternoon.

"Yes, Lester, we're going to take the jungle tram here in Costa Rica. We have paid for it, you've killed the bad guys, the explosives have been removed, and it's time for some fun," Debi said, handing him a towel as he stepped out of the shower.

"You know there are still Islamic killers out there waiting to turn us into hamburger meat."

"Let someone else be a hero for a while—we, my dear, will be in the jungle learning about the flora and fauna of the beautiful Costa Rican rainforest. Saddle up—the bus is awaiting our adventure," Debi demanded.

"All right, but if the terrorists jump out of the forest and grab you—I told you so."

Once seated on the bus, Lester held his small backpack in his lap. He had brought Salama's pistol along, just in case there were jungle jumpers. Everyone on the bus seemed relieved to get off the boat, and a few had booked early flights back home.

Lester's phone rang, and he could see it was Jim.

"Lester, we have the tour set for tomorrow. Jordan and Maria are joining you. Where are you now?"

“On a bus going on a rainforest adventure,” Lester said with very little enthusiasm.

“One would think you already had enough adventure in your life,” Jim said, laughing.

Debi grabbed the phone away from Lester. “Jim, can we have a little play time here for God’s sake?”

“Certainly, Debi. Oh, good luck on the baby making.”

“Lester tells you too much. Here he is.” Debi handed the phone back to Lester.

“Listen, Lester, when the men dug through the rubble at Dastyari’s place, they found something disturbing.”

Lester turned the phone toward the window, so Debi couldn’t hear.

“They have some equipment we never believed they would have,” Jim said with concern.

“What is it?”

“Helicopters—a lot of them.”

“Where are they keeping them?”

“Costa Rica!”

Chapter Fifteen

Monte and Simone asked the captain if they could have some time off after everything that had happened. All they wanted was to go to shore and get away from the ship for a while. He agreed and gave them a free excursion to the same jungle tram trip that Lester and Debi had taken. They were on another bus, however, and weren't aware the other couple was there until everyone gathered together for the tram line. Debi spotted Simone and Monte and invited them to sit with them in the green-caged apparatus that would take them 2,000 feet above the jungle and back down. Lester was on the phone and could only wave at them and smile.

"Jim, we have to do something. Do you have assets here in Costa Rica?"

"That would be the CIA, and I have no idea. I'll call and get back to you," Jim said and started talking to someone else as he was hanging up with Lester.

Lester put his phone away and greeted Monte and Simone, who were in the next row of seats in front of them.

"Monte, how would you and Simone like to see a little more of Costa Rica when we get off this thing?"

"Lester! What are you talking about?" Debi asked, angrily shaking a fist at him. "We're here to have fun—and you will have fun—or else," she said with her fist closer to his nose.

"I'm having fun. Can't you tell?" He pointed to an elongated smile on his face placed there only a second before.

A guide was on the tram explaining the varieties of plant and tree species, along with the history of the tram and how it was built in the jungle. She explained the need for steel cables that were attached to some trees leaning inwards to prevent them from falling across the tram and its metal tow lines and frame in the future. They were concealed nicely and required a good eye to even see them. The metal cable car reached its highest point and made a left turn and headed back down. It had gone a couple hundred feet when the quiet of the jungle was interrupted.

"See the macaw!" the guide said loudly, pointing to a bright red parrot-like bird flying high in the trees.

Cameras and cell phones clicked as the huge bird landed on a limb at eye level with the people on the tram. It was a scarlet macaw and was likely the only time most of the jungle visitors would ever witness one in the wild. There would quickly be more excitement.

"Toucan! See the toucan! It just landed in the big fig tree next to the macaw!" the guide yelled.

The toucan's huge bill could be seen and photographed easily through the sparse foliage of the tall trees. For a moment, Lester forgot about a squadron of helicopters primed and fueled for an attack on all the ships going through the canal. He focused briefly on the beautiful birds, noticed the thrill on Debi's face, and then returned to his visions of helicopters dive-bombing ships stuck in locks at the Panama Canal.

"Isn't this great, Lester?" Debi said and hugged him.

The birds finally flew off, and Lester wondered if they were trained to show up while people were descending from the highest point of the tram trip. It was the perfect ending to the jungle voyage. Once they unloaded, there was a souvenir shop blocking the path to the area where lunch was being served. Two T-shirts and a refrigerator magnet later, they were seated for a buffet lunch. Jim Webb timed his call to the moment Lester loaded his first bite of cheesecake in his mouth.

"Lester, the copters are at the Puerto Jimenez Airport, which is at the southern tip of Costa Rica. Too fucking far to drive. Bad road—not enough time. We'll have a van pick you guys up in one hour. It will take you to Chacarita Airport close to the cruise dock. The plane is a six-seater, so all four of you guys will go. You've got to dream up ways to disable these birds. Five of them are there. The others are believed to be at a private airfield close to the Atlantic side. Good luck. Any questions?"

"Is this a time where we can accept or reject the mission?" Lester asked laughing.

"All missions at this point are non-rejectable. Any real questions?"

"Not really a question, but tell your van driver to look out for an auto supply store on the way to the airport. Thanks, Jim. We'll come up with something," Lester said.

"Sounds like you already have some ideas. The van driver is some kind of spook, maybe CIA–maybe NSA—doesn't matter, and he's your pilot. I believe he has some kind of weapon, but you guys need to sneak in and out in a hurry. Don't need a gunfight at the OK Corral. Be careful and trash a bunch of helicopters," Jim said amid phones ringing in the background. "Also, the word is that the pilots and gunners are sleeping nearby. Don't know how many, but most likely they'll be sensitive about you guys fucking with their helicopters."

"That was Jim, wasn't it? So, what does he want you to do now?" Debi asked, exasperated but resigned to Lester continuing as an unpaid lawman.

Lester looked at Debi and smiled, then continued smiling as he addressed Monte and Simone.

"He wants us to go sabotage a bunch of helicopters. You guys game?"

"Can we all get killed doing this thing?" Simone asked

"Of course—what fun would it be if there was no danger?" Lester said.

"Sign us up!" Monte said.

"Do we get to shoot someone this time, dear?" Debi asked.

"Well, we only have one pistol with an extra clip, but if the opportunity arises, I'll certainly let you blast away. Keep in mind—most people throw-up the first time they kill someone. How's your stomach?"

"I assure you if someone is trying to kill me, and I shoot them, it's unlikely I'll barf afterwards. I believe that I will live for that moment," Debi said, as she remembered a couple of shootouts she and Lester had participated in back in the South.

Thirty minutes later, a Ford Explorer pulled up in the front of the

Jungle Tram office. A handsome, dark-haired Latino man wearing a polo shirt and Levis stepped out of the vehicle. He had a slender but muscular build and sported a thin mustache. He introduced himself as Gus Martinez. They all thought he could have played a charismatic leader in an action adventure movie.

Lester took shotgun, and the rest took seats in the second row. Gus took off and headed in the direction of the airport.

"You need to stop at an automotive place first, I understand," Gus said.

"Yes, you know of one on the way to the airport?" Lester asked.

"We'll be there in ten minutes, unless you want to stop and see the crocodiles in the river on the way."

"We saw them out the bus windows on the way here, so we're good," Lester said.

Lester had been sitting next to the window when he saw a bridge crossing a river and happened to look down to see huge alligators lying on the bank of the river. Anyone could stop their cars and walk down to get a closer look since they didn't seem to be fenced in.

After a short time, Gus pulled up in front of a small auto parts store with a sign above it saying "Auto Repuestos Diza." Gus explained that "repuestos" means "parts."

"Here's my idea of stuff to screw up helicopters. Oil filters to make into sound suppressors for the pistol. We'll try to shoot holes in the gas tank, engine, and controls. We don't want excessive noise. I'm thinking windshield wiper fluid would do a number on the fuel for the choppers. If there are any bicycle locking cables, we could tie them at the base of the rotors and lock them in place. Also, we need duct tape and a file. Anything else you see in here will be great," Lester said, as he eyed both FRAM and STP oil filters from a distance and hurried to where they sat on a shelf. He held both brands of spin-type filters in opposite hands.

"Let's get one of each, then write an article in Guns and Ammo magazine expounding on both of their virtues when used as an illegal silencer. Something like, 'Both filters held up well, but in the absence of a decibel measuring device, we would say the FRAM unit kept the sound down better than the STP filter,'" Lester, said chuckling.

When it was time to check out, Gus took over and charged everything to his credit card.

Lester asked, "Is that a CIA Visa card?"

"It just has my name on it, but I could buy a small city with it. It doesn't have a limit," Gus said. "Also, you both know you need an adapter that screws into the filter and also is attached to the barrel of your gun for it to work properly?"

"Fully aware of that, Gus, but we don't have time to order one. So, what we intend to do is to put duct tape on the barrel until the filter fits snugly. If we hold the pistol directly against the body of the helicopter, it shouldn't rocket away from the gun," Lester explained.

"Might work. I wish you had a forty-five instead of the nine-millimeter. But you go to war with the weapons you have," Gus said, smiling broadly. "At least you will have more rounds in your magazines then if you had a forty-five."

"Gus, we're depending on you for the location of the fuel ports and where to shoot for best results," Lester said.

"I tried to qualify for helicopter training once," Monte said. "It was during the time my wife was sick with cancer. I didn't get to finish the course, but I can help you with finding vital parts. Pretty easy since the gas tank and motor is dead center under the main rotator turret for weight distribution purposes. Refueling caps are marked with warning signs, so they vary in location but are easy to find."

"I didn't know about your wife. I'm sorry if she didn't make it," Lester said.

"Thank you, and no, she didn't make it. She was so young, too. I signed on for the ship job as an adventure to get away from everything that happened. Sort of a new start," Monte said.

"Monte, if the adventure starts with you and Simone, then you're off to a good start," Lester said.

"You're sweet," Simone said. She gave Monte a hug.

Gus pointed his SUV toward the coastline and the highway that would take them to the airport. It was a couple hours until dark, which was the way Gus wanted it. He planned to land at Puerto Jimenez airport just as it was getting dark for his plan to have a chance to work.

Gus found his way easily to the Chacarita Airport and parked his vehicle in the grass across from the runway and next to a brand-new King Air 350 twin prop plane.

"Holy shit! You don't mess around when you guys buy an airplane, do you?" Lester said.

"I believe these planes are about six or seven million. Is that right?" Monte asked.

"I think that's about right. I told them what I wanted, and they flew it over to me about a year ago," Gus said. "There are times I 'd like to have a fighter plane. Flew those in Iraq and Afghanistan, but so far my requests have been ignored."

Lester noticed another group of people boarding a King Air 200 a short way off. He yelled at them, and Lance and Holton waved back. Apparently the two computer experts were being pulled back into service because of the Panama raid.

"I'll guess we'll eventually see them back on board," Lester said to Debi as they started up the steps to the plane.

The group boarded and were surprised to find a fully-stocked bar, plenty of snacks, and bottles of Mountain Valley Spring Water from Hot Springs, Arkansas.

Lester and Debi were pleased with his water choices and set some aside while they drank rum and cokes to bolster their bravery for the mission ahead. While the plane was on auto-pilot, Gus came back and explained where the troops would be, his part in the operation, and how they might be able to complete the mission without being killed. There were no promises.

Chapter Sixteen

Jordan and Maria got the clearance to go to Panama City, but not without great resistance from both of their department heads. It took a call from Jim Webb, who let their section chiefs know the two were among the most knowledgeable law enforcement agents in the world concerning the situation at the Panama Canal. Once they got the go-ahead, their offices made reservations on Air France going from Le Havre to Paris, and then set them on a fourteen-hour trip to Central America.

First, they had to go shopping for tropical vacation clothing. It would be their first shopping trip together and a chance to test their budding relationship. They only had a couple of hours to shop since their flight left at 1:00 p.m. from Le Havre airport and then 3:30 p.m. from Charles De Gaulle Airport in Paris. With the time difference being eight hours earlier in Central America, the flight would get them to Panama City at about 10:00 p.m. the same day.

They googled shops in the area and found one called Printemps, which carried both men's and women's sportswear. It didn't take them long to find it.

"I think I'll get a couple pairs of walking shorts, a tropical shirt or two, and sneakers. Sound okay?" Jordan asked Maria nervously. He didn't want to expose his total inability to be comfortable in comfortable clothes.

"Do you think we'll be able to go swimming while we're there? I need a new swimsuit anyway. I'll get tropical—maybe linen blouses, shorts and flip flops. How's that sound?" She was confident with her clothing needs, but hadn't thought everything through.

"Can't do flip-flops. We may have to run, and I don't want you killed over your choice of footwear."

You're right, Jordan—no sandals or flip-flops."

Both headed in different directions but agreed to try on their selections for each other before they bought them.

Maria was first to show off an outfit. Even though she had put on an open-fronted, flimsy beach cover-up, there was no preparing Jordan for the orange micro-bikini beneath it. He gasped when he saw it.

"My god! Won't you get arrested in that thing? I'll say this—you're totally rocking it. I knew you had a great bod—but this—this is amazing."

There was no doubt in Jordan's mind that Maria could be a swimsuit model. She was beautiful, tall, and slender, with great breasts and gorgeous legs. He was beginning to realize how lucky he was to have her in his life. Now, if he could just not screw it up like he had numerous times before in relationships. Historically, he didn't bypass opportunities when they drifted by, but he needed to rein in his lustful ways.

They modeled clothes for each other and came out once with matching colors. They quickly changed out the twin look and selected non-matching outfits.

Their final choices would brand them as tourists in most any country. Pleased with their selections of palm-tree-plastered apparel, they drove the car to the rental agency at the airport, dropped it off, and headed for the terminal. They were shocked when they found first class seats all the way to Panama City were purchased for them. They felt important and wondered what kind of deadly mission warranted this special treatment. It had a Last Supper feeling to it.

*****

The runway lighting could be seen a couple miles out, and although it wasn't completely dark yet, it would be in a matter of minutes. Gus had instructed the entire crew on their individual jobs and how to complete the mission with the least chance of getting shot.

As the plane landed and taxied to the secluded and dark part of the fenced property, the door opened, and the boarding ladder was engaged. The helicopters were there in the dark at the end of the runway. Gus let them out, pulled the ladder back in, and taxied towards the main terminal, which was opened to the elements at both ends. It resembled a World War II metal hangar converted to a terminal, and that's exactly what it was.

Gus deplaned and checked in at the pilot's desk. He paid to have tie-down space and was told to go near the helicopters and tie down there. First, he would gas up and grab a bite to eat. The terminal only had prepared sandwiches and cold drinks and beer. Very few people were around, and at first, he couldn't find a single Muslim pilot. However, after he walked outside the terminal to the street, eating his sandwich and drinking his beer, he spotted two men with dark complexions sitting beneath a palm tree with AK-47s over their laps. Gus slowly walked over to them and tried to strike up a conversation but got a response of head-shaking and "No English."

He decided to move his plane down next to the helicopters. After he taxied there, he put quick release bungees on both wings, then reached into his plane and came out with a M4A1 rifle with a long, thirty-cartridge magazine. It would fire singles, three round bursts, or fully automatic. It was a shorter version of the well-known M16A1 and very popular with pilots. Gus took a position behind the back fuselage of his plane.

Breathing hard, the four-man team hunkered behind the farthest of the five helicopters from the terminal. Monte found the fuel intake, unscrewed the cap, and poured in half of the windshield washer fluid. Lester held the pistol next to the fuselage that everyone hoped housed the gas tank. He started to pull the trigger as he placed the FRAM oil filter directly against the aluminum skin of the aircraft. Debi said, "Not yet," and collected Simone's sweater and Lester's windbreaker, and donated her sweatshirt. She wrapped them around the gun and filter. Only then did Lester pull the trigger.

The gun made more noise than they had hoped for, but it was definitely muted. The Sig Sauer P226 held fifteen rounds, and now eight were left. Lester had used a couple of rounds on the first two terrorists on the ship, and Salama, the former gun owner, had fired five rounds at the government men who tried to arrest him on the ship. Lester had a full magazine in his pocket and eight rounds left in the weapon. He didn't have enough to put five rounds in each helicopter. To be safe, he decided on four in each aircraft, twenty rounds total with three left over.

Gus watched carefully from behind his plane and noted that no one was stirring in the almost-empty terminal. He had seen only three people working there when he walked through to the street side. The gunshot sounded like a muffled firecracker at his position and probably less to the two armed guards out front. Someone in the terminal was playing Latino music but only at a low volume.

Lester placed three more rounds in the chopper, one towards the motor, one behind the control panel in front, and one in the rotor assembly at the rear of the aircraft. This was repeated on the next two helicopters. The filter was then changed to the STP model. It seemed quieter than the FRAM, but then everyone's ears were compromised. They worked in teams of two. Monte and Simone took care of finding the fuel caps and putting in the soapy fluid, Lester and Debi picked out the spots to fire a round into the plane, and Gus guarded them from his plane with the M4.

They reached the fifth helicopter and found they had used up most of the washer fluid. Gus yelled at them to hurry up because the guards had come out of the terminal and were looking around.

"Look, we need more fluid for the gas tank. I suggest we all pee in the plastic jug and stuff our under wear down in the neck of the gas tank," Lester said as he started cutting the top from the plastic jug. He and Monte went first but it wasn't easy to urinate in such a tense situation. The girls went next with the men holding them steady while they helped fill the jug to about half full. When it was Debi's turn, she reached in her shorts and pulled out a small oblong box and removed a flat plastic object about five inches long. As she was peeing into the jug, being steadied by Lester and Simone, she stuck the object into her stream of urine.

"Is that what I think it is?" Simone asked.

"Got to see if Lester's powerful sperm hit pay dirt," Debi said, laughing.

"You are unbelievable," Lester said, as he watched her insert the pregnancy test stick into the shorts she was holding in her hand. "I don't think you would be far enough along to detect it if you are pregnant, would you?"

"Thought I'd try anyway, dear," she said, smiling. "We started trying a week or two before this trip, as you recall, and we only need a few days before a missed period to detect it."

It was a strange sight to see everyone holding their shorts in their hands, naked from the waist down, as they handed over underwear to be stuffed down the neck of the fuel intake after the now-smelly fluid was poured down the tank.

Before anyone could get their shorts back on or place more pistol rounds in the helicopter, bullets started buzzing over their heads. Then they heard the reports from firearms coming from outside the terminal. Everyone hit the ground, except for Lester, who quickly ran between his shooting placement zones and fired off the four rounds into the fifth helicopter. More bullets flew overhead. Shorts in hand and bare rears glistening in the moonlight, all four ran towards Gus's plane. Three times they had to fall to the ground to avoid incoming rounds from the two guards.

"Come to the plane! I'll cover you!" Gus yelled. He then fired off about 20 rounds with the assault rifle towards the shooters.

As the four rose from the ground and covered the distance to the plane, Gus finally realized they were half naked.

"What the fuck?" Gus murmured in shock, seeing the collection of penises and vaginas headed to his plane.

"No time to explain," Lester said. "We need to take these two guys out before we take off."

"I'll get the plane ready. Should I take off my clothes first?" Gus quipped.

"No need at this time. We'll let you know when. Can I use your M4 and the extra clip?"

Gus took the steps into the King Air with the bare asses of Simone and Monte right behind him. Gus made the preparations for takeoff as his two passengers pulled on their shorts. Lester and Debi crawled under the airplane's fuselage. The two could see the guards in a prone position. Debi pulled the homemade STP silencer off the end of her pistol but left the tape on the barrel.

"How many rounds are left?" she asked.

Lester only took seconds to answer as rounds started coming in around them, hitting the grass and throwing up tuffs of grass. A few were striking the rear of the fuselage, but so far hadn't struck anything critical.

"You have three rounds from the Sig—I am guessing that I have about ten left in this M4 magazine and thirty in the extra one Gus gave me. They're about fifty or sixty yards out. If you get a shot, aim at the head and just move down from there a little bit. I'm going to see if I can get them to stand up and retreat. Once I get them up, you take aim and fire two taps at a time."

Just then dirt flew all around them and Lester noticed the look on Debi's face again—no fear, just anger. She did not like being fired upon.

"Get ready, sweetie. I'm going to finish this mag and start on the other. I think they'll get up to run for cover."

"I'm ready!" Debi said.

Lester took aim at the prone objects that appeared as mere bumps in the grass through the sights on his weapon. They were illuminated only by moonlight, since they were too far from the terminal to be caught in the reflection of its lighting. He began to fire in bursts of three rounds with each trigger pull. He could see them squirming around, but they didn't get up. Lester slammed in a fresh magazine, while the two guards took the opportunity to open fire again. A bullet grazed Lester's shoulder and cut into the dirt next to Debi's arm, leaving a small gash in her forearm. Lester looked over at her, and from the expression on her face, she might rip out their guts with her bare hands.

"You ready, my dear?" Lester asked.

"You have no idea!"

Lester took aim and fired ten fully-automatic rounds right into the bump where they lay. He could see they were moving, so ten more rounds hit right on top of them. He heard them scream and both stood up. Before Lester could motion to her, Debi double-tapped both figures, only getting one round out on the second tap as she was out of ammo. The one on the right fell and the one on the left staggered. Lester put his final ten rounds in him.

Gus greeted them as they got on the plane, still holding their shorts in hand. The rest of the crew clapped as Lester and Debi fought to get their shorts back on against the force of the plane moving down the runway to gain position to take off. Both were bleeding from grazed bullets, so Simone and Monte grabbed a first aid kit to patch them up.

"Good shooting, babe! You took down the one on the right and hit the one on the left. If you had been using a forty-five APC, both would have gone down. But you did all right. Proud of you," Lester said. He hugged her and gave her a quick kiss on the lips.

Gus gunned the King Air, and it lifted up over the airfield, where two terrorists lay dead in the grass next to the tarmac. They could see a group of cars and trucks pulling up at the terminal. Some of the men fired their weapons at the King Air as it left the airport but were too far away to do any damage.

This skirmish was just a small prelude to what they all would face the next day in Panama.

The cruise ship had already sailed, so Gus had no choice but to take them to Panama City to stay in a hotel. Lester's phone rang during the flight. It was Jim, who had already talked to Gus. He was pleased with the mission.

"You will meet your counterpart from France tonight at the hotel. Tomorrow will be really rough. Congratulations on a job well done.

"Oh, did you guys really pour piss into the helicopters, then fight off a couple of guards half-naked?" Jim asked, chuckling.

"Where did you hear such a tale?" Lester laughed.

Chapter Seventeen

The foursome from the cruise ship landed at the Tocumen International Airport and then took a van downtown. Gus was not with them, as he had different orders. They were taken to a classy, old hotel called the Bristol in the heart of the banking district. They would later find out why this hotel was chosen. When they arrived, a hotel valet met the van, puzzled that they had no luggage.

"Fella, we're lucky to be here. At one time tonight, we lost our shorts," Lester said, laughing. The hotel valet backed away slowly, giving up on trying to be of assistance.

Once inside, the hotel manager met them and showed them the way to the front desk. When they identified themselves, they were given keys to two rooms and a duffel bag each. All was taken care of by Jim Webb.

"You are to meet your friends from France at 10:30 in the bar. Some food will be prepared for you then," the hotel manager said.

Their rooms were on the third floor, so as they rode the elevator up, everyone opened their duffel bag. On top was a bathroom kit with toothbrushes, combs, makeup for the women, condoms and shaving kits for the men. They also found boxer shorts and briefs for the men and Victoria's Secret panties for the girls. All had shorts and tropical shirts in the right sizes. At the bottom of the duffel was a machine pistol and a small backpack to carry it in. They were all MAC-10s .45 caliber with pullout metal shoulder stocks. He had provided several magazines of 32 rounds each. Lester got extra 9mm rounds for his pistol, and everyone got concealable .45 caliber pistols with extra clips. Lester looked at the small pistol and smiled. He knew they were all giving up almost half the rounds' capacity to have the extra knockdown power. Jim knew him well.

"Crap, how did he do this?' Simone asked.

"We're a gun-loving country," Lester said. "If he had sent MAC-11s, everything would be 9 millimeter, but he knew I liked a little more stoppage in my bullets. However, if you guys set those on auto, it will walk you up to the sky. They are blowback designs and really hard to hold on fully automatic. I recommend you set it on semi, and it will fire as fast as you pull the trigger. Fully-auto means we're being overrun and need to get out of Dodge," Lester said as he zipped up his duffel bag.

"No, Lester. I didn't mean about the guns. I meant how did he get our sizes on all these clothes?" Simone said.

"Don't know about you guys. He knows us well enough to guess, but he probably asked the ship captain about approximate sizes. He's good at what he does—damn good," Lester said.

"A hell of a nice guy, too," Debi added. She suddenly remembered the testing strip and pulled it from the pocket of her shorts as they got off the elevator and stared at it. A smile wrapped around her pretty face. "My God! Holy shit! I'm pregnant!

"Congratulations, sweetheart! We're going to be parents!" Lester hugged and kissed her, then helped her wipe the tears from her face. He didn't say it, but was thinking he no longer had to have sex because of the results of a thermometer reading or a timetable set by an obsessed partner. He knew she would be just as fanatical as a new mother, and he felt that was a good thing.

Simone hugged her, as did Monte.

They noticed their rooms were adjoining and Lester had to comment.

"Oh, no! Listen, you guys, Debi is a screamer, so I hope she won't affect your sleep," Lester said and felt a blow to his ribs from Debi.

"Simone moans, but you probably won't hear it unless you hold a glass to the wall," Monte said, laughing.

"You know that suggests you've done that in the past?" Lester said.

"Heck, yeah!" Monte said.

Lester opened the door to their room, and Debi rushed past him to the bathroom.

"I have another test kit. Let's see if we get the same reading," Debi said excitedly. She pulled her shorts down and ripped the tester out of the box. She was using a Clearblue model because it actually displays the results in words.

"When was your last period?" Lester asked.

When confronted with issues in his life, Lester would research them until he exhausted all the reading and online sources possible. Debi would tell him he knew way more about pregnancy than was necessary.

"It was about two weeks ago. It's been enough time, Lester."

"You're right. The levels of Human Chorionic Gonadotrophin would be measurable by now."

"Quit it, Lester. I don't want the science—just a baby, please."

She held out the tester, so Lester could read it as well. A blue digital light blinked in three little windows for about three minutes and then abruptly stopped. It flashed the word—Pregnant.

"I'm a happy guy," Lester said.

"And I'm a happy girl," Debi said, trying to hold back tears again.

Lester pushed her beautiful long, black hair from her eyes and held her. "I love you, and I know you'll be the best mother in the world. Your mother will be the best grandmother. And your dad and my dad will be awesome grandfathers. This will be one lucky baby."

After a quick shower and change of clothes, all four headed down to the bar to meet the couple from Europe. Jordan and Maria stood up as the group entered the bar area and greeted everyone. Introductions were made, and Lester had to comment.

"Jordan, I don't see how you get any work done with this gorgeous lady next to you."

"Thank you for the compliment, Lester, but you aren't too bad looking yourself," Maria said.

"My God! Simone, Debi, and Maria—all could be on the cover of Sports Illustrated," Jordan said.

"Look, I haven't yet seen Maria's naked behind, but I can assure that both Debi and Simone are sporting some really fine bottoms," Monte said. "You see, we work certain missions naked—it really confuses the enemy."

"I'm sure you'll get around to explaining all that," Maria said.

"Later, after a few drinks," Lester grinned. "Oh, and Debi just found out that she's pregnant."

There were rounds of congratulations for her, and Lester and Debi explained to everyone they had tested for the second time.

The restaurant was empty at the late hour, but a large table was set with salad and bread. A man in a suit who looked American seated them at their table and told them they had the choice of spiny lobster tails or New York Strip steaks. He took their orders and a pretty bar server asked about drinks during the meal and took those orders.

As they were settling in, a US Navy officer dressed in a formal white uniform approached the table. He was flanked by two men in suits. He pulled out a chair and barked at one of the men in suits to get him a steak, rare, and a Jack Daniels on the rocks.

The naval officer looked the part, probably in his mid-fifties, close-cut hair and silver around the temples. He was stocky but not fat and average height of about five-nine. His expression as he looked around the table said, "These are sissies who will only run away when the first shot is fired." He didn't think that about Lester, but wrote off everyone else. A folder was placed in front of him, and he flipped pages while the table went silent. His opinion was quickly changing as he read. The others at the table knew they were being judged.

"Quite a record from your time as a lawman in the South, Lester, and two good takedowns on the ship and one hand-to-hand in Niagara. Debi, you took down one at the airfield—wounded another. Monte and Simone, both did well on the mission, showing where to place the rounds into the helicopters. Jordan and Maria, you have really helped us put this thing together and almost got killed in the process. All of you are quite remarkable." He had reassessed his "sissy" thoughts.

"Tomorrow will be the moment of truth. There's a reason you are at this particular hotel. The man who helped design the placement of explosives on the ships is a naval architect by the name of Aafrin Shareef. We discovered he was staying here. We sent in a SEAL team to capture him alive, which was successful. He is being held on the lower level of this hotel and is being interrogated as I speak. We are out of time. He must talk. Thousands of lives are at stake. As soon as he does—and he will—we can finalize our countermeasures.

"Currently many naval vessels are headed to both sides of the canal from the US and other countries, but most won't make it in time. The Navy can't take all the cruise passengers, and there is a fear that explosives will take down ships in deep water. We need as many as possible in the canal locks, so they will only sink a few feet if sabotaged. For now, let's enjoy our meal. Oh, I'm Frank Hearnsberger, Rear Admiral and Commander of the Pacific Fleet." Only then did he shake hands with everyone at the table.

*****

His first degree in Naval Architecture was obtained from Massachusetts Institute of Technology, then on to Southampton Institute for a master's degree. Finally, Aafrin Shareef obtained his doctorate from Florida Atlantic University, where he also taught on the staff for five years. This was an impressive educational feat, given that he was born to poor farmers in Mosul, Iraq and saw his parents killed by a round from a US tank in 2003. Relatives in Boston brought him to the states and put him in school. Later, his much younger sister would be educated in London: an education that was paid for by relatives in England.

Aafrin's brilliant mind helped him overcome cultural and language barriers. He graduated at the top of his high school class and was awarded a scholarship to MIT. Afterwards, he got scholarships and grants for the rest of his education. His personal life consisted of occasional visits by hookers and short relationships with strippers and barmaids. Women were just for pleasure—like a bowl of ice cream or a good massage.

He did some work alongside Joe Farcus, the famous naval architect for Carnival Cruise Lines, and then he hopped over to JMS

Naval Architects for two years. Next, he moved to London and worked directly for the Royal Institution of Naval Architects, where he took clients from all over the world. It was there that Dastyari contacted him and offered twice his going rate to help in their cause. He quickly made it his cause as well.

Now he was naked and lying on a small cot with a wet towel over his face. A pitcher of water was being poured over his face. Aafrin was terrified of drowning, and his captors were well aware of his fears. They hoped it would just be a matter of time before the waterboarding broke him and made him give up the location of all the explosives hidden on the ships and around the canal locks. If the waterboarding failed, they had a more powerful method they hoped they wouldn't have to employ.

*****

Lance and Holton sat in front of computer monitors at the NSA center in Bluffdale, Utah. In front of them was the world's biggest, fastest, and most powerful computer on planet Earth. Every ship's position for the 104 infected vessels was pinpointed. The numerous takedowns, the resulting explosions, total crews at risk, and the location of all known jihadists on the ground, on ships, and as crews manning aircraft had been stored in the giant electrical brain.

On several huge screens, which looked like IMAX quality (because they were), all the ships were outlined on both sides of the canal and in the locks. Those showing a green glow were free of explosives and not part of the Islamic terrorists' infiltration. Yellow lighting defined those where the militant Muslims were neutralized but all explosives may not have been found. If any were glowing orange, it meant there were active terrorists still aboard, but they were being engaged by military forces. Red meant a totally hot ship or person that hadn't been boarded or neutralized yet.

These same color codes were applied to personnel on the ground and known aircraft at airfields. There were four Muslim names at the top of the screen in red letters for the missing graduates. The two locations for helicopters were listed in yellow for the five at the airport where Gus's team struck earlier in the night, and the five helicopters near the Atlantic side all glowed bright red. As information came in, such as placement of enemy positions on the ground, they glowed red for the work station given to them from management of the Panama Canal Authority. If information reached them about explosives placed in the Canal Zone, they were to use purple on those areas. No purple lights were on.

"Lance, you know the reason those helicopters are yellow is because of Lester and his team earlier tonight," Holton said as he watched another ship go from red to orange.

"I understand the naval architect who told the extremists where to place the explosives on the ship for maximum effect has been captured in Panama City," Lance said, and began to enter incoming information in his earphones to the computer.

"Once we get all the intel in, we'll will ask the computer to solve for defense of the entire Panama Canal and its personnel. They have asked for size of locks, depth of the water in the pooling area outside of the canal, depth of the two lakes inside the zone, and drafts of all one hundred and four ships. All information on the locks, dimensions, height, weight of the doors to the locks, and the supercomputer was asked to locate the most effective placement of explosions," Holton said and pushed a solve command with existing information. The computer whined a little and placed black X marks on places it determined would be effective for maximum damage. Naval architectural blueprints of all the ships in harm's way were scanned into the computer. The letters APE, for architectural plans entered, was placed on the ships registered with the most current information on the skeletal blueprint of their structure.

No information could be any more important than Aafrin Shareef's testimony concerning the placement and quantity of explosives in those ships. He knew every explosive device and exactly where they were on each of the one hundred and four vessels. He might also know other plans in place. There was so little time left.

Chapter Eighteen

Aafrin resisted for several hours, but the interrogators were relentless. He was not being questioned in the US, and the people conducting the questioning were from a Middle Eastern country ally, where rules could be bent and broken if needed. He would not talk, so a TV screen was placed in front of him. Desperate times called for desperate measures. A direct feed came in from London, which immediately caused Aafrin to yell "No!" at the top of his voice. He knew the men that held them would do exactly what he would have done.

Aafrin's younger sister's image flashed on the screen. Her hijab was pulled off and most of her clothes. She was naked to the waist, exposing a very beautiful, young body. Her breasts were perfectly-shaped, and it was unlikely anyone had seen them since she wasn't married. Her name was Rashida, and Aafrin could see the absolute terror in her eyes. There was no one in the world he cared about more than his little sister.

"Your little sister is very pretty, isn't she, Aafrin?" the interviewer said. "Gorgeous tits!

"In a few seconds, the men holding her will begin to cut off the left tit, then the right—after that—well, I don't think you want to know what we'll do next. She will be dead when we finish, but so will you. We want to know the location of any other explosives on the ships and how they will be detonated. Where are they placed at the canal? What other weapons will they use besides the helicopters?"

Aafrin was watching a horror story unfold in front of his eyes. The man on TV moved a huge knife next to his little sister's left breast and cut it enough for blood to trickle down the side of her breast. The pained look on Aafrin's face let everyone in the room know they just about had him. Rashida screamed and fainted. Aafrin had seen enough.

"Stop it! Stop it! Leave Rashida alone! Put her clothes back on her, and I will tell you what you want."

Aafrin watched as they replaced her bra and top. Then they put her hijab scarf back on. She was conscious now and was sitting in a chair crying, her hands still tied behind her. It was the time all the personnel in the room at the hotel had been waiting for. Several people were on computer terminals ready to relay the information he was about to give up to Bluffdale. From there, it would be relayed to every command center designated for the canal attack.

*****

Admiral Hearnsberger did most of the talking at the table, letting the rest of the people eat their meal and have a few glasses of wine. He took big hunks of his steak and talked as he chewed. Normally, he was an officer who exercised great decorum at the dinner table, but on this occasion, he was obviously excited and periodically allowed pieces of blood-red meat to slip from his mouth. It was as though he were reverting to warrior status. No time for manners—it was time to kill somebody.

He seemed excited that there was a little war going on. He lived for war, even though he said he hated it. He didn't hate it—he loved it. He had trained for it all his life and saw very little action on the Pacific side. All the action was in the Middle East. He had offered up his ships numerous times but was told to stay put.

Admiral Hearnsberger was responsible for North Korea, and he got some excitement there, but it had so far amounted to a lot of gesturing and sword rattling. This attack was real and unconventional, as most wars had been lately. No attack by waves of uniformed soldiers. Those days were over. It was the day of the Improvised Explosive

Device, or IED. It was the day of the small pickup trucks on hit-and-run missions. It was the day when air strikes killed more civilians than the enemy and more than the senior officers wanted to admit—and a time when their very own troops or troops of an ally got blown to bits by the most ludicrous term, "friendly fire."

"Admiral, do you think we can go down where the interrogation is taking place?" Lester asked.

"Only when they break him. They 're using techniques that, quite frankly, I don't want you to know about—I don't want to know either." He wiped his mouth with a cloth napkin and left a red streak. "These are Arabs doing the questioning. They will kill babies if it makes someone talk—hearts of stone," the admiral said, making a face that looked as though he had bitten into a piece of spoiled food.

Maria and Debi were sitting next to each other during the meal, talking quietly. They were becoming fast friends. Debi really admired a single mother who could hold down an Interpol Intel Officer's job and raise a child at the same time. As a speech therapist, she had more predictable hours than someone in police work. She knew that from Lester's former job in Hot Springs.

"It's easier now that she's older and at a boarding school," Maria said. "She is fourteen and living in Paris. I take the train to see her most weekends. It takes less than two hours on the Eurostar, and usually I can get special rates—less than one hundred Euros round trip. Sometimes she takes the train ride home. Trains are a big deal in Europe." Maria brushed back her frizzled blonde hair. "I so wish we had time to get our hair done."

"I'll treat you both at the ship's spa if we live through this trip," Simone said. She had been listening to their conversation from across the table. She pulled on strands of her own shoulder-length blond hair and made a disgusted face. "I need it, too."

"Simone, you're a doll. We accept," Maria said, and Debi nodded and smiled.

One of the admiral's assistants came over and whispered in his ear. The expression on Hearnsberger's face was one of pleasure.

"They have broken him. Let's go downstairs and collect some intel."

*****

"Holton, let's do searches for those four names at the top of the screen since we're caught up on everything else. These guys supposedly went for advanced training. It would be nice to know the reason why," Lance said as he clicked on the first name and didn't wait for his partner to respond.

"All right, but any minute now, that Aafrin guy will talk, and we'll be slammed," Holton said.

The first name in was Fatin Amrani. The computer gave a little whine and then started streaming information. The Gorilla coughed out school information, past travel information, and then nothing. It was as though he had dropped off the face of the earth. Lance asked for home addresses. The computer gladly gave out three addresses; the first was his parent's home in Yemen where he went to visit the first year he was in school in Australia. After that, he spent his summers in Latakia, Syria.

"What's in Latakia—maybe there were girls on the beach or a Muslim Disneyland?" Holton snickered as he typed in the question.

"It's a port and naval base for the Syrians and the Russians. I bet they've got these dudes training for a naval combat mission. All the ships stationed there were listed along with ones that had been decommissioned, which outnumbered the ones that were active. It doesn't appear to be a major port. More like a graveyard," Lance said.

The next name was given to the supercomputer. The name entered was Buhan Dukali, and similar information was spit out. He was from Afghanistan, went home at first, and then spent his summers in Latakia.

"I'm seeing a pattern here, folks," Lance said as he typed in "Ali Reza El-Zein." Before he could click his finger on the keyboard, the emergency screen came on with a loud buzzing noise. They were told to prepare for information from Panama City. But that's not what happened. Instead, information came from the Australian authorities.

On a couple of slivers of paper found at the bombed-out Muslim headquarters, the words "scud missiles operative" were found on two separate occasions.

"Holy batshit! These fuckers are trying to blow up the world!" Holton said. Both men dove into their keyboards and started the search for countries that might sell a group of radical terrorists a couple of medium-range missiles. Launching sites and drone searches could be launched from just about any place on earth by the computer and take in live information on the search.

The screen lit up again with the loud buzzer sound. This time it was information from the hotel in Panama City, Panama.

*****

Aafrin Shareef was allowed to dress, have a bite to eat, and a cup of hot tea. His handcuffs were off. The mess caused by the waterboarding was cleaned up, and he sat in a comfortable arm chair with a room full of people sitting and standing, as they intently tuned into what he was about to say. The interviewer was a linguist from a US agency, most likely CIA.

"Mr. Shareef, I understand you are a naval architect. Is that correct? And please use English, unless you can't find the right words; then in that case I am fluent in Arabic."

"Yes," Aafrin said calmly in English.

"As we understand it, when it was decided by Mr. Dastyari to place explosives inside certain cruise and cargo ships, you were consulted as to where those charges would be most effectively placed," the man asked in a gentle voice.

"Yes."

"Let us start with cruise ships. Please tell us the places where the explosives were placed."

"As you are aware now, they were placed under welded panels in the boiler rooms so both hulls would be penetrated. In the bow of the ship, powerful shaped charges were placed under fire extinguishers, which were mounted on the port and starboard hulls. The charges were shaped so they would penetrate both hulls," Aafrin said without emotion.

"Were explosives placed anywhere else on the ship?"

"Yes."

"Please tell us where."

"Lifeboats and tenders," Aafrin said.

The crowd around him gasped. Someone in the audience said, "No fucking way!"

"Rear hull under a metal box marked 'auxiliary electrical panel. Do not remove.'"

"What kind of explosive device?"

"A small shaped charge meant to compromise the hull below the waterline."

"Aafrin, were any of these charges booby trapped or set to go off if they were tampered with?"

"Not the stern or life boat charges. All of these have cell phone detonators with antennas, with a range of a few miles or from anywhere if you call the right number. There are bow charges, and they will detonate if they are removed."

Flurries of phone calls were being made, computer laptops were blasting information to Bluffdale, and the giant supercomputer there was going nuts. Holton and Lance tried to keep up.

"How do we get around the booby trap?"

"I suggest a bomb expert. The back of the fire extinguisher is bolted to the inner hull. Once the bolts are removed, the charge and wiring will be visible. A series of wires are attached: two reds, two greens, two blues, and a black ground wire. Cut one of the red wires, but only the one going directly to the cell phone. Cut anything else and it blows," Aafrin said, acting a little relieved to be able to share this information.

Phones, laptops, and sat phones warmed up again. Bomb experts were on their way to nearby ships. Many of the experts were at local airports awaiting orders. Helicopters would be shuttling that night and all the next day. They all knew the terrorists could use their phones at any time to set off these explosives before they were removed, or even worse, while they were in the process of dismantling them. Everyone knew it would be almost impossible to remove all the devices from over a hundred ships and thousands of lifeboats.

"Can we take a short break? I have an emergency phone call," the interviewer said.

Chapter Nineteen

Once the interviewer, an army intelligence officer named Captain Sweeny, got off the phone, he walked with the admiral and a couple of men in suits to the corner of the room. His mode was somber when he addressed the crowd again.

"Bluffdale has informed us that the Islamic terrorists may have some scud missiles."

"What the fuck?" Jordan said, loud enough for the whole room to hear him. "Do we know where they are?" How many do they have?"

"We guess that they are in an adjoining country—probably hidden in the jungle, with portable launchers. We think two or three at each location. There isn't time, we don't think, to get an anti-missile battery installed in the Canal Zone. We will load a couple of Patriot anti-missile systems on a C-130 tonight. Have it here in the morning and try to get them set up in time. Meanwhile, all our SEAL teams are engaged at the moment getting the bad guys off the ships. We are going to ask some of you here if you will volunteer to help take them out. We will send a munitions expert with you or a CIA operative, but you will most likely face a well-armed battery at night. Come see us after the interrogation for further orders." He then took his place across from Aafrin and restarted his questioning.

"Mr. Shareef, how are the explosives placed on the container ships?"

"Essentially, the same way, except the architecture of the vessel is a little different. Both ship types are double hulled. The cargo ships are thicker steel, so the explosive charge is a little stronger, but the placement will be the same."

"Is there more than one person assigned to the cargo ships?"

"Only one. The married couple arrangement was to allow martyr status for the wife who would wear a suicide vest and kill a lot of passengers on cruise ships."

"Aafrin, how long ago was this attack planned, and who funded it?"

"The idea came up right after 9/11. The US and its allies were out to destroy Al Qaeda, so a huge, well-thought-out plan was put into motion by recruiting and masterminding from a distant base. Dastyari was perfect because he was in Australia and would not be constantly bombed and harassed as were the members in the Middle East.

"Osama bin Laden's seven-million-dollar-a-year-allowance stopped coming five or six years before the 2001 attack on the US. But he had several million dollars available to him at any given time. Less money came in later on, but his funding paid for numerous weapons for the Panama Canal attack, including the funding for the education of all the students at the marine academies all over the world. It was an extension of the pilot training done for the 9/11 attack. Every aspect of the attack had been completely funded before Osama was killed."

Lester said to Debi, "Honey, are you ready to go in the jungle and get shot at?"

"Hell, no, but I will if you will."

"Jordan, you ready to take your girlfriend into the jungle?"

"No, but I'll go if we have to."

"Monte, are you and Simone ready for some jungle love and a fun adventure?"

"Lester, it has been nothing but danger since we met you guys. Is it like this back in Arkansas?" Monte asked.

"Yes, only worser."

"Is 'worser' a real word?" Simone asked.

"In Arkansas they probably use it in spelling bees," Lester said.

"Aafrin, did you know about the scuds?" Captain Sweeny asked.

"Yes. I was present when they were being discussed, but I don't know a lot of detail. I know they had at least six of them from either Iran, Syria, or Russia. I think they even talked to North Korea. They are on mobile launchers, so I don't know exactly where they are. I heard them say placement will be one hundred miles on each side of the canal in Panama. They only have a range of one hundred and eighty miles. I do understand they are Class B scuds made in the late 60s, so countries were trying to dump them and get the new Class D that have the built-in visual aiming features. They told me the B types are only accurate to about fifteen hundred feet of the target, so, I doubt they will hit anything they are aiming for. The new D ones are good within fifty feet of the target. I don't think they could afford those, and I doubt anyone would sell them if they came up with the money. The B types were cheap.

Before the interviewer could ask another question, he was stopped because of another call coming in from Bluffdale. He was handed a piece of paper from one of the suits. They talked to each other for a moment, and then Captain Sweeny turned again towards Aafrin.

"I'm going to read you the names of four graduates of marine academies who didn't take jobs but went for supposed additional training. They are Fatin Amrani, Buhan Dukali, Ali Reza El-Zein, and Jarrah Youssef. Tell me everything you know about them."

"I have never met them, but I have heard their names," he said, squirming in his seat.

"Why did they go to Latakia in Syria?"

"They went there—uh—they went to the Port of Latakia for training."

"Don't make me pull it out of you. We can bring your sister back out, you know."

"Submarine training," he said and lowered his head as though he was in pain. This was the big secret he could not tell, or it would mean immediate death when the other jihadists found out.

"This is like the end-of-the-world-type shit!" Admiral Hearnsberger blurted out. "Captain, ask him what kind of submarines and how many."

Aafrin heard him loud and clear and didn't wait for his interviewer.

"Four Russian 'Whiskey Class' diesel-electrics. Cold War German U-Boat-designed subs bought from Russia for a song by bin Laden's people way back in 2009. They have worked on them for over six years to get them running. Stripped down derelict subs for parts. I understand they have pieced together some torpedoes—I don't know how many. Sir, they are really planning to make a statement at the canal. Two of the subs went around the tip of South America to get on the Pacific side of the canal. I have heard Dastyari making them say over and over again on the phone, "One torpedo, one ship," Aafrin said. He slumped in his chair and held his head in his hands.

The crowd was stunned. It was quiet for a moment as everyone tried to take all this in and find ways in their minds of combating all these threats.

The admiral quickly got his staff together and briefed them on how to find these subs. "We'll use all methods to find them and track them. Call all my commanders and captains to start search and destroy. You CIA guys get your teams ready to locate and take down the missiles."

Everything Aafrin said had been piped into Bluffdale. Now the people there wanted to talk to Aafrin directly about the placement of explosives in the locks, how the different explosives would be detonated, and where the ground forces would be hidden at the canal site. They also wanted to know what kind of weapons their enemies would use in the attack. Aafrin was patched into an interviewer at NSA headquarters. The man they chose was Skip Jackson, a former marine officer and veteran of Vietnam and the first Gulf War. He was also an advisor in Iraq and Afghanistan. Skip was now in his early seventies and knew the questions to ask. His questioning would be a live feed to Bluffdale and to Panama City.

*****

The gang of six was asked to get their equipment and assemble in the lobby, prepared to go into the jungle. Rick Summers, a Navy SEAL officer, and veteran of both Iraq and Afghanistan, stood in front of his pitiful commandos. He knew about Lester from the admiral, but the rest were really questionable. He had one Panamanian policeman, who had no combat experience, to go with the group, but needed more fighters desperately. None were available. It was this group or no mission. He was stuck with the worst squad of irregulars he had ever seen, but he noticed they all had good weapons. He bore down hard on them, barking orders and asking questions. He was surprised at their experience.

"Any of you fuck-ups ever been shot at?" To his surprise all of them raised their hands.

"Ever shot anyone?" Lester, Debi, and Jordan raised their hands.

"I'll take it a step further—anyone ever kill another person?" Lester, Debi, and Jordan raised their hands again. Lester looked over at Jordan who answered a non-verbal question. "I was in a couple of shootouts in London—took a few of them out," Jordan said quietly.

"Lester, do you take your wife on a lot of shootouts?" Rick asked, smiling.

"Her mother thinks I look for gun play on every date," Lester said, laughing.

"I expect you guys to be brave mother fuckers on this mission. We'll be in the jungle at night. Starlight binocs and night-vision scopes will be placed on your Mac-10s. You will be issued communication devices, munitions, and explosives. We will have a couple of RPGs with plenty of rounds. One other soldier will be with us. He is a Spanish-speaking Panama police officer. Call him Juan. He's never been shot at and certainly hasn't killed anyone. I hold out hope that he will be helpful at finding the best barbecue and taco place in the vicinity.

"You will wear Kevlar vests and helmets. What else you wear, I don't give a shit. Except for shoes—ladies wear sneakers that will hold up in the jungle—hiking shoes if you have them. Oh, each will have a backpack and canteens—lots of water—you'll need it. You will be hot, scared, and miserable, but you'll have water—that's right -you'll have that going for you.

"In the helicopter, I will show you how to use the RPGs. Try not to shoot down our aircraft during the demonstration. I will show you how to use the mics, the C4 explosives, and for those of you who have never used the MAC-10s, I will demonstrate those. Pay attention or you will fucking die.

"Close range—all of you have pistols and knives. Someone jumps you—pull out that fucking knife and cut their throat, run it through their gut, or between the ribs into their heart. If there are guards posted, we need to take them out without any noise. If you see me point to a guard and then slice across my neck with my finger and point to you—then goddamn cut their throat.

"Nothing goes as planned on a mission. Improvise and stay alive. Everything you've seen in the movies is bullshit. It's chaos. It's crazy. Try to not be dead. These guys are like us and want to live. We act quickly. Never—never hesitate or you will be holding your guts—having a conversation with your guts. It will then be too late. Let's get in the van and catch the helicopter. We have intel on the location of some of the scud portable launchers. Here is an infrared picture taken by the drone that located them. We don't yet have weaponized drones in Panama, they're on the way, but we can't wait on them."

The photograph was of blurry, red human forms, about seven or eight of them next to a tall object partly lit. A truck could be seen in front of the raised object and other vehicles were parked to the side. There were probably other missile launching trucks on site.

"Here is the location on a topo map and this is the road they took in. About two miles up the road is our LZ."

"What's an LZ?" asked Simone.

"Uh . . . maybe a landing zone?" Rick said sarcastically, shaking his head in disgust.

"Sorry, Rick. Do you know what a landing strip is when you're doing a Brazilian wax job?"

"What are you talking about, Simone?" Rick was irritated.

Simone laughed. "The landing strip is a thin strip of public hair, trimmed nicely, that runs right above the vagina. You know—so dumb guys can find their way to the Promised Land," she said.

"From now on, the LZ will be an LS. It certainly will bring happier thoughts," Rick said, chuckling quietly.

On the way to the airport, everyone was putting on flak jackets and helmets. The group wrestled with straps and looked at the strange things in their packs. There were some plastic dough-looking explosives with timer switches on one side. It appeared to be set on one minute, and there was a toggle switch under a safety cover. There were grenades, extra ammo, a utility belt with first-aid pouches, and a combat knife with a sheath.

And there was water. Two huge liter bottles were in the pack, and a canteen fit on the utility belt. The gear was heavy—thirty or forty pounds. Everyone loaded on the big helicopter. Some had seats, and some sat on the floor of the aircraft. It took off and the ones who had earphones could talk and communicate. The others could hear nothing but the rotors.

Lester had ear phones and announced, "I hope no one has pissed in this gas tank." Those who heard him laughed. Jordan and Maria didn't know the story yet.

The flight took about forty-five minutes and landed about a mile below the missile battery, as quietly as possible. Had they been in a Cobra or Apache, there would have been no need for boots on the ground. The helicopter would just hover and blow the place to bits. This helicopter landed, and eight people scrambled off and hunkered down in the tall grass. Rick had explained about the other ways they could die on this mission. Snakes, jaguars, pumas, spiders, scorpions, poisonous plants, and even little, colored frogs would kill you.

They saw the dirt road after a few minutes. Rick took point with Juan in the rear, with Monte and Simone with him to the right of the road. He had all the inexperienced ones to look after.

Lester led Debi, while Maria and Jordan took up the rear on the left.

There was a moon, but clouds were moving in, threatening to obscure it. As they walked along the road with guns at the ready, everyone heard Simone say, "I just don't know what to say to my guts." The entire group almost fell to the ground in muffled laughter. It was indeed the humor they all needed to relax.

Chapter Twenty

The radar and sonar operator, who had just retired a month before from the US Navy, where he had done the same job, could not believe what he was viewing on his screen. He had to report it quickly. It was nighttime, so he couldn't confirm it by line of sight.

"Captain! Captain! Torpedo hot and fast, amidships, take evasive action NOW!"

"Full right rudder! Full speed ahead! Swing her fast!" To everyone on the bridge, the former Navy commander did what had to be done, but a 1200-foot-long behemoth wasn't a ski boat. It did turn enough so that the projectile heading directly for the center of the giant ricocheted off the monstrous hull. A few minutes later, it turned away and the proximity fuse caused the aged torpedo to explode. The ship actually rocked from the concussion wave that followed.

Captain Kirby Petersen had retired from the US Navy twelve years earlier. The conflict in Iraq had put his Perry Class Frigate in the thick of battle. He had sent cruise missiles into downtown Bagdad and targeted attacking aircraft with tomahawk missiles. Now he effectively had a large bathtub from which to fight. No guns, no submarine depth charges—nothing but a wheelhouse filled with radar and sonar screens and a crew of twenty-three seamen armed with Penthouse magazines and iPads.

Maybe he should have fled, but Kirby's next move was to head directly towards the submarine by following the path of the torpedo. His ship was the *MV COSCO Development*, and it had a draft of forty-six feet. If the submarine hadn't begun her dive yet, he might ram it and sink it. If he didn't try, the sub would send more torpedoes until they sent the big vessel to the bottom of the sea. If the submarine captain had sent two deadly torpedoes initially, it would have been over quickly.

Jarrah Youssef had been following the torpedo through the ancient periscope. Suddenly there was a colossal vessel heading right for him. They were at periscope depth. His orders were clear. One torpedo. One ship. He just realized that philosophy would get him killed.

"Dive! Dive! Dive!" Jarrah yelled, and ballast tanks started blowing, but he didn't have much time.

Kirby's ship was doing over 20 knots, which seemed impossible. He could only maintain that speed for a few minutes or he would burn up his engines. Even through the blackness of the night, the experienced captain could feel the presence of the old sub. He had chased them before. His men must have thought he was crazy chasing a streamlined U-boat type with a fat-assed freight humper the size of a small city.

Jarrah didn't think he was crazy. He knew what the cargo captain was doing and admired the maneuver. His submarine was nose down as the huge ship passed over. He felt he was in the clear, then suddenly a horrible scraping sound reverberated at the stern of the submarine. The propellers and rudder had been ripped off. Jarrah's whiskey class submarine wasn't going anywhere. It wasn't going to sink, but he would have to bring it to the surface for repairs.

But there was no one around who could repair an antique. The Russians had reverse-engineered the last models of submarines designed by the Nazis for this type of submarine. They served pretty well at the beginning of the Cold War but fell behind the Americans very quickly. The scud missiles were basically German V-2 rockets with a better engine. The Russians took apart a B-29 that had an emergency landing during WWII and refused to give it back to the Americans. After reverse-engineering it, they built one so closely a duplicate that their model had the same mechanical problems the Army Air Corp had experienced. After a while, the Soviets built their own war machines that began to rival the Americans. They had long abandoned the Whiskey Class submarines.

Kirby knew he had struck the submarine. If he came around and faced the sub from a T-bone perspective, then all he would have to do was wait till it surfaced, head towards it, and crush it. What if the sub's deck guns worked? Kirby knew the submarine came with 57mm rapid fire cannons. The thought of having those shells exploding in his wheelhouse made him respect, even fear the weapon. What if they had a way to move the boat around to face the cargo ship, then fire off more torpedoes while on the surface? The enormous size of the *COSCO Development* might be able to dodge one torpedo but not multiple ones. He got on the sat phone and marine radio and asked to be patched into the nearest naval vessel. He was only a few miles from the Balboa entrance to the Panama Canal on the Atlantic side, so he knew the removal of the Islamic militant from his ship by SEALs meant the Navy couldn't be that far away.

*****

Lester led his group of four along the edge of the road and took steps that were brisk, but soft and soundless. They hadn't planned a great deal for the attack. He and Rick had said such things as, "You take the people on the south of the road and we'll do the north." They had also discussed the element of surprise. Both the road warriors were to file out in the jungle and slowly go through the foliage until both sides were at the edge of the clearing. They would use trees as shields from incoming rounds, while they hid and took down their prey. Jordan and Monte were to toss grenades towards the back side of the missile launcher to clean out the personnel there. Rick kept pointing out that charges needed to be placed on the missile and the launcher. He changed the delayed detonator to ninety seconds, to give them more time to clear the area. If, for some reason, the missile's warhead exploded, nobody would survive unless they were over fifty yards away. Even a missile full of liquid propellant would be hard to escape from during the explosion. Lester and Rick were to fire an RPG at both the upright missile and the launch vehicle. Even though everyone had communication devices, no one explained to the rookies that after the first explosion, everyone would pretty much be deaf. Chaos is a hard thing to visualize or explain, but the entire group was destined to experience it in real time.

They had walked about thirty minutes when they could make out the clearing in the distance. Lester and Rick could see men with flashlights about 150 yards out but couldn't see what they were doing. Lester and Rick moved into the thick jungle, and the rest fell in behind them. The vegetation was mainly big, wet leaves that would slap the person behind them in the face unless it was eased back. It concerned Lester that the trees and plants were not mature and seemed to consist of saplings and young palm trees. There would be very little protection from AK47s.

Rick noticed that there were few trees on his side of the road. He said, "If there are no trees, we will take the prone position and shoot to kill. I'll give the command to fire once everyone gets in place."

The movement through the jungle was very slow, and after another ten minutes, they could see the clearing in more detail through the piles of brush. It appeared to Lester that the open space had been bulldozed recently, and all the cleared brush was pushed to the edge of the clearing. It might have been a good thing, except it was so high the group couldn't see over it. To climb on top of it would give them a great vantage point, but they would give themselves away if branches were snapped on the way up.

"Lester, you and I will carefully climb to the top and hit them with RPGs and grenades. The rest can climb up after us and start shooting," Rick said, as he carefully started his stealthy ascent.

"Safeties off; be ready to join us," Rick said softly and heard several safeties click. He wondered to himself if anyone would have gotten their weapons in a ready mode on their own. He had checked to make sure there was a round in all the chambers, and the guns were set on semiautomatic.

Five minutes later, Lester and Rick had mounted the pile of brush. They could see several men milling round the huge rocket. Two more missiles were in a prone position on portable launchers behind and some distance to the left of the one preparing to launch. Vapor seemed to be forming around the missile. Most of the personnel appeared to be moving to the safety of the cab of the launch truck. Neither Rick nor Lester had ever seen a missile launch, but it appeared it was about to happen. Rick keyed his mic. "Lester, you ready?"

"Yeah, I'll take a shot at the missile if you get the cab of the launcher."

"Roger that." A few seconds later two rockets flew through the night jungle air. One hit the missile but bounced off to the left and exploded at the edge of the clearing south of the road. The other rocket left a red-orange streak of exhaust gases and hit at the back of the truck cab, blowing it off the chaises. Both then tossed grenades where the men were milling around the launch area. The men dove for cover and heard screaming even through the ringing in their ears.

Debi, Maria, and Jordan moved to the top of the brush pile and started shooting at warm red blotches they saw in their scopes. The fire from the burning truck made objects hard to distinguish, so they tried aiming without the scope and using three-round bursts as they were taught. Lester loaded another round in the RPG launcher, but laid it aside to use his MAC-10. He saw two men get up, return fire, and jump behind the missile pad. Four men ran to the right of Rick's position to try to flank him. Rick called on everyone to take them out. Simone and Monte stood up and killed two, and Rick got the others. Rounds were still coming in on both sides, but it was hard to find the targets. Lester saw a muzzle flash under the burning truck. He clicked his weapon on full auto and sprayed under the truck. There was a momentary muffled scream. As he reached for another magazine, a spray of automatic gun fire peppered his team. Debi and Maria had hits on their Kevlar jackets. Jordan and Lester were nicked, both minor shoulder wounds.

"Jordan, did you see the muzzle flash?" Lester asked.

"It was by all that equipment, dead center of the clearing," Jordan said. "Maybe a real machine gun."

"I'm going to light it up," Lester said, and fired a rocket directly into the equipment pile.

Bodies flew into the air, and still more incoming rounds exploded from behind the missile launch pad, and all four of Lester's team threw grenades in that area. More deafening explosions.

Suddenly, fire began to emit from underneath the huge rocket. It became stronger and more powerful.

"Rick, they're launching the mother fucker!" Lester yelled into his mic.

Let's try and shoot it down before it gets much off the pad," Rick replied.

Lester reached for Jordan's pack, which had a couple rounds in it, and found one to shove in the launcher.

"Rick, all these people need to get behind the brush pile if we do hit it—all that fuel could kill us all."

"They need to get off the hill and run like hell—which is exactly what I plan to do," Rick said.

Both men readied their rocket-propelled grenades, as both teams were blasting out of the jungle and down the dirt road.

The reverberation of the big rocket's engine was horrific and the blast from the missile nearly reached the brush pile. The three-story tall rocket lifted of the pad—slowly at first but began to pick up speed.

"Rick, you ready or did you leave with the others?"

"No, like an idiot I'm still here."

"I don't want this fucking thing blowing us up, so give it a minute to get going. How many rounds do you have—I've got two."

"Two," Rick answered.

Lester sent his round after the missile and grazed it but didn't cause it to explode. He watched as Rick's missile went right into the fire from the propellant, and the powerful exhaust turned it away to explode in the jungle. They had two more shots left. Lester and Rick fired at the same time and both hit the missile as it rose several hundred feet in the air. The rocket-propelled grenades exploded on opposite sides of the missile, causing it to change direction and fall south of their position several hundred yards in the jungle. The explosion was unbelievable and knocked Rick and Lester off their perches.

As they recovered, they saw the whole area around the missile launch light up. Sitting on the other side of the clearing and on the dirt road leading away from it, were two more missiles lying flat on launch trucks. Rick grabbed a small pack containing C-4 bricks and scrambled over the brush pile, running toward the trucks, with Lester directly behind him providing cover fire if needed. Lester saw one wounded man moving towards a weapon under one of the trucks and double-tapped his weapon to take him out.

Quickly, the two attached detonators on the C-4 putty on both missiles, set the timers, and turned toward the underbrush. They grabbed their backpacks and guns and ran through the jungle until they met the others on the road. It was only a few moments until the explosions lit up the sky from the last two scud rockets.

Once they were at their pickup, LS, as Rick called it now, they began checking for wounds. Rounds hit Debi's and Maria's Kevlar vests but didn't penetrate. Other than bruises, they were okay. Both Lester and Monte had shallow shoulder wounds but nothing serious. The ladies patched them while they waited to be picked up. Rick had a nicked ear to match the other banged-up ear he got in Iraq. Simone didn't have a scratch, but Monte had a minor head wound and a bullet hole in his helmet. Juan had the worst wound. A round went through his thigh. They stopped the bleeding, but he would need a doctor.

Maria poured some water over her head to cool down as everyone watered up. Rick heard a sound in the distance and grabbed Lester's arm. "It's that other vehicle we left there." It was louder now and coming right for them.

"Into the ditch—guns ready. Anybody got an RPG round left?" Rick asked

'I do!" Juan said and pulled it from his pack.

Lester was sitting right next to him, so he grabbed the round and put it in the launcher, just as the jeep rounded a curve and started shooting automatic weapons. From the ditch, Lester took careful aim, as rounds kicked up the dirt around him. Debi was next to him with her MAC-10 on fully automatic, sending thirty-two rounds into the jeep. Lester pulled the trigger and watched the jeep drive right into the path of the rocket propelled grenade. The whole vehicle was lifted off the ground. The concussion from the blast and the automatic fire from Debi killed all three men aboard.

Everyone was okay, except Rick, who got another nick in his ear.

"What's this thing about ear nicks?" Simone asked.

"Girls think it's sexy," Rick chuckled.

In about twenty minutes, the helicopter picked them up along with the automatic weapons they salvaged from the jeep. The conversation on the helicopter on the way back was constant, even though some didn't have earphones. They were on an after-combat high. Rick said he was proud of his kick-ass warriors and glad that Simone didn't have to talk to her guts.

Chapter Twenty-One

Rick's success with his team may have inadvertently caused the failure of the other scud removal team. As soon as the attack started with the RPGs being directed into the missile launching area, the militants contacted the other scud team some two hundred miles away. They had not yet been attacked. An hour later, when the second team attacked, a full-scale counter attack squad was ready for them and a missile was launched only minutes before they arrived. They also had two more missiles on trucks which were destroyed during the attack. The Islamic terrorists were eventually subdued but at a cost. The attack team lost two in their team and four were seriously wounded. They were flown to Panama City where another died on route. The team destroyed three missile launchers and confiscated a huge number of weapons. Eleven militants were killed and two of their wounded escaped into the jungle.

Ships had never quit going through the canal except during the down time, when the ships reversed direction; if anything, the process was moved into a more rapid process. If ships were going to be blown up, then sinking only a few feet in a canal lock was preferable to sinking to an endless depth and having the ship's lifeboats blow up, full of terrified passengers.

It was about midnight when the Ocean Phantom reached the Miraflores Locks, a set of two chambers accessed from the Pacific side of the canal through the Port of Balboa. Nearby, and south of the locks, was a railroad track that ran parallel to the canal. Suddenly, from the northern sky, they could see a bright object moving through the clouds at tremendous speed. At Mach-5 speed, the scud missile bore down on the canal. Notoriously inaccurate, the scud fell from the sky much like the V-2s did in London during World War II. These missiles gave birth to the scuds, and the fear held the same intensity as it did back then.

At a distance of about a thousand feet from the ship, the giant projectile exploded between an auxiliary track and the cruise ship. The train track was ripped apart, and the concussion wave tore through the ship. Windows were blown out, and the ship crashed against the canal wall, damaging both, but it was in no danger of sinking. The Ocean Phantom was one of the first ships to be totally cleared of stern and bow explosives. Her lifeboats were now also explosive-free. She continued through the locks at Miraflores and then sailed into Miraflores Lake en route to Pedro Miguel locks. She would clear those locks and sail across Gatún Lake and their locks until she reached the Port of Colón and the Caribbean Sea and the Atlantic Ocean.

She would be free except for one formidable obstacle, a refurbished fifty-year-old Cold War submarine piloted by a fanatical Muslim jihadist named Buhan Dukali. He was very unhappy that a ship supposedly sabotaged by his Muslim brothers had escaped with only a few broken windows and a big dent on one side of her hull. Still in relatively shallow water, he laid in wait for the ship to clear the locks. He wanted to sink her in the path of the locks as an obstruction to other commerce. Dukali had hopes he would not meet the same fate as his brother-in-arms Jarrah Youssef. Jarrah had been dead in the water after being struck by a huge cargo ship, when a Navy patrol boat came by to investigate. Jarrah's deck guns opened up on the Navy vessel, hitting it with exploding 57mm shells. The patrol boat's armor held up and one tomahawk was launched from her collection of deadly rockets. It struck at the water line below the conning tower and dealt a killing blow to the old ship. Automatic .50 caliber guns raked the deck and wiped out all the personnel not killed by the explosion. She sunk fast in about one hundred feet of water and would make a nice dive site once the unexploded ordnance was cleared out. One of two submarines on the Pacific side were now neutralized, but both subs on the Atlantic side of the canal were very much operational.

Dukali saw no one in the immediate vicinity except the big cruise ship. It was barely deep enough right outside the Port of Colón to submerge the vessel more than 70 to 80 feet, but it didn't matter because he was going to brazenly take the shot from the surface. Buhan Dukali turned the glorified U-boat to a position that would allow for a shot dead-center of the Ocean Phantom's hull, directly below the piano bar. The Muslims in the submarine could hear decadent music playing. It was the evils of the West and needed to be destroyed. He called for an "all stop" after surfacing and asked for torpedoes to be loaded in the lower two of her six tubes. Just as he was about to give the command to send the mechanical fish toward the cruise ship, he noticed two helicopter gunships, which seemingly came out of nowhere. Each one fired two missiles, and all struck the submarine with a tremendous explosion, lifting it out of the water. There were secondary explosions, most likely caused by the sub's own torpedoes going off.

The two Super Cobra helicopters flew over the top deck of the cruise ship and then circled, looking for more submarines. Two more were left, one on each side of the canal. Hopefully, they would be found and taken out in time.

*****

Lance and Holton hadn't had a break in almost six hours. They left their terminals and entered the NSA canteen. It was not completely stocked since the Bluffdale site wasn't fully staffed yet; however, it still offered an incredible selection of food and drink.

"Holton, do I see lobster and snow crab legs listed on the menu? Maybe they put it there as a joke."

"Test them, dear," Holton said as he spotted river shrimp and Kobe steaks on the digital menu above the front counter.

"Sweetie, would it be possible for me to get a lobster? Is it one of those little tails—rock lobster thingies?" Lance asked, feeling he knew what the answer would be.

"Whole Maine lobster—pound and a half to two pounds—steamed, with corn on the cob and new potatoes—comes with drawn butter. Should I order one for you?" an attractive lady behind the counter asked.

"How much?" Lance asked nervously. He loved lobster, but it always busted his budget when he ordered one.

"All food and drink here are no charge for our associates. Just a perk to keep you from going over to the Russians," she said, laughing.

"I hate the Russians, don't you, Holton?"

"I despise the fuckers!" said Holton.

"Plus, the only other place to eat in Bluffdale is a Dairy Queen about four miles away," the counter girl said.

"If you have ice cream and malts, I don't see the need to go to DQ," Holton said.

"We do have them, with real ice cream," she said.

"I do love the blizzards—maybe every once in a while," Lance said.

"You can go, but security goes with you," she said.

"You must be kidding me!" the men said simultaneously.

"Yep. Top secret site. Even I have top secret clearance," she said. "We have overnight housing here, and our own airport to shuttle people back and forth to their homes and other airports. We don't really want interaction with the locals."

"Is it like a hotel room—the place we stay?" Holton asked.

"Each of you will have a separate cabin. A really real nice cabin."

"We're a couple, so we'll only need one cabin," Lance said.

"I see," said the counter girl, trying to not sound disapproving.

"Okay, we'll take two lobsters and one cabin," Holton said, smiling broadly.

*****

Maria and Jordan couldn't get in the shower quickly enough. There was no fooling around since they needed sleep. They wanted sex, but sleep was the priority since they had to meet in the lobby at 9:00 a.m. It was past 3:00 a.m. now. They dried off and climbed into bed naked. Jordan looked into Maria's eyes before he turned off the bedside lamp.

"Baby, you did a great job tonight. I'm very proud of you. Maybe you belong in the field rather than in Interpol. Wait—I take that back.

I would worry about you being shot at all the time. Forget what I said. You stay safely behind your desk," Jordan said.

"So far, it's been the most exciting time in my life, Jordan, but I know lots of cops, and from what I've learned they rarely get shot at or shoot at anyone else for that matter. I do have a daughter to look after. Oh, if anything happened to me—and you could interpret that to mean I get my ass blown off—my ex would take care of Leslie. Have you seen a picture of her? No, I didn't show you one."

Maria got out of bed and walked to the dresser, where she had laid her purse. He watched her body as she walked away from him and saw how well-proportioned her beautiful buttocks were to her slim waist. Then she turned, and he had full view of her breasts and pubic runway area. He was smiling so broadly that she had to comment.

"What? What are you so happy about?"

"I was just not believing how beautiful and sexy you are. I am so lucky to be with you. I'm also damn glad to be alive."

She opened her billfold and began to flip through a plastic picture holder. Then she found the picture.

"There she is," she said, and pulled a picture from the protective cover and handed it to Jordan.

"This is a picture of you!" Jordan knew it wasn't, but Leslie looked just like her mom, except she had long blonde hair.

"I can't deny she is my daughter. Much more beautiful than me and smarter than I was at fourteen. Boys chase her around Paris, but her father keeps a close eye on her since he lives there now. Even though he's remarried, he has her over a lot and goes by the school to check on her. I go there as often as I can."

"What happened to the marriage?" Jordan asked.

"He met someone at work. Back then, he traveled a lot for the French Government, and she was assigned to him as an assistant. She was gorgeous. I told him it wouldn't work traveling weeks at a time with her. He fell for her and admitted he had had an affair with her. Many French men have mistresses, but don't fall in love with them. I would have forgiven a mistress, but he really fell in love with her. They're married now, and she's pregnant. I don't blame him or her.

Humans are humans. Males are attracted to females, and vice versa. They can stand only so much closeness without touching each other, kissing each other, having sex, then becoming involved. The problem with their relationship was they "liked" each other before they fell in love. I couldn't fight that. If he had gone looking for someone, I would have been more upset. The first time he introduced her and said they would be working together, I knew it would just be a matter of time. We're still very good friends—without benefits of course."

Maria took the picture back from Jordan and laid it on the night stand. As she moved next to him, she felt his erection.

"We shouldn't waste that, you know," Jordan said and slid over and on top of her. She smiled and placed it inside of her.

"What's tomorrow going to be like?" she asked.

"Finding bad guys in the middle of a bunch of good guys," he said.

"Are you a good guy?"

"I'm a guy that likes you a lot."

"I think that's a good start," she said as she moved faster toward an orgasm.

*****

"I can tell they're screwing because their bed hits the wall timed with the thrusts," Debi said.

"Let them have fun. Why aren't we doing the same thing?" Lester asked.

"We will. I'm just so wired up. I find out I'm pregnant, a bullet hits my Kevlar vest, and we get sprayed with bullets from an escaping jeep. Help me calm down. Can I have a glass of wine?" Debi asked.

"You know the answer to that. No alcohol until the baby comes. Lie on your stomach and let me work on your back."

Debi took off her pullover top and both examined the big bruise she had above her left breast. She had a bandage on the right upper arm and another on her right calf. She dropped her sweat pants and laid face down. Lester couldn't resist playfully spanking her naked bottom. He massaged her back very professionally. The community college in Hot Springs had offered a night course in massage therapy a few years back, and Lester had taken advantage of it.

"You're good at that. Feels great. Is there anything you're not good at?" he asked.

"Sky diving. Scares the shit out of me to jump out of a plane."

"Do you know that I've done it before?" Debi asked.

"You and Brad?"

"Just me and a bunch of sorority sisters. We were drunk, of course—did the tandem thing. Cute instructor," she said, feeling good that she had done something Lester hadn't had the courage or stupidity to try.

"I don't think I could get drunk enough to try it." Lester was now sitting on her buttocks and was erect.

"I guess my massage is over?"

Lester didn't say anything but raised her buttocks up and entered her from behind. He wouldn't tell Debi it was a favorite position, since she had told him she liked to look at him while they made love. It seemed tighter and more sensitive from behind, and he loved holding her butt cheeks as he pushed into her. He realized this was the first time they had sex after finding she was pregnant. It was better, much better. In a few minutes, he released in her, knowing that his semen was not going to battle its way to an egg. It wasn't wasted because it had made two tired warriors feel good.

After they finished, Lester called down to the front desk and asked for a wake-up call at 7:30—only four hours away.

Chapter Twenty-Two

Abdulhasan Askari was the leader of the fighting forces at ground zero in the Panama Canal Zone. Most of his forces were either two-year graduates of the marine schools, or drop outs. Most were Sunnis, but a few were Shias, as was Askari. Their religious interpretations of the Quran differed greatly, but no fighters were fiercer than a motivated Shia.

Askari had been under the command of Dastyari in Australia and had been supplied weapons and explosives from headquarters. He had been praised by his superior and now it was up to him to direct the final objective. Even though he had taken a two-year associate degree from a marine school in Australia, he held an undergraduate degree in chemical engineering from the University of New South Wales and a master's degree in computer science from the University of Sydney. He easily qualified for the position of supervisor for computer operations at the Miraflores locks on the Panama Canal.

Most of these Muslim militants went to work in 2014 and had three years to plant explosives, put men in positions where they could do the most harm, and develop a weapons cache any self- respecting Muslim fundamentalist fighter would be proud to dip into at a time of need.

The Muslims would be hard to spot among the Panamanian workers. For the most part, Muslims had darker skin than whites, as did most Panamanians. Askari told all his men that beards would give them away, so they were all clean-shaven. It was difficult to spot them by their clothes, since they all wore the work uniforms of the Canal Zone.

Askari knew about the subs that had been sunk, the removal of all the explosives from some of the ships, and the damaged helicopters. Of course, the six scud missiles being taken out hurt a great deal, but Askari had worried the missiles would take out his men, since the scuds weren't accurately aimed at anything. They were just meant to be a terror weapon, but now they were gone.

He would have to do the best he could. He was the leader now of all the remaining forces, which consisted of six helicopters, two submarines, and fifty armed and well-trained men. Askari also had a secret weapon he was saving until last. He was hoping he didn't have to use it. He also had an escape plan for his family if everything collapsed on him but felt everything was ready for whatever happened during the day. This had been planned for so long and so well. It would stop much of world commerce to the West for a year and let the world know that Al Qaeda was still a force to be reckoned with.

*****

Monte and Simone woke at 6:30 am. First it was Simone who wrapped her long, tanned legs around Monte and squeezed him firmly. He responded by pressing a large erection on her stomach and then slid it down and entered her free hands. It found its way into her through self-direction.

"Went in on its own accord, my dear. Just proof I'm very talented, I'd say," Monte bragged.

"I'm so impressed. We must have collapsed last night. I don't even remember going to bed," Simone said, rubbing her eyes, then grabbing Monte's rear and pulling him hard into her so the penetration would be deeper and more intense. They came quickly, then showered together and went down to the first floor to meet the others for breakfast.

An excellent buffet was set up for all the fake tourists. The room was full of tropical shirts—palm-tree-imprinted shirts that covered the waistline and any guns placed there—and all types of shorts. The ones that bothered Lester were the men whose shorts exposed very white legs, whose feet sported black socks, and then completed their ensemble wearing dress shoes. Lester assumed these people would be shot first, and deservingly so. What did impress him were the beautiful legs of Simone, Debi, and Maria. He stared at them, trying to judge which were the most attractive. Simone's legs were very tan and long. Debi's legs had long been a sight that gave Lester great pleasure and were long, slender, and matched her olive complexion. Maria's were French legs; they were shapely, tan, and made to look so sexy with the tall, casual heels she wore. All the legs were different and wonderful. Lester's roving eye didn't go unnoticed by Debi.

"Put your panting tongue back in your mouth, Lester," Debi said and jabbed him in his ribs.

"I'm sorry, babe, but I was just doing quality control on our troops."

"You're such a pervert. A handsome one, but still a pervert," she said, managing a crooked smile.

Lester knew he wasn't a pervert, but he felt guilty he was so attracted to beautiful women. Since he was very young, he had found it easy to catch them. There were no more chases, no more sexy conversations, no more slipping his hand on their back as he talked to them, and never again would there be an unwrapping of the package when they were alone. He had Debi, a drop-dead gorgeous Greek Goddess, and now he was going to be a father. A damn good one, he told himself. He tried very hard not to stare at Simone's and Maria's legs. They had spotted him looking at their pretty limbs and both just glanced at him and smiled. Women have the strongest weapon. They control sex and pleasure. Always have and always will.

Rick had been placed in charge of all the fake tourists going in today to the visitors center, the museum, and the observation and viewing platform. He was a hell of a soldier, but many doubted his skills as a tour guide. He didn't want to stop and smell the roses, nor would he point out volcanos or give the people information on other landmarks. Just wasn't his style.

"This operation is fly-by-your-ass—don't know where the crazies and Hodgies are and where they are going to attack, but I have word it will be while the ships are coming through. Even though there's a brand-new canal for the big fucking ships, they can still only go one way at a time because of the Culebra Cut. Huge-ass ships can't pass each other in there, so one way at a time.

"Listen up. Every six hours they change directions, but from 10:20 a.m. to 2:00 p.m., no ships will be coming through. If we can find the militants and engage them during that time, the ship will be clear of the locks; then most can be taken out before any ships or passengers will be in harm's way," Rick said, as he ran his hand through his buzzed haircut. His muscles could be seen bulging out of the surf boards and woody cars on his shirt.

"In the two lakes, there will be plenty of ships, but the Navy should be patrolling both Miraflores Lake and Gatún Lake. After 10:30 a.m., the vessels going through the locks will change directions and new ships entering will be sent through the opposite end of the locks. This switching-around procedure means there is no ship traffic through the canal for about three and a half hours. They go from north to south, and then south to north in six-hour shifts, but there is down time to get all the ships coming from the Pacific to the Atlantic, and then the other way around. During a full day, each group of Pacific and Atlantic ships going in each direction gets twelve hours in the canal—in theory, but down time has to be subtracted.

"We have explosives to dismantle and defuse, weapon caches to capture, and bad guys with RPGs and machine guns. Guess what? We only know where a few of them are located. Your weapons are in your backpacks along with your vests and helmets. Inside the museum, there is a movie theater, a good place to put on your vests under your shirts and emerge ready to fight. The movie is about the building of the Panama Canal—hear it's pretty good, but don't think we'll have time to watch much of it. No tits or asses anyway," Rick said, getting a round of laughter.

"I'm going to pass around the intel from NSA, which points out where we think the bad guys will be positioned. Also, it shows us where the explosives might be that our overnight Special Ops people may have missed. They've been at it in all three locations during the night, and they reported that huge amounts of explosives were neutralized, but they felt sure others were still there. Our bomb specialists said that all were set to go off from cell phones."

Lester walked with the group outside the hotel and noticed three big Mercedes tour buses parked by the curb. Rick pointed to the first bus for Lester and his group.

"Lester, I keep putting you at risk. Hope our Special Ops guys took a notch out of their firepower. NSA says five helicopters from the Atlantic side got up, and one of those you sabotaged got off the ground. I'm guessing it's the one you guys pissed in the gas tank of. Super fuel is what you gave 'em. Ha!" Rick said, laughing.

Everyone got on and put their back packs in their laps. Simone and Monte were directly behind them, and Jordan and Maria were directly across the aisle from them.

"Our cruise ship will start through and will be at Miraflores locks at about 2:00 p.m. All the passengers have been told to be somewhere on the ship where rooms or other walls will protect them. No one is to be out in the open, or on any of the top decks. The captain will not be at the wheel since the Canal Authority sends a pilot aboard. Hope we have things under control by then," Monte said.

"Girls, hair and nails on me when it's over. Monte will sneak you on board, won't you, dear?" Simone said.

"You bet ya ass," Monte said.

"Can I get my hair done, too, Simone?" Lester said, laughing.

"How 'bout we dye it blond?"

"Cool! Wait a minute! It's already blond," Lester said, running his hand through his thick hair.

Rick barked out instructions and paired teams so that the non-military participants would take a support position behind SEAL teams and Black-Ops guys, all wearing cheap tropical shirts. The military were given the names of those going with them, but there would only be three teams that had civilians tagging along. Each fire squad had from five to seven people in it. Lester and Debi were paired with a SEAL team leader named Tank. He looked the part. The other three in his team were Buck, Herb, and Liggett.

Rick had a map of the area and there were numerous outbuildings to secure. Some of these were huge, like the visitors building and the main Miraflores control building, located between the two canal locks. Maria, Jordan, Monte, and Simone were split up into two groups with five Navy SEALs each. The SEALs probably didn't want any of the group until Rick explained they all had seen combat—alongside him—and did well. Some of the SEALs were fresh from training and had never been shot at. Now there was respect for those who had.

"Okay! Listen up! You people have your assignments. You will be backed-up by Super Cobras, Blackhawks, and Apaches—some distance away, but should be in the theater soon. Blackhawks first, since they are close. They will take out the known gun emplacements but only after we get started. When you emerge from the movie theater, you will have your gear on and will proceed with your teams to take out and secure your assignments. All non-Muslim personnel should have been notified to stay in the visitors center and take cover. They will be needed later when the ships come through the gates. Notifying them without alerting their Muslim friends has been a bitch. A good chance they will be used as hostages if we don't protect them, and there's a chance they might become collateral damage. These wackos have had a long time to hide weapons and explosives—be careful. Please don't turn this into a Charlie Foxtrot and, for you civilians, that stands for CF or Cluster Fuck. I will be on the visitors observation platform and will coordinate airstrikes and the firefights. Keep miked up. You are now in the hands of your squad leaders," Rick said, and walked to the back of the bus to talk to some other officers.

*****

Holton answered the phone while inputting numbers into the giant behemoth of a computer. Lance leaned in to hear the cell phone conversation between his partner and Lester McFarlin.

"Holton, I'm on a bus on the way to the canal where we are going to engage a bunch of dug-in Jihadists around the Miraflores Locks and Visitors Center. You got some info that will help us? I'm worried about in-place snipers and explosives the Navy SEALs might have missed."

"It's good to hear from you, Lester. Be glad when we're back on the boat choosing between cheesecake or ice cream for dessert. Here's some info you can use. You'll have snipers from the roofs of the visitors center, main depot roof, and the forested area across from the railroad tracks. There are six helicopters that will show themselves at some point. We are still dealing with two submarines, but I believe they're located and hopefully we can take them out. The SEAL teams who went in after dark removed a bunch of C-4 and Emulex® from the hinges on the locks and on a couple of the electric mules which pull on the cables to stabilize the ships as they go through. Should have been more, but they only found three with explosives on them," Holton said, as he handed the phone to Lance.

"Lester, you have to watch out for something. We don't know why, but Askari has rented the tourist train that goes almost the whole forty-eight miles of the length of the canal for the entire day. There is a tunnel a little southwest of the locks. We think the train will come back from Panama City and stop in the tunnel. Above the tunnel, and it's the only one on the line, is inscribed 1909 Cusa 2001 Neosho. It is seven-hundred thirty-six feet long and about twenty feet tall and fifteen feet wide. Apparently, new tracks were laid down in 2001. All of us here think he's hiding something in there. You guys are getting help from the air. Some Columbian and US Blackhawks will get there from our Quasi-base at Tolemaida, Colombia.

"The US doesn't have any real bases in Panama or Central or South America anymore, probably the primary reason the Jihadists decided to attack it. Instead of bases, America keeps small detachments of military forces to combat drug cartels. Also, they're stationed there for Special Ops missions. Apaches and Super Cobras on their way from California—may be late. Hope this helps. Good luck to you guys!" Lance said and handed the phone to Holton to say goodbye to Lester.

"Lester, let those crazy SEALs and jarheads take the lead on this, and you and Debi back them up. Call us if you're on a position and need intel. We're here to be your eyes. Keep your ass down. See you soon," Holton said.

Chapter Twenty-Three

Submarine Warfare

In World War II, the US led the world in submarine-chaser vessels. Most were only 110 feet long and were deployed along the US coastline. Later in the war, a bigger version, a 175-foot craft, came into service. Together these small ships took out around 67 German U-boats in the Pacific theatre alone. The Germans were winning the tonnage war, and so the Americans gained an advantage by building liberty ships faster than the U-boats could sink them. None of these brave little sub-chaser boats are used today.

Instead, all submarines, surface craft, and airplanes use a heat signature detection system called FLIR or Forward Looking Infrared Radar to pick up the locations of other countries' nuclear submarines. The US usually knows the exact location of all of Russia's subs at any given moment, as they most likely know in what waters the US is operating their submarines. It is said they all can be tracked by satellites. It is a comfort to have this knowledge, but by designing location systems to track nuclear subs, a far less sophisticated detection method might have been overlooked. German U-boats ran on electric systems while submerged and diesel engines on the surface. While they lay on the bottom at 150 meters and everything was silent, even the most advanced vessel might just overlook them—a mistake that might be costly. Some countries still use diesel-electric powered submarines, so the US has detection methods to find them if they are moving or not. They use acoustic and magnetic anomaly detection devices, as well as modern radar and sonar. However, if an old U-boat type lay down by a reef and no sound was coming from it---all the detection systems in the world might think it was an unfortunate old wreck sent to the bottom by a storm. This was the hope that Ali Reza El-Zein held in his heart.

*****

Captain Fred Divers paid little attention to the jokes given birth from his last name.

"Dive 'em, Divers!" "Divers-dive-dive-dive, Diver man!" "Do we dive, Divers?" "Are you a diver, Divers?"

His men didn't tease him. It would amount to disrespecting an officer, but his fellow officers knew they would only get stern looks, and many times he laughed along with them. He had brought his nuclear submarine the USS San Diego, a new Virginia Class attack sub with the latest technology available—some available only on his vessel. It was loaded with Tomahawk cruise missiles, fly-by-wire and standard torpedoes. He could support SOF (Special Operations Forces) and lay mines if necessary. His big sub was agile, streamlined, and as modern as was possible. The USS San Diego had a champagne bottle busted on her bow just six months ago. Fred loved his boat and didn't feel bad that he wasn't assigned a "boomer" sub that carried nuclear warheads attached to big missiles with the ability to blow up much of the world.

During World War II, Fred's grandfather flew in a hunter-killer squadron around convoys looking for periscopes making trails in the water. Barney Divers would swoop down and drop depth charges in their path. If he timed it to where the charges would go off before the U-boat dove out of range, he could sink them or drive them to the surface, where he could strafe their decks or release a torpedo of his own, blowing them out of the water.

Barney told his grandson Freddie that he usually ran out of gas before he finished the job. He never understood why his grandson wanted to be, and these were his words, "a goddamn sneaky-ass submarine jockey." Fred understood his disapproval, but his master's degree from Annapolis in Nuclear Physics caused the old man to swell with pride, regardless of the boat his grandson chose to pilot.

Fred Divers looked like the movie star who would be assigned to play his role. He stood six-foot, one inch tall, polished, shined and creased all over. His face was chiseled, with steel gray eyes and cheek bones high enough for him to claim he owned the entire Indian nation. Handsome was an understatement. Since he was the captain of one of the most expensive submarines in the Navy of the richest country in the world, the first place people would look when staring at him would be at his temples to see if there was the mandatory required gray hair. It wasn't there, just well-trimmed, dark brown locks. "Way too young to captain this vessel," many people said after meeting him for the first time.

What people didn't know about Captain Fred Divers was his level of brilliance, and how quickly he had mastered the skills of his profession. He was number one in his class at Annapolis, passed Navy SEAL training and went on every Special Ops gig that he could find. He rescued kidnapped victims in Iraq and Afghanistan. He was awarded the Navy Cross for one harrowing mission where his chopper was shot down in Iraq. He saved several lives on board, taking out over twenty attackers while he sustained numerous gunshot wounds. While licking his wounds, he asked if he could enter submarine training, something he had always planned to do, and the reason for his college major. His experience in combat and possession of a master's degree in nuclear physics allowed him to gain rank quickly—faster than anyone in history who had commanded a nuclear sub. He was only thirty-five.

The USS San Diego found that the Pacific entrance to Balboa harbor and directly out from the entrance to the Miraflores gates were extremely congested. All the big ships were looking for shallow water in case their vessels were blown up by munitions overlooked by the bomb crews. Their deep drafts against a shallow bottom left little room for Fred's submarine to maneuver. Forced to deeper water, a patrol perimeter was set up in waters about 80-to-150-feet deep. All devices on board were turned on to look for an old Whiskey Class Russian sub inspired by the Nazis and spirited into use by Stalin himself. The US sub directed much of its search at the sandy bottoms between coral heads. It was a good plan, but they wouldn't find it there. Ali Reza was much too clever to be found in such an obvious spot.

*****

Submarine battles have been the topic of many movies and books. The truth is that it has only happened twice in the history of the submerged vessels. Once in World War I, a German U-boat took out a British submarine while both were submerged, and in World War II, a British sub took out a U-boat crippled by a noisy diesel engine. The German sub had gone to snorkel depth to replenish the air supply and charge its electric batteries. It dove, but not quickly enough as it switched from diesel to electric, giving the torpedo enough time to find its mark before the evasive maneuver could take place. The German sub was on a mission to take jet engine parts to Japan for their research in designing a new fighter plane. Because the Nazi enigma code had been broken, the British were aware of the mission and went after the U-boat. There are numerous cases of submarines taking on others while on the surface, but underwater, the use of hydrophones, sonar, and other new sophisticated detection systems makes it unlikely they will get in each other's way while submerged. Submarine commanders have many other weapons coming at them from the air to worry about instead of easily detectible submarines.

Ali Reza El-Zein had read every book he could lay his hands on about submarine warfare and felt sure his nemesis aboard the attack submarine had as well. He had just heard the monstrous vessel go right over his U-boat. After searching the waters outside the Port of Balboa for many weeks, he had found what he needed for his sub. It had appeared on his radar screen and was confirmed by his crew who had donned scuba gear and gone down 100 feet to verify the site.

Most coral heads rise from the bottom of the ocean, usually only twenty or thirty feet, and are covered in sponges, sea fans, and colorful varieties of coral. Most are somewhat rounded on top and taper down to sandy valleys between them. A sub lying in the sand might appear to be an old wreck, but a good sub captain would certainly check it out anyway. Ali Reza had found a glory hole. Scooped out much like a banana split bowl was a large opening perfect for dropping a small 270-foot-long sub into, concealing it except for the conning tower and snorkel. Not a real target for sonar and almost impossible to see even in line of sight. It was just a matter of time before the big, stealthy American submarine would come overhead and downstream from the U-boat.

The American sub was longer than the U-boat by 100 feet and fourteen feet wider, not nearly as large as the boomer subs, but not at all tiny. There are no portholes on either ship, so both have to depend on what equipment they have aboard to detect each other. Up close, both vessels' sonar readouts have a baffle or blind spot that requires they move out of a straight line sporadically to clear it.

Ali Reza's equipment was a hodgepodge of retrofitted electronics, and some actually worked, while others only came on if a big wave hit the side of the craft and jarred the needles loose for an infrequent reading. It was a tribute to Ali Reza's genius that anything on the scrap yard boat worked at all.

Ali Reza El-Zein lost his parents in a bomb strike by an Iraqi warplane in 1988 as the Iran-Iraq war was coming to a close. He was passed around to relatives from the age of four until he finished high school at age 15. He was the brightest and most gifted student in his high school. After applying to King Fahd University of Petroleum and Minerals in Saudi Arabia, he was offered a full scholarship to study at the university considered the best in the Middle East. Since only males were accepted at the university, he had no distractions from his studies.

At age 23, Ali Reza became the youngest student to ever earn a PhD in chemical engineering. Teaching wasn't what he wanted to do, but he accepted a position at the university for a while—until the Iraq war dragged on and on. It bothered Ali Reza that Americans had been in Iraq longer than they should and much longer than he could tolerate. It would seem he wouldn't want to defend a country that had killed his parents, but this was larger than two Muslim countries fighting each other; it was Western infidels trampling on sacred soil. He had to intercede.

Ali Reza left the university and joined a group of militants fighting the US and their coalition forces in Iraq. At age 33, he was piloting an antique submarine against the most elite underwater vessel on earth, but he felt he could win. He didn't look the part. He was about five feet, five inches tall, with a stomach that looked like he had swallowed a pillow. He had a beard, but it was short and stubby and didn't appear it would ever bust out and become a majestic, long growth that could be a source of pride. As a grown man, he was the polar opposite of an athlete, but his brain was superior to almost anyone he had ever met, and there was no question of his bravery. He was willing to die and take as many people as possible with him.

*****

The San Diego moved slowly across the bottom of the Balboa's outer harbor area. Captain Divers knew the U-boat was hiding among the coral, and it would be their move first. The bigger attack sub would act as a decoy until Ali Reza fired on them. Fred Divers felt their countermeasures would be comprehensive enough to handle WWII torpedoes. His assumption would soon be tested.

With all the sonar and acoustic devices searching in a 360-degree area, an alarm was sounded when Ali Reza's sub rose from its hiding place in the coral almost directly behind the San Diego. When it had leveled off, a full six torpedoes rushed out two at a time, spaced only by about ten seconds a pair. The nuclear sub spotted them immediately and launched underwater sputter drones which went starboard and port away from the vessel. Three of Ali Reza's acoustic torpedoes followed them. They were designed to veer off in a straight line, move downward, and take the torpedoes into either the bottom or a coral head. It worked perfectly. The big sub was now running silent, so its own props would not attract the incoming torpedoes.

One torpedo was on a heading that would take it dead center of the large conning tower, since the sputter drone sent for this underwater missile malfunctioned and merely floated silently in space. Just seconds before the conning tower was struck, one of the torpedoes on the starboard side of Fred's sub exploded against a nearby coral formation, sending a shock wave that both rocked the conning tower momentarily out of the path of the torpedo. As the conning tower rocked back in place, it struck the torpedo on its long body sending it towards another coral head nearby. The resulting blast sent people flying around in the sub. Divers was knocked to the floor and slammed against the bottom of the chart table.

Ali Reza knew the sub would try to lock on a firing solution for him, so he tried an old trick. Spotting what looked like a Navy cruiser heading in to help, he swung his sub directly underneath the large ship and tried to match its speed. The noise of the cruiser would mask out the sub's diesel engine sounds. This method of almost shadowing a ship to get in a harbor undetected was used a lot in WWII until the sonar started looking for ships that appeared to have drafts of 50 or 60 feet. The term of hiding under ships was called the "tethered goat" maneuver, and Captain Divers and his crew spotted it quickly and set up a firing solution.

"This guy is trying everything he's read in a book or seen in a movie. Set a firing solution for directional fire-by-wire torpedoes. Fire sets of two, each five seconds. Depths of thirty, forty, and fifty feet. Warn Cruiser to stay pointed at us and to be alert for runaway ordnance," Divers said, and watched his sonar screen as the six big fish blew out of the tubes. Now it was a video game for the San Diego. The controllers used joy sticks to counteract anything the U-boat might do.

Ali Reza headed his boat towards the surface as fast as possible. If the torpedoes weren't "smart" ones, he would be okay. If they were, he didn't stand a chance. As he watched his screen, he saw the jerky motion of the torpedoes moving and correcting as he tried to maneuver his craft out of their direction. He only had time to empty his six bow tubes before the San Diego's modern torpedoes slammed into him. The boat lifted out of the body of water, exploded, caught on fire, then sank in about eighty feet of water.

Six more torpedoes were headed toward the San Diego. "Six fish! Hot and heavy! Countermeasures now!" Divers fired six intercept torpedoes which had been loaded as soon as the one that brought the U-boat under were fired. Fred had guessed these latest rounds would be proximity torpedoes and would go off when the timing device triggered it. Again, five of these intercepts worked and destroyed their targets, but the sixth just grazed the old submarine underwater rocket. It was still on course and was aimed about 20 feet above the conning tower—and that's where it exploded.

The snorkel, periscope, and antennas were ripped off. It took a while for the crew to gain access to the conning tower once they surfaced. They worked on it from both sides, having come up through the deck hatches. Finally, it was freed, but all the equipment was unusable. Captain Divers assessed the damage and received orders to go to the nearest submarine base for repairs. The San Diego cost $3 billion to build, and it was almost done-in by an old sub designed about 70 years ago and purchased mostly for scrap.

"To the crew, listen up! It's the captain speaking. We are lucky to be alive. If it was not for your brave actions, we would be in an untimely watery grave. We met a worthy opponent who pushed us to our limits. We discovered that we have flaws in our systems that need to be corrected. Stopping five out of six torpedoes means we have work to do. We'll go in for repairs, and you men will get a little R&R. Thanks to all of you. Captain out."

Chapter Twenty-Four

The forces commanded by Abdulhasan Askari were in position, but they didn't have the information their leader possessed. Askari now knew about the three submarines that were taken out, yet took great pleasure in hearing Ali Reza had damaged a US nuclear sub before being killed. Six helicopters were on their way; five were Vietnam-era Bell UH-1 Hueys with M-60 machine guns mounted front and back on the sides of the aircraft. Four other helicopters sat in a field in Costa Rica riddled with bullet holes along and with gas tanks loaded with soap. He was in communication with his troops but wouldn't tell them they had lost most of the explosives so carefully placed during the past few years. The SEAL team had come in, dismantled the explosives on the locks, quietly killed several guards, and destroyed two hidden machine gun emplacements. They left without introducing themselves. Even though the other locks were not so well-guarded, SEAL teams also took out explosives on all the other locks. They would be back.

A large group of what appeared to be tourists had gone into the film theater, which was the common starting place for the tour each day. The lookouts for Askari did notice that there were mostly men and only a few women, but didn't report it as unusual. Some of the women were either FBI or undercover ATF agents who had posed as tourists on the Tropic Queen, along with Debi, Maria, and Simone. The movie about the construction of the Panama Canal came on automatically, and the lights were dimmed in the theater.

While the movie was still playing in the background, Rick turned up the lights and had one of his men go into the theater control room and turn down the sound.

"In the lobby are several cartons which we had delivered this morning. They are marked 'Display items,' but they are our larger weapons—machine guns, RPGs, etc.," Rick said, as he gestured to a few of his men to retrieve them.

"The US forces will be using FGM-Javelins, and our Panamanian police forces will use Russian RPGs. May be a few of those left for other members of our group. The Javelins require a lot of training since they are infrared lock-on and 'fire and forget' guided weapons. RPGs are monkey weapons—aim and pull the trigger.

"I have given each fire squad an objective. I will work my way up to the fourth observation platform to oversee everything. Expect heavy fire from the big lock control building that sits on an island between the two canals. Our intel has identified it as the headquarters for Abdulhasan Askari. It appears that all the outbuildings are occupied. All workers should be treated as Jihadists. If you capture men, use nylon ties on hands and feet and leave them for interrogation later. Each fire team and frog team should have a medic. We will medivac the wounded as soon as possible.

"Some of you might not be coming back. Any civilians who are having second thoughts and don't want to go can stay here in the museum. Let's stop a minute from putting on our gear and bow your heads. Pray with me.

"Heavenly father, please place your mighty hands over these soldiers to protect them as they go into battle. I thank you for your gift of eternal life. I ask for your divine protection for my nation, my army, my family, my soldiers, and myself. I appeal to your divine justice to grant us victory. I ask this in the name of our heavenly father. Amen."

Several "amens" were muttered by the group, and Debi looked at Lester without smiling.

"Well, if that doesn't scare the shit out of you, I don't know what will."

"I tend to be more afraid when the actual bullets whiz by my head," Lester said.

"I don't know—I've seen you go into your Zen state and become a statue when the bullets hit all around you," Debi said.

"Doesn't mean I'm not scared," Lester said, smiling at Debi and giving her a hug and a quick kiss on her forehead.

"I expected a lightning bolt to come into this room and strike me dead for even being in a room where a prayer was spoken. Not been in a church in so . . . so long," Jordan said to Lester.

Maria overheard and replied to Jordan's confession, "Honey, if we live through this, we're going to Mass as soon as we land back in France."

"How about we go to a church that would accept us if we got married—a nice Presbyterian or Episcopalian church? The Catholic Church would require us to get an annulment from our first marriages, which is a little ridiculous, don't you think?" Jordan said, before he realized that he had stuck the "marriage" word in the sentence.

"I agree with your assessment of nice churches to attend, but did I hear a veiled attempt to ask for my hand in marriage?" Maria said, smiling and pressing her nose to his, with her eyes wide and locked on his.

"Maria, I hope the end result of our time together will be marriage, but I am capable of a much better proposal—one that includes a ring and me on a knee. Also, I'm a traditionalist, which means I would call and ask your dad's permission to marry you."

"You got to know that my church accepts anyone unless they don't pay for their meal," Lester said.

Maria had read about Lester's church café. "I like the idea of your church, Lester, but it doesn't seem to lend itself to weddings and funerals."

"Nonsense! Move a couple tables out of the way, lay out a buffet of fried catfish and frog legs, and have the owner do the ceremony. We can get her a 'preachership' real quick on the web. Won't be fancy, but it'll be the talk of Kirby," Lester said in his most unconvincing voice and holding back a laugh.

"Fried frog legs? Can I list them on the invitations going out? It might cut down on attendance," Jordan said.

"The very purpose of listing them—only your true friends will show up," Lester said and watched Rick cringe at the talk of mistreating frogs. All the SEALs called each other frogmen, most likely as a reference to their origins in WWII.

"Listen up! Make sure your tropical shirts cover your vests. Your resort wear will identify you as a friendly. The Panama Canal workers will have on work clothes. Shouldn't be any non-jihadist workers here—they were told to stay away until 2:00 p.m. Get with your fire teams and good luck to you. Let's move out," Rick said.

Monte looked at Simone, smiled, and muttered, "Stay frosty, my girl—stay frosty."

The other five from the group almost fell on the floor laughing when they heard the overused phrase.

"What in the hell does that mean?" Simone said.

Before anyone could answer, each couple was called to go with their fire team leader. Tank had his team fall in with him.

"Look, in combat, the objective is not to just kill the enemy," Tank said. "The most important thing is to keep the person next to you alive. You are fighting for your buddy. Keep him or her safe. There's plenty of time to engage the enemy. Do it with your fellow frogmen in mind—and guest frogs, of course. No fuck ups.

"Our objective is a big building across the canal. To cross over, we will run across the top of the closed lock gate. You will see yellow handrails but not much room. If the canal gate is open, we have to wait until it's closed to get across.

"First, we'll need to take out the machine gun in the main control building. Intel says it's there. Far right window top floor. When you see us setting up the Javelin, you'll provide cover fire. Don't get in the way of the back blast because it'll kill you. Frogs, let's move out."

Tank sounded like someone who had been in combat a million times. In truth, he had never been fired upon. Lester and Debi got the impression he couldn't wait to have bullets zipping by him. It was what the frogmen lived for and why they became SEALs to start with.

As they moved out of the theater, down the stairs to the rear exit, they could hear gunfire from the upper floors. One fire team was moving to clear the upper front offices, so they could get eyes on the snipers in the tree line across from the visitors center. Since the big glass oval front windows didn't have access, the SEAL snipers had to break the glass on the fourth story walkway to the observation platforms. Shortly, they could distinguish the sound of the Barrett .50 caliber long range sniper rifle firing ten round clips.

"You know, Debi, that Barrett must be trying to cut down the tree," Lester said.

"I hope to hell they do their job before we take off in open space across the yard," Debi replied.

When they reached the ground floor and exited the building, they found a low concrete wall for cover. It was a patio area adjacent to the snack bar, but it was perfect to sight in the administration building on the island between the two canals. If the advanced information was accurate, then the top window on the right housed a machine gun.

"Start putting rounds in that top right window. If we get a response, then we'll send a Javelin on its way," Tank said, and helped the two-man missile team set up.

"Debi, let's send three-round bursts at that top window but don't feel bad if we don't get close. These MAC-10s are no good at that distance which looks like about 200 yards," Lester said, as he aimed and pulled the trigger as did the rest of the team.

Pieces of stucco put out little smoke signals as the building was dusted by small arms fire. There was no return fire. Above them were four observation decks, and fully-automatic gunfire could be heard on all decks as squads of SEALs moved in and cleared out all enemy personnel.

Suddenly, a large barrel protruded from the middle window in the main control building, directly above the lettering for the Miraflores Locks, with the date "1913" below it. It began firing, and pieces of concrete were ripped and blown away all around the squad of seven fighters.

"Fifty cal. Got to get 'em fast or it'll chew up our cover," Tank said, and directed the team member who had just magically produced a Barrett .50 caliber sniper rifle from a bag where it had been in a disassembled state. It looked odd to see a man wearing yellow cargo shorts and a shirt covered with palm trees and surf boards putting together one of the deadliest long-distance killing weapons on the planet.

“Buck, slap a clip in that window—move down a ways on this wall—we’ll give you a little cover fire,” Tank said.

Buck slid an extra round in the chamber and rose a little above the wall as all his team sent rounds downhill towards the machine gun barrel protruding from the window a good two city blocks away. Dust puffed in small clouds all around the window, and the machine gun opened up and erratically threw rounds all around them but not directly on their position, causing chunks of concrete to shower down on them from where the huge rounds tore into the observation platform above them. Then came the sweet sound of the big Barrett as eleven rounds were sent through the window. The machine gun went silent. Next, was the sound of the Javelin as it rocketed toward the infrared signature and then exploded, leaving a huge hole where there had been a window before. No movement could be seen in the opening.

“Ok, prepare to move out!” Tank said, with no change in his voice from losing his combat virginity. “Keep an eye out for those other windows.”

His fire team quickly grabbed their equipment to move out from the protection of the concrete wall when Tank got a message from Rick.

“Stay put a minute. We’ve got a fucking sniper.”

Chapter Twenty-Five

Abdulhasan Askari had moved to a more fortified location in the basement of the Miraflores Locks main control building after the Javelin round took out his machine gun in a room a couple of doors down from where he was observing the initial attack. His new view of the fighting, although not by human line of sight, was supplanted by a wide bank of closed circuit television cameras enclosed in a concrete bunker.

The Central Miraflores Security Center allowed the best views of the entire campus and surrounding areas. Most of his time at the Canal Zone had been spent in this office, and much of the equipment had been upgraded at his request. As the security supervisor for the entire Miraflores Lock operations, he was now the fox, and the Panama Canal was his hen house. His position had been particularly helpful when he would put on full Muslim crews, mainly at night, and plant explosives and string antenna wire for detonators during the down period when ships were not coming through the locks. He now needed to call his helicopter commander, but had his hands full with the sudden attack of tourists in flower-covered shirts carrying automatic weapons.

*****

"You are all to proceed to your hidden positions. You will hunker down there out of sight until you are commanded to advance to our objectives. We have a deficit of four helicopters, so each of you is asked to man-up and cover our losses. I know many of you are incredulous about us completing our mission. Just know that Allah is with us. God is great. Good luck and good hunting," said Romuald Farouk, flight commander of the Panama helicopter group. Farouk had served as a captain in the Egyptian Air Force, where he flew American AH-64 Apaches and French Gazelle reconnaissance helicopters. He left Egypt and the military to work for Al Qaida and the Panama Canal militants.

Farouk had gone to the same college as Askari but didn't know him well. Unlike Askari, Farouk didn't care for engineering and instead embarked on a path of study which earned him a master's degree in philosophy. Askari never mentioned it to his face but did tell some of his associates that the degree was frivolous. It didn't matter to Farouk, who was tall, well-constructed, and had an extremely attractive face. Several people had asked if he was Omar Sharif, the famous Egyptian movie star. With his physical attractiveness, women were drawn to him like mosquitos in a swamp. He currently had two wives and a selection of mistresses as needed.

He would tell his friends that he was writing a novel, but no one ever saw it. When he spoke, there was a tendency to add too many words, either to impress, or to just play with his extensive vocabulary. Arabic was his native tongue, but English was the language he liked to experiment with in elongated conversations, knowing full well most of the people around him couldn't compete verbally.

Beyond his excessive vocabulary was his love for American movies; in particular, he loved war movies and Westerns. Jargon such as "saddle-up" and "lock and load" got mixed into the sentences to the point that if Farouk didn't have a language of his own, he certainly had a unique colloquial style. It wasn't unusual for his helicopter pilots to call each other to interpret what he had just said to them as a direct order.

Askari didn't have much patience or the time to figure out his messed-up communications. Usually within a few seconds, he would stop Farouk and say, "Romuald either talk to me in short little sentences, or I'm hanging up. I don't have time for your shit!"

Fueled by a reprimand, Farouk would go into a John Wayne short-sentence routine.

"Will do, Addul—jump right on it! Choppers ready—say when."

It was apparent to Askari that nothing about his head pilot was normal. However, his skills with a helicopter had never been in question. Farouk could fly them upside down and flip them through a series of loops at critical angles that no one thought was possible for a helicopter. Most people believed if anyone else tried to duplicate Farouk's antics, they would be killed. So far, no one had been stupid enough to try.

The attack from the air was going to be after the locks were full and the opposite harbors had ships stacked up ready to go in the opposite direction. All Askari wanted was to have the canal locks full so he could do the most damage. He didn't care which directions they were going. They would begin the process of filling the locks at 2:00 p.m., and in three and one-half hours it would be full of ships. Then it would be closed again, and for the next three and one-half hours, no new ships would go through. At 9:00 p.m., the cycle would start from the opposite ocean all over again. The air war would begin once the canal was full—at exactly 5:30 p.m.

*****

Maria and Jordan were in a SEAL team ordered to clean out the four levels of observation decks above where Lester and Debi were stationed at ground level. There was more than one team going up, but they were the first. One by one, the fire team had engaged the militants on each level. Maria and Jordan had the assignment of watching and guarding for any jihadists attacking from the rear. So far, all the combatants had been in front and the SEALs took them out quickly with little resistance.

As they approached the upper deck, which included the entire back roof area along with an observation area, a dramatic change took place. Militants seemed to come out of every crack and crevice. Jordan noticed them first as they attacked from the right rear of the group. He dropped to the floor behind a large planter filled with golden bougainvilleas and red Hawaiian Ti plants and pulled Maria down beside him. Bullets buzzed above their heads and blew off pieces of concrete behind them, as they struck the wall of the observation deck. Before he hit the deck, Jordan got a glance of the two shooters and saw they were behind a patio table that had been turned on its side. The combatants were shooting their AK-47 on fully automatic, which meant their magazines would need to be switched out soon. Jordan waited for the clicks and heard them both hit empty with audible clicks.

"Now, Maria!" Jordan yelled, as both rose and sprayed the patio table with over thirty rounds each. First there were screams, then gurgling sounds, then nothing.

The rest of the fire team had taken cover nearby. They signaled Maria and Jordan to stay down, since they had taken fire from a doorway on the far left of the upper level of the building. Jordan raised his head and peeked through the leaves of the Ti plant. There was no movement on their side of the roof. A couple of closed doors and one small window were about all Jordan could see. Gunshots sounded out all over the compound, but everything was quiet on the roof for now. Maria jammed a fresh magazine in her MAC-10 after she observed Jordan reload his weapon.

"Did we waste ammo on those guys?" she asked.

"Hey, we got the assholes. One use of automatic weapons is to cover a large area when you can't see your enemy. We did that. But, to answer your question—yes."

"I'm going to use short bursts next time, if I don't freak out," Maria said, as she looked for that setting on her weapon but only found semiautomatic. She clicked the lever down for single shots as fast as she could pull the trigger. If things got hairy, she now knew where the full auto switch was located.

"I'm leaving mine on auto, and I will try to get off the trigger in a hurry," Jordan said.

Every few minutes he would rise, using the Ti plant for cover, and check for movement. Suddenly, as if timed by a stop watch, doors opened on both sides of the roof and five militants came through each door. At the same time, a machine gun came alive from the small window, raking rounds all around Jordan and Maria, providing cover fire for ten crazed jihadists as they rushed towards overturned patio furniture. Inexplicably, they all stopped and took positions behind small plastic chairs, Plexiglas tables, and fallen umbrellas.

Once they slid into place, Maria stood up a few milliseconds before Jordan and started pulling the trigger as fast as she could. Once Jordan was fully up, he pumped in short bursts through the flimsy fortification where the jihadists were huddled. Some turned to run but were mowed down. In a matter of seconds, with very little return fire, all the militants were on the deck, either dead or seriously wounded.

The couple even had time to move their weapons to the left and spray the men coming out the door in front of the rest of the SEAL team; however, the machine gun at the window on Maria and Jordan's side roared back to life now that their own men weren't in their line of fire and sent the couple down hard on the deck behind the planter. A yellow-orange trail zoomed across the deck from the SEAL team and entered the window of the shooter and exploded. The window was doubled in size and nothing more was heard from the machine gunner.

Elements of the SEAL team rushed in all the doors to root out other fighters. Maria and Jordan heard a few rounds expended, but it seemed slight compared to what they had been through. Their fire team leader came over to the flower planter and spoke to the European couple.

"My name's Grant Givings. Thanks for taking out all those assholes. Man, you fucked 'em up! We still got work to do, but you guys can be on my team any time.

"We're leaving a couple snipers up here, but we need to move out. Got other objectives. Follow us down. How's your ammo?" Givings pointed at their magazines protruding from their weapons.

"I have two mags left," Maria said.

"Me, too," Jordan said.

"Should do okay with that. Let's go," he said, and led the group through one of the secured doorways.

Chapter Twenty-Six

A few hundred feet from where Lester and Debi had been told to stay in the food court, Monte and Simone fell in behind five grizzled Navy SEALs. Actually, they were abreast of the last two men who were trying to shield them from shots coming from the rear. Dean Sharp was a Lieutenant Commander who had earned his rank in the field and was leading this battle-hardened fire team. Wounded in both Iraq and Afghanistan, he was the real deal. Even though he had been briefed that the two civilians with his group were battle-tested more than once, he knew they hadn't received the proper training for the type of combat they were about to undertake. He did need more men, however, so he would use these non-military types judiciously. One thing he knew was they were fearless and would follow orders.

"When we start clearing buildings, you two watch what the men do for covering fire, and you fall in line—take positions for cover—then advance—then cover. Over and over again. Advance—gun pointed to protect—move in—stop, aim, and protect—next man moves up," Commander Sharp said as they neared the rear of a large maintenance shed.

A bullet struck at the corner of the shed exactly where Simone had stood not two seconds before. "Fucking snipers still active," Dean said. "Somebody needs to take them out before all the patrols head out across the yard."

The shed was much like an oil change facility with a rack to lift vehicles and a pit below it, so the undercarriages can be examined. Small electric train locomotives, called mules, were being serviced there. Usually, as many as eight mules are used to stabilize a ship from hitting the sides of the canal walls or crashing into the gates. There was only one mule in the shop, along with two pickup trucks, and a tractor with a grass mower attached. There were stairs leading to upper areas and two doors with glass panes. As soon as the SEAL team turned to enter the lower area, automatic gunfire erupted from the upper platform. Rounds hit all around them as they took shelter behind the electric mule.

"Johnson, Valdez, and Monte, give us some supporting fire. Simone, cover us from the rear; the rest of you pipe hitters pour it on now," Dean said, stepping out and firing in the direction of where the shots had come from only seconds earlier.

As soon as the three giving support fire stepped out, a barrage of bullets hit all around them. Rounds struck Monte's and Valdez's vests, knocking them to the ground. Johnson sprayed the shooter with M-4 rounds, killing him as one popped his head open. Dean's men were now headed up the metal stairway towards the office. Monte, Valdez, and Johnson stood out and gave covering fire into the door at the head of the stairs.

Simone now watched all the downstairs area, as the rest were working their way to the two doorways on the upper balcony walkway. She thought she heard a noise near the tractor, then saw a man rise behind the big mowing machine. He began to bring a weapon up from his side. She didn't hesitate and poured two bursts from her MAC-10 into the upper torso of the man. He fell in a lifeless lump over the top of the mower, as she heard the clanking of his AK-47 hitting the concrete floor.

Dean threw her a quick salute as he moved to kick in the first door. He and two of his men blew through the doorway and opened up with full automatic weapons. There were two armed men there, but they didn't stand a chance against the SEALs. The militants nicked a couple of Dean's men, but the wounds were superficial and would be patched up later.

Now it was time for Monte, Valdez, and Johnson to clear a room. Johnson was a huge man from Louisiana, so large that he had played football at LSU as a defensive end. He attacked the door with his size thirteen boot and went in with his two fighters firing at all areas of the room with their M4 and Monte's MAC-10. At first it seemed no one was there.

Suddenly, two dark figures rose above a thick wooden desk and began firing with AKs at a close distance. Johnson and Valdez dropped to the floor and took cover behind a metal file cabinet. Monte found a support pillar that went upwards to the ceiling and was wide enough for him to press his body against. He could feel the vibrations of the rounds hitting the steel support and was glad they weren't slamming into his body. The shot he had taken in his vest earlier may have broken some ribs. He would worry about that later. As soon as he heard the clicks of empty weapons, Monte slid out from his post, waited as they jammed in fresh magazines, and then rose to fire. His timing was perfect, as he riddled both their heads with .45 APC slugs.

They all went back to the lower area where wounds were patched, and their next objective was discussed. Dean called Rick and gave him an update. He particularly wanted him to know about an active sniper.

"Sniper?" Rick said. "We've heard from the other men that one's still active. Any idea where the shot came from? Where were you when the round came in?"

Dean explained that it seemed to come from the tree line in front of the building. Rick said he would get on it. As soon as Dean had clicked off his com mic, he saw two Black Hawk helicopters heading for the tree line. Explosions could be heard along with the whine of the Gatling guns.

What the helicopter couldn't see was a man on a cell phone tower south of the tree line. He was so well-camouflaged, it was impossible to see him. The man had a big poster of the metal struts in front of him duplicating the structure, background, a blue sky, and covering him completely. He was basically invisible until he leaned out for a shot. His weapon was a US M21 rifle with a big scope. The gun used a 7.62 NATO cartridge, which had been picking out targets at a thousand yards, but very close to the far end of its effective range. He had barely missed Simone as she moved into the maintenance shed. At night, the infrared scope would find him, but most likely he knew that and would be down by then.

*****

Lance and Holton had instant battlefield information. They had seen the team that had gone into the shed, and they watched as the Javelin took out the machine gun in the administration building. They didn't know which teams their friends were fighting in at first, but as they watched closely, they could see three teams with one woman in each. Where security cameras were close by, they could make out the faces. Satellite images gave broad overhead views of the entire battle ground. They knew exactly where all the people from the cruise ship were positioned. The supercomputer could tell the type of weapon by rate of fire, velocity of the bullets, type of the rounds, and the measurements of the weapons they held. All this information came from security cameras, drones, satellite images, and helicopter camera footage. The big gorilla was tapped into everything available. As they were pointing out possible enemy positions to Rick, their phone rang. It identified the call as from Lester.

"Boys, enjoying yourselves in that air-conditioned room while we're getting shot at?"

"Oh, Lester, my dear—so wish I could be there—gun in hand, but someone has to tell you where the bad guys are hiding," Lance said.

"Well, the very reason I called you. Got a sniper somewhere beyond the tree line directly in front of the visitors center. Blackhawks just turned most of that area into a post-apocalyptic wasteland. Can you find him?"

"Hold on, and we'll search for anomalies," Holton said. "Big ass cell phone tower, but it looks empty. Perfect spot, however."

"Holton, if you were going to hide in plain sight on a tower with metal braces, what would you do?" Lester asked.

"Well, sweetie, I'm afraid of heights, so I wouldn't go there. But if I could duplicate the braces with a picture of the braces—shit! There he is! Lester, about halfway up, a guy is hiding behind a picture, poster, or whatever. It's goddamn clever what he's done. Tell Rick—you guys take him out. I'll watch from my air-conditioned room. Good luck!" said Holton.

"Debi, Holton, just called me 'sweetie,'" Lester said, laughing.

"I think he has the hots for you—can't blame him," Debi said, smiling ear to ear.

Lester quickly turned his attention to his squad leader.

"Tank, there's a sniper in a cell phone tower about halfway up. He has a poster of the struts hiding him," Lester explained.

"Buck, ease around the side of the building and see if you can get a shot at that bastard. Lester, can you spot for him—take my scope," Tank said, and ordered the rest of the team to watch for movement from the locks control building since Lester and Buck were exposed from the rear. As they set up to search for the sniper, rounds began to come in from two of the windows across the canal. Tank asked for coving fire from his group. All the openings in the big building across the canal were peppered with rounds. It slowed the rate of fire but didn't stop it.

Chunks of stucco were raining down on the two men sent to kill the sniper in the cell tower. Just as Lester spotted the sniper in the powerful scope, a round hit his vest and two rounds blasted Buck's, all in the upper right shoulder area. The rounds didn't penetrate but knocked them to the ground and would result in serious bruising. They hit the ground, moaning and trying to breathe as the air had been pushed out of their lungs. They were in too much pain to hear the first Javelin take off towards the window where the shots emanated. They were getting back on their feet when the second Javelin rocketed towards the building. The explosions rattled the windows behind Tank's team as he assured his sniper team that they would not be molested again.

Buck put two .50 caliber rounds dead center of the strut poster. The sniper fell a few feet below his camouflage and hung there, attached to a safety strap. Most of the force of the rounds must have hit the struts of the tower. He held fast to his rifle and brought it around to shoot. Buck found him in his sight and fired a burst of three rounds, but as he fired he saw the muzzle flash of the M21 and instantly felt the round go through his helmet and crease his forehead.

All was black for a few seconds. He came to as Lester was putting some gauze on his heavily bleeding wound. Tank and the rest of the team rushed to his aid and helped carry him back behind the wall at the patio. Although he bled a lot, he was going to be okay.

The sniper on the cell phone tower didn't fare as well. One round took off half his skull and the other two left large holes in his body. As he watched the shooter drop his rifle and go lifeless, Buck said, "That man was a hell of a marksman to go for a head shot on me while he was hanging from a strap."

With Buck patched up and the sniper dispatched, they could now search the smoking remains of the canal control building and see if anyone remained alive. They moved out on the grass that covered the area between the two largest buildings locked at the Panama Canal. The administration building was a much larger structure, but it wasn't directly at the canal site.

Askari was in the main Miraflores Locks Control building, and he was waiting on them.

Chapter Twenty-Seven

Fatin Amrani knew that anti-submarine warfare (ASW) had come a long way from the developments put into service during WWII and during the time when his aged vessel was built. However, it was still a game of cat and mouse, which was keeping Amrani moving forward with his plans to blow up a shitpot of commercial vessels before they entered the Panama Canal. His three predecessors had made mistakes and died, along with their crews. Ali Reza had been brilliant but lost to a superior submarine and a very competent captain.

Amrani had no delusions of being a strategist or an escape artist. He had accepted his fate. He would die this day, but people would go down with him. His old submarine was nothing more than a large suicide vest loaded with torpedoes packed full of time worn Torpex explosives rescued from surplus munition dumps. It sat silently on the bottom in 80 feet of water, just outside the Port of Colón on the Atlantic side of the Panama Canal, next to the wreckage of the *Lyon,* a sunken schooner from Jamaica, and an unidentified vessel from Havana, Cuba. They collided in 1818, and although there wasn't much left of either of them, it was a perfect place to park a submarine and not get noticed. Amrani had researched wrecks in the area and found this spot to start his attack. He knew the wrecks would be listed on all the modern submarines' computer charts.

A large cargo ship, part of the Maersk fleet, was crossing directly in front of Amrani's Whiskey-class sub. It had a forty-eight-foot draft and made an easy target, even for a ghost vessel of a once mighty wolfpack of the German navy. Fatin Amrani blew ballast and rose to the depth of thirty feet, leveled out, and sent two remanufactured torpedoes directly broadside of the monstrous container ship. Both found their mark and at least one penetrated the second hull, causing instant flooding. Shortly after, it began to list. Even though Amrani didn't get to see it, the Maersk ship sunk in sixty-five feet of water. Only part of her superstructure remained out of the water. The crew of twenty-one seamen survived with some injuries.

*****

Within minutes of the torpedoes striking the Maersk ship, Commander Richard Somerville got the bad news. On the previous day, England had sent the Royal Navy Type 23 Frigate Warspite II to help ferret out the last remaining jihadist submarine and sink it. It was the perfect ship for the job since its main purpose was submarine detection and warfare.

Regardless of his rank, the men on board called him "Captain Somerville," out of respect for the position he held as head man on board.

"Look at old wrecks—that's where I'd hide if I had an old German U-boat. Ping 'em, drop acoustic buoys, and check the computer histories of the shape of the old wrecks," Somerville said. He walked over to the sonar operators station and looked at the screen for a while. Meanwhile, he directed the ship on a course that took them directly over the site of the two 1818 wrecks. As soon as he got there, he ordered the Warspite II to drop four depth charges right on the wreck. Of course, the sub had moved, but it sent a clear signal to Fatin Amrani that this British ship was out to kill him. If he were spotted, there would be no throw-back depth charges sent overboard; instead, they would launch homing torpedoes, which would be guided to the target. Great Britain had just purchased new Mark 48 self-propelled torpedoes with 650 pounds of explosives in each from the US Navy. Along with the underwater hardware, the British Government had also installed the American Aegis tracking system which could lock on 100 targets at one time.

Richard Somerville knew nothing else besides the Navy. So many Somervilles had been officers in the Royal Navy, going back two hundred years. He was born to do this job. One of the youngest commanders at age 28, this assignment would either propel him to captain's rank very quickly or glue him to his current rank forever, if he screwed it up. Standing six-feet, three-inches tall, with a handsome face and striking blue eyes, he looked the part of any rank he might strive to achieve. The ocean, ships, war, and the navy ran through his veins, put there by generations of Somerville men.

The explosions right under his ship made him cringe momentarily. One of his great-great uncles had piloted the *Lyon* at one time, and here he was erasing it, or at the least, disturbing a graveyard of a once-fine vessel. It had been an ostentatious move on Somerville's part. Make some noise and rattle some sabers. Let your enemy know there is a big, bad ship after you. He wondered if Amrani felt any fear. There should be no doubt that Somerville was out to kill him.

*****

Amrani was treating this mission as one with suicide being the end goal, but only after all the torpedoes had been exhausted, and he had rammed his submarine broadside of any ship unlucky enough to be close by. Now he was by another wreck, recently sunk for divers to explore. All the dangerous doors and hatches had been removed, along with anything else that might snag a diver. He didn't have to wait long as a huge cruise ship passed by overhead. He moved above the wreck and loaded his forward tubes with four torpedoes, took aim, and ordered the first two torpedoes to be fired.

The cruise ship *Mother of the Seas* took evasive action, turned in the direction of the torpedoes, and watched as the two fish traveled along each side of the ship and missed it entirely. Both the torpedoes continued on and struck a small cargo ship, sinking it within minutes. Her small crew of nine lost one man. He appeared to have been below when the vessel was struck.

The sub maneuvered out to have another shot at the cruise ship.

Amrani's vessel achieved a perfect set up for two more torpedoes. He fired a T-bone-type strike that couldn't miss. It couldn't miss as long as an anti-torpedo chaser hadn't been launched from the Warspite II. Faster, more accurate, and guided by a system the German submarine captains couldn't have imagined, the two aged torpedoes were intercepted and destroyed about 100 yards before they struck the cruise ship. The U-boat had already headed down and out. Amrani quickly moved to shelter behind an enormous container ship, submerged just about equal with the big vessel's draft. It took a little while for Somerville to find it. When he did, four torpedoes were headed his way. Amrani was determined to use his entire arsenal before he was finished. The Warspite II sent out anti-torpedo devices against them and fired one round at the U-Boat, which was diving for cover.

Once close to the bottom of the harbor, the U-boat fired two rounds at the big container ship and two torpedoes at the approaching Royal Navy frigate before the M48 torpedo split the old cold war relic in half. Somerville was able to defend against the two fish traveling towards them, but one of the U-boat rounds found its mark right below the bow of the ship. It began to take on water, but water-tight compartments kept it from both listing and sinking.

Richard Somerville and his crew hovered over the wreck of the U-boat for an hour. Bodies were recovered, but there were no survivors. There were no more jihadist submarines. They were doomed from the beginning due to better-equipped ships and modern equipment. The effort was a gallant attempt, but the militants were woefully outclassed in all areas. They did some damage, but an overall disaster was averted, and all the cruise ships were left unscathed.

The threat of submarines and scud missiles had been eliminated and the battle for the Miraflores was going well, but some of the deadliest weapons of the jihadists' plot against the Panama Canal had yet to be released.

Chapter Twenty-Eight

Askari had been in contact with his submarine captain right until the end. Fatin Amrani had called out the trajectory path of the torpedoes headed towards the container ship. He also called in the proximity of the guided torpedo fired at him from the British frigate Warspite II. When his mic went silent, Askari knew his man was in Paradise, looking over several virgins to ravish at his convenience, since he had eternity to make his choices and an erection that stayed hard forever. Back on earth, a person with that condition would be required to see a doctor.

Currently, he had pressing problems of his own. Askari wasn't convinced the seventy-two virgins promised was real, so he took his chances with the here and now. There were service tunnels under much of the canal gate area, and he made sure his office had an escape hatch to the entrance of the underground passageways. The time was near for him to go. The supervision of the final attack could be done offsite.

Lester and Debi moved across the grassy area and across the closed canal gate until they were against the east wall of the Lock Control building.

"Babe, how're you doing?" Lester asked.

"I think I like this combat shit a little too much. Why is that?"

"Don't know, except you get mad when you're in danger. Most people are scared—you try to kill the people shooting at you and fear is lost in there somewhere. A Rambo brain locked in a beautiful girl's body. Damn sexy!" Lester said.

"Cover me when I go around this corner," Lester said. He, Buck, and Tank moved around to a closed door, while Debi held her weapon aimed at it. Buck and Tank decided to open it and fire a few bursts to soften up the area. No one fired back.

Covering each other as they entered the building, it was slow going as they crawled over the piles of rubble left from the three Javelin rounds. There was no resistance. It was easy to find the canal security room, but not so stress-free breaking through the steel door protecting the entrance.

"Buck, put a block of C4 near the handle on the door and set it for fifteen seconds. The rest of you get behind something," Tank said, and moved into an adjoining room for cover.

Buck did as he was told and yelled "Fire in the hole!" after he set the timer on the detonator. The door came off, but a secondary explosion took place inside the room, which destroyed all the monitors and communication equipment.

"Hey, there's a trap door with wires running out of it," Lester said. "Might be dummy wires to delay us—maybe we should blow it just in case."

Rick agreed and had Buck set another charge. There wasn't a secondary explosion, and everyone rushed into the tunnel. They all had to duck-walk to avoid banging against the low ceiling. As they saw daylight ahead they heard a noise.

"Is that a helicopter?" Tank asked, even though he already knew the answer.

"Yeah, and it looks like his family is aboard," Buck said, as he crawled out of the tunnel into the bright sunlight.

There was a Vietnam-era helicopter with a single Browning machine gun pointed in their direction. A woman wearing a hijab and two young girls pressed their faces against the window directly behind the pilot.

"We can't shoot—might hit the kids," Tank yelled, and watched the aircraft turn and head east.

As the fire team wandered around the partially demolished canal control building there was a message to Tank from Rick.

"Area secure. All teams assemble at the visitors center for debriefing," Rick announced to all squad leaders. "Be aware—Cobras, Apaches, and Blackhawks landing in area."

The Blackhawks had been around for a while, but now they were joined with Apaches and Super Cobras from the states, all carrying fresh troops. All knew there was a threat still out there from six old Hueys. No one knew what kind of damage they could do but were ready to take them out if they showed up.

Lester and Debi walked across the grass towards the visitors center when they noticed a cruise ship coming up to the first gates at Miraflores.

"It's almost three o'clock and the canal is back in business," Lester said, looking at his TAG dive watch.

"You do realize that the canal will be the most vulnerable when the locks are full of ships. I can also see from here the super Panamax container ships are moving," Debi remarked. "Does Rick realize this?"

"I'm sure everyone here realizes the danger. I wonder what the optimum time will be for some sort of attack," Lester said as he dialed Rick on his cell phone.

"Yeah, Lester. What's up?" Rick said, sounding busier than usual.

"What's the prime time for an attack?" Lester inquired.

"We figure about 5:10 p.m. All locks will be full, and I'll have all the birds either in the air or set on ready."

"What can we do?" Lester asked.

"Be ready to shoot down some helicopters. I'll position all the squads where they'll do the most good. Just relax until then."

"What's up with the train they rented for the entire day?" Lester asked.

"Forgot about that—could be they wanted to escape in it. I'll send a squad in the train tunnel shortly to see if anything is going on in there. No trains have run today," Rick said, with a dismissive voice.

"Right. Well, if nobody is handy, I'm sure Tank will take the job," Lester said, pointing to Tank and smiling at having volunteered him for more action.

"What did you just sign me up for?" Tank asked. "I need something to do."

"The train that normally goes up and down the canal was privately rented for the day. Tunnel needs to be checked out. No hurry," Lester said. He saw Jordan, Maria, Simone, and Monte in the beer line at the food patio. The drink cooler had miraculously survived the onslaught of bullets.

It took a while to exchange war stories, but it was obvious all saw considerable action. Lester discussed the tunnel assignment, and for some reason all of them wanted to go check it out.

"You guys really want to be shot at in a dark tunnel? A bunch of fucking adrenalin junkies, I'd say," Lester said.

"You can round up whoever you want for this patrol, but we can't spend much time on it. Everyone needs to be in place at around five o'clock around the locks. We've got teams at the other locks with choppers standing by. There are some jeeps and trucks that will take you to the railway. It's about a half mile or so to the tunnel. It's over seven-hundred feet long—could be anything in there. Train doesn't have a station or stop here—only two stations—one in Panama City and the other at Colón. You need to finish your beers and go begin your new career as tunnel rats. Lester, you and Buck take the lead on this. I'm going to line out our positions for protecting the ships. Join us when you get back. It's 1530 hours—be back at 1730 hours. Got it?" Tank said.

"Got it. Grab your beers—we can drink them on the way," Buck said. "We'll get this over in a hurry."

The six people from the *Queen of the Seas* followed Buck down to a small military-type truck with police markings on the side. The driver already knew where to take them and pulled off the road to a small gravel path used as a service road for the railroad tracks. They saw the tunnel in the distance, and as they got closer, they could read the two dates carved out in the concrete: 1909 Cusa 2001 Neosho.

"I was told they replaced the track in 2001—different gauge—more modern," Lester said.

"And before we go in, I want to call our buddies at NSA," Debi said. "They know this battle from all angles."

Lance answered on the first ring, "Debi, my doll—see you made it through the battle."

"Doesn't pay to piss me off," Debi said. "We're about to go into this damn railroad tunnel. How does it look through your cameras?"

"Just fly-by pics. The main train is still in Balboa. I'll call you if it moves," Lance said.

"Thanks. Can you guys find out who paid to rent the whole train for the day?" Lester asked as he pulled the phone closer to his ear.

"A group called Friends of the Canal paid for the whole day," Holton said. "Looks like it was reserved by a Nadia Askari, and the payment was in cash."

"How do you find out this crap?" Debi asked.

"We're good at secret shit. It's our calling," Holton said, laughing.

"I doubt we'll find anything, but we're going in," Lester said,

Buck told the driver to stay put and had the group break into two rows to cling to the entrance sides of the tunnel. Lester was teamed with Debi and Simone.

"Damn, this is the threesome I've always dreamed about," he said.

"Down, big boy. She's spoken for," Debi said. "Besides you're worn out from making babies."

"I could garner the energy—if you two would be gentle with me." The two girls laughed and snuffed out his fantasy.

They slowly began to see the light at the end of the tunnel. In the dim light, they could see something lying next to the tracks. It appeared from a distance to be rags—several stacks of rags on each side of the tracks almost halfway into the tunnel. When they got closer, they turned on flashlights and cell phones to make out the objects. Maria, Jordan, and Monte were first to examine the rags only to discover they weren't rags but fine Muslim garments. Maria held one set against Jordan for prospective. When the garment unfolded, a beautiful full-length abaya and hijab draped across the front of Monte's body. All the outfits were black and made of a rich fabric. There were forty-two neatly-folded Muslim dresses and scarves.

"Buck, you've been to Iraq and Afghanistan. Is this the proper dress for a woman to attend a funeral?" Lester asked.

"Women normally don't attend funerals in the Muslim world, but if they did—yeah, this would be proper," Buck said. "I don't know why they would be planning a funeral dress for inside this tunnel. We've seen enough. Let's get back to the visitors center. We'll have your buddies keep an eye on this place. It's goddamn creepy!"

Chapter Twenty-Nine

The helicopter carrying Abdulhasan Askari apparently held extra fuel tanks and didn't stop until it was in the jungles of Guatemala, some 800 air miles from Panama. The two Blackhawks followed them as far as their fuel would take them, but turned back after a few hundred miles. Under normal circumstances, the Blackhawk would have a range of well over 1000 miles and the Huey about 300 to 400 miles. The Blackhawks had flown in from Columbia using some of their fuel and needed fuel for any action at the canal. So, they abandoned the chase and let Askari be tracked by satellites and a drone.

The drones had just arrived about noon aboard one of the Apaches. They were unarmed, small surveillance aircraft with a long range and held the ability to upload information to satellites. The singular drone launched on this mission from the Blackhawk reported back information containing the location of the landing site and a quick view of the jungle compound where Askari was headed. The drone retreated when it came under fire from the security detail at the compound. It compiled a great deal of information given the short time it hovered above the structures. The NSA had the information in seconds.

*****

Jordan and Maria kissed briefly as they sat next to each other at the food patio on the top floor of the visitors center. Both had minor cuts from pieces of wood and concrete blown into their flesh from bullets striking objects around them. They treated each other's wounds with bandages and antibiotics. From a distance, they looked like two well-dressed chimpanzees preening each other. They had been given some sandwiches and soft drinks by the staff, who had filtered back in after all the shooting was over. Occasionally, they would look out over the grassy area and watch the Super Cobras and Apache helicopters land. Sitting on the field were a total of twelve attack helicopters, and more were expected.

"Maria, I want to say you were incredibly brave today. You handled yourself like a veteran Special Forces soldier," Jordan said. "I'd like to think we both made a difference in the fight."

"You know we did. I hate it people died, and I hate I made it happen to some of them—it was them or us—because they were damn sure out to kill us," Maria said.

Deep inside, she was trying to reconcile killing the Muslims in the firefight. Those people would never see their wives and children again, and their loved ones would never welcome them home. It was a profound sadness few people experience. She tried to ignore it, but the pictures of flesh flying away from the ones she shot flashed again and again in her mind. She watched the movie in her head that showed them fall to the ground in agony, or even worse—the ones who fell lifeless with their eyes still staring ahead looking at nothing. She wanted it to stop but knew it would affect her for the rest of her life—no matter how many times she tried to block it out. She started to cry and felt Jordan's arm around her. He knew the same feeling but masked it much better. Her sobs, he felt, would be therapeutic, so he let her cry and gently rubbed her back.

Monte and Simone sat and drank beers on the bottom floor of the visitors center. They both had some issues with the combat but hadn't internalized the carnage as did Maria and Jordan. They were recovering little by little—beer after beer. As they enjoyed the respite from the fight, Lester and Debi dropped by.

"Buy me a beer, Monte?" Lester asked.

"Of course. I'll buy both of you one, since they are free today," Monte said, and got up to pull out a chair for Debi as he gave her a kiss on the cheek. Lester kissed Simone but always aimed for the lips on pretty girls, and usually wasn't rejected. He wasn't this time either.

"I understand Maria and Jordan had it pretty bad," Lester said. "Rick told me they killed about twenty of the bad guys—almost got overrun. Maria isn't handling it well. We'll give them some space, but the action might be over for them."

"Shit, I hope it's over for all of us," Debi said.

Out of nowhere, an old Huey rose from the tree line in front of the visitors center and opened up with M-60 machine guns on each side of the aircraft. The two shooters were clearly strapped into monkey harnesses and had their weapons on a bungee cord, so they could move the guns around to rain bullets down on their prey Vietnam style. The four friends dove behind the concrete patio wall and tried to get off some shots before they were out of sight. They could hear returning fire from the upper observation area.

Jordan had seen the gunship turn behind the visitors center, bank at eye level, and open up on the personnel on the upper level. He quickly pulled Maria on the other side of the concrete flower planter and both opened up on the Huey. Some of the personnel on the roof took hits.

"Eat these bullets, you assholes!" Maria said. She saw that several of her rounds from a full magazine found their way around the right-side gunner. He dropped the M60, and it hung by the bungee cord as the shooter looked after his wounds which were numerous.

Jordan had concentrated on the pilot, but wondered if any of his rounds had penetrated the Huey's protected armor. The glass was bullet resistant but could be penetrated. He saw the pilot shield his eyes from the full magazine Jordan sent his way. The helicopter turned and sent 7.62mm machine gun rounds into two of the Super Cobras on the ground, then banked and headed out the way it came in. An Apache attack helicopter had been approaching for a landing and immediately pursued the Huey. After a short distance, it overtook the old helicopter and blew it to pieces with its Gatling gun. Upon close inspection, there was minimal damage to the gunships on the ground. A repair crew got on them instantly and medics were working on the casualties on the roof.

"Maria, you okay?" Jordan asked as he put his arm around her again.

"I'm fine . . . damn fine. I'm over that little spell I had. All it takes is to have one of those motherfuckers try to kill you, and you come back to the job at hand. I can do it as well as anyone here, but I'm down to one magazine. How about you?"

"Same here. I'll call Rick," Jordan said, and dialed his cell.

"Rick, you guys have any MAC-10 45 APC ammo on hand?"

"Go inside to the theater and look in the duffel bags we left there. Might be a few mags left. You guys are doing great. Let me know if you need anything else."

"I would like to sign up for post-traumatic syndrome counseling," Jordan joked.

"I'll put you guys on the list, but you're far-fucking away from 'post' anything, and you may have to teach the course. Got to go. Stay frosty, my man. Ha!" Rick laughed.

"He loves this shit, doesn't he?" Jordan said, more or less to himself.

"Babe, it's the highest-high and the lowest-low," Maria said, taking Jordan's hand to go inside and down the stairs to the theater. On the way, Jordan called Lester to tell him about the ammo and to let him know they were headed there.

"Lester—meet us in the theater—we're headed that way," Jordan said.

"Thanks, Jordan, we'll meet you there," Lester said, and directed his group inside from the lower patio. They all met and exchanged war stories as they looked into the duffel bags strewn around the aisles of the theater. Only one duffel bag contained the correct ammo and magazines, yet it was packed. It contained a few clips with ammunition loaded in them, but mostly it was boxes of .45 rounds. Most everyone had saved their empty magazines, so it was just the matter of putting in the rounds one by one. Debi and Simone gave Maria a hug and asked her if she was all right.

"I'm fine. The last magazine I emptied felt much better. I was more mad than scared. Debi, I'm getting like you, girl," Maria said.

"Hey, I get plenty scared, but for some reason, I convert it to anger. But none of us had the amount of combat you and Jordan had—don't want anything that intense either," said Debi.

The men were more interested in what came next.

"So, we have five choppers left to come in—is that right?" asked Monte.

"Yeah, that's what I understand," said Lester. "We can guess they'll look like the one that buzzed through. Seems like a suicide mission, and they have to know that."

"They must have them for a purpose other than to sacrifice a few Muslims. It must be the ships loaded in the canal gates they're after," Jordan said.

"Rick said that prime time is around 5:15, so we're about an hour away from a full-scale attack, if the ships are their targets," Lester said. "I don't see how they can do much damage with a couple of machine guns on each chopper. We're missing something."

*****

The five Huey helicopters couldn't be seen from above. They were beautifully draped with realistic jungle camouflage; the men were underground, hiding their heat signatures, and God knows where all the drones had landed. It was certain the NSA had several sites picked out where something might happen, but they probably couldn't differentiate the landing site for the Hueys. Romuald Farouk had faked out the satellite surveillance by flying several large drones of his own in many directions, while he dropped these five Hueys down and covered them immediately.

Farouk received a call from his boss, Abdulhasan Askari, shortly after the helicopters were secured.

"Farouk, listen to me carefully. We lost the chopper we sent in today—shot down by a Super Cobra. It sent back video of all the aircraft on the ground. We have a tough task ahead. Here's what I want you to tell your pilots. Two are to come in from the east and two from the west, one minute apart, and one from the north—all at 5:30 pm. The locks will be full. Every one of the detonators are set on the same frequency, so if any of your people get within a hundred yards of the ships, they should be able to trigger them. Remember, they don't explode immediately. They will float up from the floor of the locks once the signal releases them, then the magnets will attach themselves to the hull of the ships. Once attached, they will explode in five minutes. You got that, Farouk? You should—we've been over this a thousand times," Askari said, reminding his helicopter commander to follow orders just this one last time. He still wasn't confident that Farouk wouldn't screw up the mission.

"Roger that, boss. Crystal clear. Ready to rock and roll," Farouk said, and prepared to instruct his men on what would most likely be their final flight on planet Earth. In the process, there was a good chance he would bludgeon the English language and completely baffle the troops under his leadership.

"My invaluable and intrepid troops, may Allah bless you forever. Praise the name of Allah. We are about to embark on a Herculean adventure where we will rain down a vociferous and catastrophic hellstorm on infidels who hate us and our way of life. To our great alacrity, the Americans will feel our rancor and taste our venom. They will witness our truculent warriors and will fall in droves. Be jubilant in your coming victory. Each helicopter has a set of instructions. So, saddle up and let's get this show on the road."

The camouflage was ripped off the five Hueys, and they began to warm up the engines. One pilot leaned over to his copilot as they lifted off.

"Do you know what that fuck he just said?" he asked.

"No one does. 'Vociferous'—my ass!"

Chapter Thirty

"Lester, it's Lance. Can you hear me?"

"Barely—all these helicopters are taking off—must be fourteen or fifteen of them," Lester said.

"Sixteen—to be exact. We are tracking the five bogies coming in. It appears they will hit east-west and from the middle. Also, just wanted to warn you that the train is moving in from Panama City and should be at the tunnel in about twenty minutes. Keep an eye out for it," Lance said.

"Thanks. I think we'll leave this helicopter raid to the attack helicopters and sit back and watch the show. Where is the *Tropic Queen*?" Lester asked.

"Lester, sweetie, it's Holton. Our ship has gone through the canal and is in the last lock gate at Gatún. Should be going through the gate and into the Port of Colón, then the open ocean in about ten minutes. Hopefully, before the attack starts."

"Great! Keep us apprised. We hope there will be five old Hueys smoking and crumbled on the ground pretty quickly," Lester said. "By the way, are those ungrateful bastards going to get us back on the ship?"

"Probably they will fly us to Aruba, so we can catch up then. But nothing official yet," Holton said.

"Thanks. Keep us informed. We're a little tired of being shot at."

*****

No one had ever blown up any part of the Panama Canal. The Germans had plans to send a ship through loaded with explosives to mirror the successful St. Nazaire Raid of German dry docks in World War II by British commandos. It never happened. Then there was the Japanese plan to launch float planes from a nearby aircraft carrier to torpedo the locks. The issue for all the warring forces in World War II was that it wouldn't really affect the US Naval forces that much. It would have been a minor inconvenience but not a game changer. In addition, during that era, there were many military forces very close to the canal. Today's security forces were limited and what forces were around had grown complacent. Soon they would pay the price for their lack of vigilance.

*****

Farouk was in the lead Huey and would be the lone helicopter to pass from the north to the locks at Pedro Miguel, which lies twenty-three miles to the Gatún Locks and less than two miles to the Miraflores Locks. He had a bold plan. All his aircraft was to get in position to move on the ships in the canal, but not until they had dropped down and hidden close to where they started their run at the ships. All the pilots knew they were no match for the Gatling guns of the Super Cobras, Blackhawks, and Apaches. These superior aircraft were expecting to see them exposed and then shoot them down with ease.

Farouk wasn't that stupid. He would ambush the big attack aircraft when they came looking for them. The two Hueys coming from the Pacific side set down in a park outside of Panama City, rotors turning, and waited until one of the attack helicopters came looking for them. As soon as they spotted one nearing their area, they both ascended and split up in different directions. Whichever direction the attack chopper gave chase, the other Huey fell in behind and opened up on them with their two M60 machine guns before the big aircraft could return fire or change directions. The first to get shot down was a Blackhawk with a very inexperienced pilot. It smoked from the engine damage and landed hard in a grassy area outside the city with considerable damage and wounded personnel.

The two Hueys headed for the locks and flew crisscross patterns over both the new and old locks at Miraflores. It looked as though nothing was happening. As they approached the area of the Panama Canal Visitors Center, they met small arms fire from the center and strafed the area with their machine guns. Both aircraft were tailed quickly by Apaches. The efforts of the old Hueys to outrun the modern attack helicopters were almost humorous, except for the knowledge that real people would soon die a violent death.

One Huey dove his damaged aircraft into the *Mother of the Orient* cruise ship, hitting it between Decks Eight and Nine. A large explosion and fire followed, along with general panic on the ship. Knowing they were still in dangerous waters, the crew of the *Mother of the Orient* was ready with fire hoses and portable extinguishers. The fire was subdued quickly, but the injured were slow to get the care they needed. The small medical staff on the boat was overextended. As they opened a gangway platform to carry the wounded off the ship, the first ambulance could be seen pulling up next to the giant ship. Several ambulances had been called to care for the wounded during the fighting that took place a few hours before.

The first explosions from the locks at Miraflores were muffled since they occurred underwater. The explosive devices were not foolproof but were most certainly ingenious. The explosive charge was placed on the floor of the locks completely submerged in water-tight containers. Since high-frequency radio waves can't penetrate water more than a couple of feet, an antenna had to be rigged to pick up the signal. The militants had to hide the wire in the creases in the concrete walls of the locks. They accomplished this feat during the nights when Askari had fielded all Muslim crews. Once the underwater device captured the signal, the bomb was released with enough buoyancy to float it upwards. The bomb was still incased in plastic, so it wouldn't foul the explosive and strong magnets that surrounded the mechanism. Once it was released from the bottom, a timer engaged and set a five-minute delay before the initial charge set off the main explosion. There was enough C4 to tear a hole in the outer hull, but it was unlikely it had the power to compromise both hulls. All the Huey pilots had to do was to fly over the locks with their button down on the detonator signal. If they got within one hundred yards, they had a good chance of floating some magnet bombs upward where the device would take over from there. A few would bounce off the ship and float to the surface. Once they went off in the water, little damage was done to the ships since the water acted as a buffer.

One Huey flew over Lester and his friends as a Super Cobra raced after it. Lester instinctively raised his weapon and unloaded a big clip into the helicopter as it screamed by.

"Take that, asshole!" Lester said, as he saw several of his rounds hit a machine gunner who was holding on to the bungee cord that held his weapon. He had already been wounded and was not long for this world. The chopper was attempting a turn towards the canal, so he could crash into a waiting ship. The Cobra was not going to let that happen and opened up with his Gatling gun and 20mm cannons. The old Huey went down in a heap of smoldering rubble on the grass behind the visitors center.

The two Hueys that came in from the Atlantic side to the Gatún gates pulled the same maneuver on a couple of Super Cobras. They weren't fooled, and unlike the unfortunate takedown of one of their helicopters on the Pacific side by two Hueys, they instead found themselves locked in a battle that amounted to a helicopter dogfight. The Hueys were smaller and more maneuverable but lacked the firepower and sophistication of the aircraft chasing them. The Hueys inflicted damage to the Cobras, but superior armor and a missile package unavailable to the old Vietnam-era choppers eventually did them in. All the flying over the locks done by the Hueys had released the hidden bombs on both the old and new canal locks at the Gatún gates.

The pilots of the Hueys probably didn't know the moment their aircraft, which undoubtedly cost more than their old helicopters, were struck with missiles. Once they crashed, there were large secondary explosions caused by crates of C4 onboard. One Huey was above a Maersk cargo ship when it went down, and the deck was almost cleared of containers from the huge charges on the helicopter. A huge hole was blown open on the main deck, exposing the cargo stored below. The crew quickly covered it with tarps until they could get to a repair facility. Six of their crewmen were injured and two were killed, but their bodies were never recovered as they were on deck when the Huey dropped down on them.

"Askari, it's Farouk here. Guess I'm the only dude left." Farouk couldn't resist trying to use modern street talk even at the point of death. "Gotta do the most damage possible. What I want to do after releasing all the floating bombs—gotta hit the canal with a crate of C4. Might fly directly into the gates," he said.

"Farouk, you are a martyr for sure. Thank you for your service to Allah. Enjoy your virgins," Askari said, and clicked off his radio. He had one more attack up his sleeve; then he would have to coordinate his escape for his family.

"*I don't believe that seventy-two virgins shit. I'll stick with the wife I have*," he said to himself.

*****

Lester and Debi had watched as explosions occurred under the two ships that were in locks directly in front of them. The *Ocean Goddess* was lucky. She was in the lock on the far side from the *Mother of the Orient*, which was still dragging off wounded from the Huey suicide crash. The bomb directly below the *Goddess* floated up from the bottom of the canal and popped up between the stern and the first gate, failing to attach itself to anything. The explosion rocked the boat but did little damage other than throwing people around on the lower decks.

The opposite was true for the already-damaged *Mother of the Orient*. She unfortunately took the full force of the magnetic bomb amidships, rupturing the outer hull, leaking diesel fuel, and filling the water-tight compartment with water. All the personnel had evacuated when the crash on her upper deck had occurred. The big ship dropped lower in the water but did not bottom out in the canal. She could still float and would dock somewhere in the lake ahead and wait for a temporary plate to be welded on the four-foot-wide hole in her hull. Once that was done, the water was pumped from the compartment, and she completed her canal crossing and found her way to dry dock for extensive repairs. She hadn't been refurbished since 2009 and was due for a facelift anyway.

The success of the magnet bombs was about 50-50. None were powerful enough to breach two hulls on any ship, but the designers knew they wouldn't completely sink a ship. The Muslim militants had hoped, however, that the compromised water-tight compartments would drop the ships to the bottom of the canals, stopping traffic for a while and temporarily disrupting world trade.

The first captain to be affected and to report the bombs was on a cargo ship in the Miraflores Locks. The *MSC Taranto* was making her maiden voyage through the newly-expanded canal when a bomb floated to the surface directly in front of the ship's stern. The captain, Fritz Müller, had to step aside for a Panama Canal pilot during the transit, as did all ships. It was a time for him to relax and let someone else do the driving. He had walked to the stern and was looking over the forward gunnel when he saw the bomb float to the surface directly in front of the ship. It looked so tiny from his vantage point on the ship. He took his binoculars from around his neck and focused in on the object. It appeared to be plastic and elongated, maybe a foot long, with large magnets glued all around it. He could even see a red, blinking light inside the object. Suddenly, it exploded. The shock wave knocked Fritz Müller to his knees, but there was no damage to his ship or the canal gates. He called the canal headquarters, which in turn called Rick as the leader of the military forces there. Rick made sure all the captains knew the danger and had all personnel removed from the lower decks after the water-tight doors were employed on all the ships. This advance warning from Captain Müller undoubtedly saved many lives.

*****

Romuald Farouk was a great pilot, in spite of his over-confident attitude and his love of big words and American slang. He knew he was the last of the Hueys and was determined to do the most damage possible. He had timed his flight over the Pedro Miguel Lock to catch a large cruise ship making her transit. It was possible the single-chambered lock was the most vulnerable since there was only one lock. If it were damaged, all traffic would stop and back up from there. All Farouk needed to do was to blow up one set of double-gated locks.

Two Super Cobras spotted the Huey as it rose from hiding behind a tree line close to the Pedro Miguel operation. Farouk made one pass over the locks, releasing the bombs by hitting his detonator switch, then banked for a return pass at the gates.

Two missiles were released by one of the Cobras but missed as Farouk shot his aircraft straight up and then flew it upside down long enough to escape the first barrage of rockets. Maybe it was luck or good piloting from Farouk, but as he straightened out his chopper, there was a Cobra right in front of him. His men on the two M60 machine guns unloaded on the Cobra and hit enough vital areas to cause smoke to blast out the engine and send the mighty attack helicopter to the ground. Now, the other Cobra was behind him in hot pursuit, firing both Gatling guns and missiles.

Farouk was determined to have a successful death. His thoughts were of his two wives and many mistresses. He had been so successful with women here on earth and had no doubt he would be rewarded in heaven. Without a second's hesitation, he dove his helicopter straight down at the forward gates at Pedro Miguel. Two missiles hit the rotor area of the aircraft as it sped downward, causing the helicopter to veer slightly away from its target. Farouk's helicopter struck the outside gate, exploding the crate of C4 onboard. The crew was vaporized, and the outside gate was totally destroyed. He had completed his mission, yet the outside gates were there as a safety mechanism to stop runaway ships. The canal could still operate with one set of gates. Nevertheless, someone had destroyed a gate on the Panama Canal for the first time.

*****

"Lester—Lester are you there?" Holton asked.

"I'm here, Holton. What's up?" Lester said.

"All you guys get to the roof. They're on the move from the tunnel. Get to the roof now—all of you!"

Chapter Thirty-One

"Rick, do you see what NSA has seen coming at us from the south? Maybe from the railroad tracks?" Lester asked while running up the stairs to the roof of the visitors center. All his friends were running with him.

"From a distance, it appears to be Muslim women in black dresses and head gear. Appears they are all about twenty to thirty yards apart. Creepy—they're walking so slowly—like ghosts or black apparitions dressed in black," Rick said. "What are they up to and what are they wearing? Lester?"

"I'm guessing here, but I'd say these phantoms have bombs strapped on them. That's seems to be all these asshole Muslim terrorists know to do—blow shit up!" Lester said, gasping for breath as he finally reached the roof. He then climbed on the roof to look south for the women in black.

He found a pair of binoculars around the neck of one of Rick's SEALs, who was already hunkered down in a prone position, and asked to borrow them. Adjusting for distance, he pulled the women in focus. Glancing from one woman to the next, he found one thing in common besides the way they were dressed.

"Most of them have their right hands closed—a few have their left hands closed. I'm thinking detonators," Lester said, as he handed the binoculars to Debi, who in turn shared them with Jordan, Monte, and the other two women. All agreed that none of the women had slim waists—a tale-tale sign the women had suicide vests on or they were all pregnant. The latter though was discarded quickly.

This time it was Lance calling. "Lester, satellite imagines show abnormal body profiles. We think forty-two women with explosive gear. Better take them out before they blow up the whole damn place."

"Rick, permission to take them out," Lester said.

"Okay, I hope you guys are right and this isn't suicide by soldiers," Rick said and started barking orders to his men to start picking them off.

As snipers started dropping the women, they would explode when they hit the ground. It was obvious there was a dead-man switch on the detonators. The explosions were horrific, suggesting a very large amount of C4 or Emulex® was under their flowing, black dresses. As the women were blown apart, leaving large craters, it seemed the bodies were vaporized, but some distance away their heads would fall to the ground, having been separated at the time of the blast. Blast investigators had found this anomaly for years but rarely did the public know about it. Not that it mattered in this case, but the identification of each of the bombers was practically assured.

The group of six tried to take down the women but found them out of range for their MAC-10s. All fired a complete magazine at several women and only brought down two of them. They put in fresh magazines and waited for them to get closer, then watched as snipers took out several of them while they were walking slowly. They were mesmerizing. Many were beautiful, and their hijabs and dresses flowed in the breeze. The women could be seen smiling as they got closer. Explosions were going off more often now as they fell from sniper fire.

Suddenly, they stopped and sang something enchanting and mysterious. One of the Navy SEALs on the roof who had Muslim relatives explained it was an Arabic Byzantine chant. It was soothing and beautiful. Because of the effect of the melody or the fascination of the whole spectacle, the snipers stopped shooting for a few seconds. Then there came even more bizarre sounds—like yelping or ancient tribal screams with strange tongue movements. The same soldier explained they were called "ululations" or "tongue trills."

"Sounds like nomadic chants you might hear in the desert before a battle—something like in a *Lawrence of Arabia* movie or the noises made before the Zulus came to stick a spear in your ass," Lester said.

The women who were left began running in a zig-zag manner towards buildings on the Miraflores campus, shouting the tribal song. Now everyone was firing at them. Two women were able to run between the buildings and were headed toward the ships in the locks. Several bullets struck them, and they exploded, leaving craters in the grassy areas. Four women ran in a serpentine pattern towards the visitors center; all were shot, but one woman recovered enough strength to run into the lobby. She was Romuald Farouk's second wife, Zyan, one of the most beautiful women Farouk had ever seen. She had dark, emerald eyes, and would have easily graced the pages of a playboy centerfold, if Muslims allowed that behavior.

Neither Zyan nor her husband expected to return home after this day. They had two sons, ages three and five, who had already been sent to live with Zyan's parents in Iran. She may have thought about them as she held her thumb above the trigger, entering the mostly deserted lobby of the visitors center. She looked at the marquee above the theater, which stated the next movie about the history of the Panama Canal was to start in fifteen minutes. She blinked a couple of times as tears streamed down her face. Blood was gushing from wounds in her right side and left shoulder. It was time.

She pressed the button on the detonator. Nothing happened. She held it to her face to examine it, but her eyes were beginning to blur. A single blue wire going to the detonator had come loose. She knew the backup plan. She looked at the industrial grade carpet covering the heavy traffic area in the hallway of the visitors center and dove to the ground. The secondary detonators on the interior of her vest clicked loudly when she fell on the carpet. Then everything went black for Zyan.

The structure above the main floor where Zyan detonated her charges were floors dependent on load-bearing columns and cross beams, directly above where the explosion occurred. Two main columns were entirely blown away, along with three cross beams. There was a cracking and crunching sound that got louder and louder. Lester and his team felt the explosion and felt the building shudder.

"Damn, we got to get off this roof!" he said and grabbed Debi's arm. "Gang, we have to get as far away from the damaged part of this building as possible."

All his group and the Navy SEALs who had been with them got up and ran to the far eastern part of the building and found concrete stairs leading down. As they flew down the stairs, the building behind them started to implode. The roof shifted to the west and began to collapse with a loud popping and hissing sound as air was pushed out of the compressed floors beneath it. At the second-floor level of the concrete stairs, all the people rushing down jumped to the ground and then ran to the open grassy area. They watched and listened to the roar as the entire building compressed to a large pile of concrete debris. They were lucky to be alive.

In a few minutes, all the forty-two women were dead. They had caused damage to several buildings and injured and killed many of the fighters with bottles of nails and screws strapped next to the explosives, which turned them into flying shrapnel. They had been the wives of the militant Muslims, the helicopter pilots, and those killed at the scud bases. Their children had been sent to relatives in the Middle East a few weeks back in preparation for their mothers' and fathers' imminent death.

"Is it over, Lester? Please tell me it's over," Debi pleaded. She had been to war and was sick of it. All three women were beginning to get the long stare not unlike veterans of prolonged conflicts. Very few soldiers ever see the combat these three women had experienced, and it was likely their lives would be affected forever.

Lester desperately wanted to tell them it was all over, but he knew there was one more task that had to be completed.

"As far as I know, that's all the combat you will see. You guys went far above what was expected of anyone. I never thought it would be this bad, or I wouldn't have let you come along. Too many surprises. Too much killing. Yes, it's over for all of you."

"What are you saying, Lester? What else are you going to do?"

Lester was silent for a while as he looked over the three beautiful women who now had smudges of dust and dirt on their faces. Their makeup was now wiped from their lips and cheeks. Mascara had long since left their eyes, but they were all still beautiful. It was obvious each of them had cried at times during the long ordeal. He couldn't blame any of them and didn't see it as a weakness. He noticed their eye colors: Debi's eyes were a warm brown, Maria's were a pretty French-blue, and Simone's were a tropical-water green. Lester loved them all and wanted no more violence in their lives.

"It's nothing for you guys to worry about." His phone rang, saving him from an explanation that Debi wouldn't like at all.

"Lester, my dear. It's Holton. Are you still alive? I saw the building come down."

"We're all okay. Just a little shocked by so much gunfire and explosions. What's going on?" Lester asked.

"Our boat is okay. It left the locks just minutes before the float bombs surfaced. It blew up as the other ship was being lowered down. It made a big splash but was entirely ineffective. I called Captain Polycron, and he said to meet us in Aruba. He has a big party planned to celebrate our victory. He said to bring Jordan and Maria along. Free cabins for them—suites to be more accurate," Holton said.

"Look, Holton," Lester said as he walked out of earshot from the group. "I have something else to do and need your help. Askari is still in hiding, and you know exactly where he is. We cannot let him live, or we will be doing this shit all over again real soon. Help me by giving out the coordinates and an outline of his compound in Guatemala. I don't want them to know I'm going in."

"You haven't talked to the SEAL team or to Rick yet, have you?" Holton asked. "If you had, then you would know they are about ready to shove off early tomorrow, and they already have the coordinates for Askari's compound. Also, Lester, you have done so much—why go put yourself back in danger?"

"So many of the SEALs were wounded. I know Rick needs me. I'm going to call him now." Lester hung up on Holton and dialed Rick as he walked even further from the group.

"Rick, Lester here."

"No, you can't go—none of your people," Rick said before Lester could even tell him why he was calling. "You've done too much, and you aren't getting paid to do this shit. Go back to the *Tropic Queen* and snuggle up to a rum punch and Debi—not necessarily in that order."

"Look, Rick, I know how many of your SEALs were killed or wounded. You need me, and don't say you don't. This bad guy will be back to take us out again if we don't kill him right now. I'm going in if I have to walk to Guatemala."

"Okay. Be here in front of the visitors center's ruins tomorrow morning at 6 a.m. You'll ride in on a Navy Apache. You'll be issued something more than that MAC-10 peashooter. It's going to be rough. You might not come back."

"I understand, and I'll be here. How many men do you have left for this mission?"

"Eight—counting you—and some of them have wounds. Have you been hit?"

"My vest a couple of times. Bruises and maybe a few cracked ribs. I'm fine."

"See you then." Rick hung up.

Lester thought, *He didn't thank me and he was especially solemn.*

"Who were you talking to?" Debi asked.

"Holton, who by the way, called me 'dear' again. I can't get used to these gay guys hitting on me. Anyway, there's a big party planned for us back on the *Tropic Queen,* which is in good shape and out of the canal headed for Aruba."

"Where are we going tonight?" Simone asked.

"I understand a bus will pick us up here in a few minutes and take us back to the hotel, along with the survivors of our other partners. A few of those people who came over with us didn't make it. They're still pulling bodies out of the visitors center," Lester said. He wasn't telling anyone about going on the raid of Askari's compound. Although he knew she would be mad, he had no intentions of telling Debi about the mission. She would refuse to let him go or want to go herself. Neither option was satisfactory.

"Debi, if you're nice to me, I'll let you share a shower when we get back to the hotel," Lester said, trying to be cute.

"You know, usually I would make you wait until I'm done, but this time you just might win me over."

"Why don't we all take a shower together?" Maria quipped.

"The French know how to live!" Simone said. "But I think I want Monte all to myself. He needs special attention."

"You people are making me horny, and guess what—I get the French girl, and you guys don't," Jordan said and laughed. He pulled Maria close to him and kissed her.

A bus pulled up and loaded the wounded first, then all the others. It appeared that everyone had some type of wound, either on their body or in the center of their brain. Everyone was transformed—no one would ever be the same.

Chapter Thirty-Two

Everyone showered, but not all together. Maybe after they all got drunk they would try that sometime, but Lester doubted it. He felt terrible about not telling Debi what he was going to do the next morning. He would rather be beat up by some thug than take the verbal tongue lashing he would get from his wife if he survived the raid.

They all met for dinner and drinks that evening. Everyone had small bandages on cuts and nicks on their faces, arms, and hands, but no one chose to speak of the events. It was a little too raw to relive.

"OK, Monte, tell us how to break into the ship on the open sea," Debi said.

"There's a small landing surface on the top deck, but several things have to be cleared to make it work for an emergency-type helicopter," Monte explained. "Now, these big attack choppers have rescue winches that will lower you without actually landing. Myself, I'm flying to Aruba from Panama City on the *Tropic Queen's* dime. Also, I failed to tell you I have tickets for all of you tomorrow afternoon about five o'clock."

Lester wondered why it was an afternoon flight instead of leaving in the morning. Maybe that was the only time they could get tickets to Aruba. Maybe it was good it was a late afternoon flight, and he could get back in time to go with them.

It was great that everyone was breathing air, and even though it wasn't said, they all were starting new lives—lives they had earned by surviving combat. They had all taken lives to keep their own. It made them different from others who hadn't had similar experiences—very different.

Lester had set his iPhone alarm on vibrate for 4:30 a.m. and woke up while Debi was sleeping soundly. They had made love after dinner.

It was intense—so intense he felt both were looking for something therapeutic and cleansing from the horrors they had seen during the day. Of course, it didn't work, but was certainly enjoyable. Debi was pregnant so nothing clinical was going to happen. Both were looking for pure joy from each other and found it briefly.

Lester tiptoed into the bathroom, dressed, and picked up his duffel bag containing his guns and vest. The vest worked. It had saved his life and that of almost everyone on his team. They were fortunate because certain rounds would have penetrated the vest. So far, he had been lucky enough not to have that happen. This time, he planned to put in the two tactical trauma plates. They slid into a pocket over the heart giving level III maximum protection there—whatever that meant. He had been told it would stop an AK-47 round, or multiple rounds, over the heart. This information was all he needed.

Outside the hotel, a taxi waited for him.

"Hey, buddy. How long to get to the visitors center at Miraflores Locks?" Lester asked the driver as he placed his duffel in the seat beside him.

"Blown up yesterday," the driver said. "But I guess you know that. Takes only forty to forty-five minutes this early. No traffic," he said, and drove away from the hotel.

Lester felt calm. It was quiet out, and the driver didn't talk. *Probably half asleep,* Lester thought. Lester dozed off for a few minutes and was awakened by the driver as they stopped by two Blackhawk helicopters between the bomb craters in front of a still-smoking, collapsed visitors center. A Super Cobra, which carried a crew of two, was warmed up behind them. The rotors were turning slowly.

He was directed to the second aircraft and jogged over to it. A Navy SEAL helped him aboard. Lester took his seat next to several other oddly-dressed individuals. They all wore Flak jackets and helmets, but something was different, yet familiar about them. One woman removed her head cover and sunglasses. It was Debi!

"How in the fuck did you get here, and why are you here?" Lester asked, then identified Maria and Simone as they uncovered and let their hair flow from the helmets. "And I'll be goddamned if all of you aren't here! I can't let you guys risk it again. You've done too much already," Lester said with tears in his eyes—one of the few times Debi had seen him come anywhere close to crying.

"You have no right to make that decision for us," Jordan said. "We all respect your bravery, but it's our decision to go along. You can't have all the fun, ol' chap."

"Fun, my ass. We could all get ourselves turned into Swiss cheese on this adventure. And Debi, don't forget my kid is in your belly," Lester pleaded.

"And, I'm going to tell him that I had a chance to help his dad and didn't go along? What kind of mother do you think I am?" Debi said.

"A wild and reckless one. But the reason we have to kill this asshole is because he will look us up and kill our families, one by one. I have no doubt," Lester said.

A man walked through the cockpit of the helicopter and stood next to Lester. "We believe the same thing, Lester. We also believe he's capable of recruiting and organizing another jihadist terror group. For those reasons, he is public enemy number one," said Rick Summers, who was the leader of this expedition. "Saddle up and stay frosty, my friends!"

He got the usual laugh with that statement. Then he turned solemn for a moment while he recited a pre-combat prayer. Now, every person on board knew how important the words were.

Once in the air, Lester asked Debi, "How in the fuck did all you guys beat me here?"

"Simple. You didn't fool anyone with that phone call to Holton. We knew you had to see this through and would call Rick. So, we called him and told him we were going with him no matter what. He had the helicopter pick us up at the hotel—sort of air valet service, I guess. Also saved on the cab fare," Debi said.

"Damn. I hope we can do this without too much drama," Lester said, noticing a strange helicopter lift off in the distance. It was sleek, black, and unlike any helicopter he had ever seen.

"Rick, what is that thing?" he asked after borrowing a headset from one of the crew members.

"It's a Comanche. Only made two of them and then canceled the program after spending seven billion dollars. It will go in silent and be our scout. They designed them to be spotters for the Apache. Very quiet and has a low heat signature. Goes about two-hundred miles an hour while the Blackhawk does about 180. It's a beauty. Pulled out of moth balls just for us." Rick smiled.

"It will need one aerial refueling to get there even with its extra tanks. Our Blackhawk may need one coming back, unless we set down at a local airport."

Lester sat next to Debi and began to examine the BAR machine rifle with several 20 round clips given to him by Rick just minutes before. He checked quickly to see if the gas cylinder had been chromed. It had. The stock had been hollowed out for weight reduction and so had the forward wooden hand hold. Any metal that could be shaved without damaging the integrity of the rifle had also been done. Lester estimated they had dropped the total weight from sixteen pounds down to about twelve to thirteen pounds.

The tripod, flash suppressor, and carry handle had been removed. Lester knew more about this weapon than most people on planet Earth since he owned two of them. He had bought one from some ATF agents and also was gifted one after a huge raid on an illegal gun store in Louisiana. He loved the weapon and took this one apart on a moving helicopter and put it back together in minutes. He knew about the Polish model that had been developed for aircraft use with a spring-loaded 91-round pan design that sat on top of the weapon. Lester knew about the experiments with thirty round clips and realized that twenty was just right for the BAR.

He passed out magazines to fellow soldiers to carry. If they wanted a fire brigade weapon with them, then they needed to help with the ammo. Nobody minded helping in WWII or the Korean War—even in Vietnam they were used and had the reputation of being the most stolen gun in Vietnam. The gun was heavy but damn dependable. The big rounds got anyone's attention and scared the shit out of most enemies. Lester hoped it would help in the raid.

The flight was long—almost four hours, which gave Rick time to sit with maybe two or three people at a time and go over the plans. He passed out headsets, so they could hear him above the rotor noise. The basic plan was to land in a clearing in the jungle behind the compound and let part of the troops out to penetrate the jungle, then attack the compound from the rear where it would be lightly guarded. The helicopters and the rest of the troops would land on a road above the compound and act as guards against them escaping from the front of the buildings. All the women, the pilots, and two SEALs were assigned that task. The rear-attacking force consisted of five professional soldiers, plus Lester, Monte, and Jordan. The Comanche would be hidden and called in to take out a target when needed.

The landing in the jungle was smooth, and the eight men started moving through the dense tropical foliage. The helicopters proceeded to the road and landed. The pilots stayed with the choppers, and the three women and two men moved cautiously towards the compound.

Debi keyed in a message to Lester. "We are down and on road. Don't see anyone."

She stuck the phone in her back pocket where she always kept it. Her hand was still on the keys of the phone when ten Islamic men moved out of the dense vegetation and pointed guns at them. Quickly, Debi typed blindly and by memory of the keys to Lester, "Captured." She then pushed send.

Chapter Thirty-Three

Lester heard a ping from his phone. He was annoyed with himself for not putting it on silent, but glad he had paid for the coverage for Central America. He slowed down a little to read the message—then came to complete stop, causing Jordan and Monte to crash into him from behind.

"Rick, our people have been captured!" Lester spurted.

"What the fuck! Wait! I have an incoming message from the Comanche. 'Ten insurgents walking our people up a dirt road. Just passed over a building with camouflage laid across the roof. Long structure with large section at the end—maybe a school.'"

No sooner had Rick gotten off the phone with the pilot, Lester was talking to Lance at Bluffdale. "Lance, do you see us?"

"I see two Blackhawks on the ground. The Cobra flew off and the Comanche is doing drive-bys. By the way, we had a hell of a time identifying that thing. Where in God's name did you get one? Only two were ever made," Lance said.

"I know. See if you can get me a schematic drawing of the building down that dirt road where they are marching our captive troops. The Comanche pilot thinks it might be a school," Lester said.

A few seconds went by, and Lester's and Rick's phones pinged again. Together, they looked at the building plans for the old Guatemalan Rural District High School, written in Spanish. The first section was a series of small classrooms across a hallway from each other. At the end was a large gym-and-auditorium combination. Outside the building was an administration building, which had been converted to a single-family residence. Lester and Rick knew instantly it was now the home of Askari and his family.

Rick barked an order to the Cobra pilot, "Take out the compound. Not occupied. Don't want to give them a place to hide."

"What's the quickest path for us to the schoolhouse?" Lester asked Lance.

A minute later, Lester and Rick had a map that led them to an old service road that went to the rear of the school.

"Lester, it looks like two guards near the start of the road some two hundred yards ahead of you, then I see about three people at the rear of the school—some armed—some not," Lance said.

"Lester, you guys be careful," Holton said, pulling the mic away from Lance.

"On one of your passes, can you take these two people out?" Rick asked, forwarding the pictures to the pilot.

"How about those yahoos at the rear of the school?" the pilot asked.

"Only if you can do it without a single round going into the building. We have hostages somewhere in that schoolhouse, or they'll be there soon," Rick said.

The Cobra pilot began a busy schedule. In one pass and one crank of his Gatling gun, the two jihadists guarding the road were ripped to pieces, not knowing what had hit them. He then zoomed to the school and hovered, pointing away from the building, and opened up again with enough rounds to kill fifty men. All of them were cut to shreds. Then he flew back to the compound to take his time with the destruction.

On the way, he passed over Rick's fire team headed toward the service road. Once at the compound, he started with a couple of hellfire missiles that collapsed the roof on most structures, and then cleaned up anything left standing with his 20mm Gatling guns, which fired semi-armor-piercing, high-explosive rounds—lots of them. Some fires were burning in the rubble as he banked and flew over the school for a quick look, and then went back to land near the destroyed jungle estate.

*****

A large, smelly Syrian jihadist named Samee, who spoke some English, directed the placement of the captives.

"Take the women into the classrooms on the left and the men on the right. Blindfold them and make them strip. Tie them to a chair with their hands behind them. I will be by to interview them. Do this now. We must know how many we are dealing with," he said.

At first, the number of captives almost equaled the captors since they had the pilots and copilots of the two Blackhawks with them. Once they neared the school, several more militants in traditional Muslim clothes came out to help. All of them wanted to see the women strip, but Samee would only let one or two people go in a room with a captor. The men and women did what they were told. The SEALs had undergone prisoner-of-war training and knew the technique of stripping the captors for maximum fear effect. They knew being naked made people psychologically vulnerable, and in many cases made it easier to break down the individual, so they would give out information. They yelled at the girls to stay strong.

Askari was in a building near the gym with his wife and two young girls. His cell phone information came in constantly and kept him abreast of the action. Runners supplemented his information from real, live sources who gave their version of real-time events.

"Sir, we have the infidels tied to chairs. Do you want to interrogate them?" the runner asked.

"I want to know how many fighters are on the ground. Do what you have to do to find it out," Askari said. "Once you know, kill them."

"Can we have the women for our pleasure?" the runner asked. "They are all beautiful."

"Only after we wipe out the attackers. When you are done with the women—kill them."

The runner found Samee and delivered the information from Askari. The questioning began in earnest. Some of the militants were trained for questioning captives; others were merely voyeurs and perverts.

Maria's interrogator was the latter. He was the only other person in the room, so he was free to be his vile self. He never told her his name and didn't ask hers. The jihadist didn't seem to have a good grasp on the English language, but it was obvious what he wanted. With her arms bound to the back of the chair with nylon twist ties, she was mostly defensive. As he ran his dirty hands over her breasts and fondled them, she found the perfect time to use the only weapon she had and kicked him as hard as possible in his nut sack, bringing him to the floor. She then stood up with the chair still attached to her back and swung the hard, wooden chair leg into his skull repeatedly until he was a bloody mess. When she knew he was unconscious, she knelt next to him, chair on her back, until she felt a knife in the waistband of his robe. Even with her hands tied to the back of the chair, she found a way to cut the ties. Then she freed her feet. Once her body was freed from all the restrictions, she drove the blade of the knife into the man's neck. He whimpered and died. She felt no remorse, only anger at having been violated.

There was an AK-47 leaning against the door, and she grabbed it first, ready to shoot anyone who came through the door. There were no clothes anywhere, but it didn't matter. Briefly, she considered wearing the dead man's robe, but figured a nude woman would create shock and awe for the rest of the Muslim jihadists, so she would use it to her advantage.

She had heard sounds from the door directly across from her. She flung it open and found a man in a Muslim robe attempting to hook up a battery to one of the Navy SEAL's testicles. Maria sneaked up behind the militant and cut his throat as adeptly as if she had done it a thousand times. She cut the ties on the captured man and found there was an AK in that room as well.

"Hi, I'm Tank. We met back at the visitors center."

"Yes, I remember you. I'm Maria," she said. "

He grabbed the gun and took the next door. Debi was there tied to a chair. A militant had undressed her and was moving toward her with an erection. In a flash, Tank grabbed his arms so he couldn't resist, and with one swipe of the large knife, Maria cut off the man's penis and let him take in the horror of seeing his manhood lying on the floor. After a few seconds, she slit his throat. He fell to the floor, alongside his severed body part.

"How you like being a dickless Arab fuckhead?" Maria growled.

Debi was shocked at the violent soldier Maria had become, but thanked her profusely. Another gun was there, and Debi took it after being cut free. The freeing of the rest of the captives was becoming easier, but Maria and Debi were worried about Simone. They heard a scream from a room two doors down from where they were standing. Hurrying there, they saw other doors opening and blasted the jihadists as they emerged. When they reached the door where the scream originated, they found two nude men, one of whom was trying to penetrate Simone, who was having none of it.

"Get these motherfuckers off me!"

She had kicked one severely, and he now had a knife at her throat, rubbing his injured scrotum. Debi put her gun to his head. "Drop the goddamn knife, you camel-fucking pervert!" He did, and held up his hands. Debi then shot him between the eyes.

The rest of the captives were freed, their captors killed, and still no one had put on any clothes. It didn't seem to matter as everyone was hugging and consoling totally nude people. Now, though, it was time to find where the clothes were hidden.

In a few minutes, one of the SEALs opened a room and found not only the clothes but their weapons as well. The men stood guard as the women got dressed first. While the men were standing outside, Rick, Lester, and the rest of the fire team burst through a door from the rear of the school right into the hallway near the men on guard. Not sure who they were, Lester wasn't sure he shouldn't shoot them, when one of them yelled out to Rick.

"Hey, Rick, it's Tank. Aren't you going to ask me how it's hangin'?"

"My god, man! Put some clothes on. You'll scare the enemy. Where're the girls?" Rick asked.

"We're standing guard while they dress," Tank said.

"Are they—you know—okay?" Lester asked.

"None were raped, if that what you're trying to ask, but it was damn close. Along with some dead jihadists, you might be lucky enough to find some important body parts on the floor in some of those classrooms. It doesn't pay to piss off these girls. Maria was the first to break loose. She freed me, and we went on a spree," Tank said.

The women came out and ushered the men in to dress. Immediately, they saw the others and ran to hug them.

"May I tell you, Lester, I don't care to be a captive. If you ever decide to tie me to the bedpost for a little fun, be prepared to die an awful and painful death." Debi was laughing, but Lester knew she wasn't kidding.

Once the men were dressed, the entire group walked towards the entrance to the connected gym building, and two men with automatics moved out firing and covering the doorway. They moved for cover behind the gym doors.

Lester could see they were behind big, solid-core wooden doors since the barrels of their weapons were protruding. He stepped in the middle of the hallway and moved a 30-06 round into the chamber of the BAR. He aimed and sent several rounds into both doors, almost tearing them off their hinges. The guards fell dead on the floor.

"Good shooting, Lester," Rick said.

"Hard to miss with a BAR," Lester said.

The group moved closer to the main doorway of the gym. There wasn't any more resistance. At the rear of the group, behind the three women, two men ran from a storage room that no one had inspected, down the hallway towards the front door. They carried guns but didn't fire them at first until Debi, Maria, and Simone showered down on them with MAC-10 rounds. Both fell and started returning fire wildly. Lester dove in front of the women and let loose with a full magazine. He could see parts of their bodies rip away and splash against the doors of the classrooms and all down the hallway. They quit moving very quickly. Lester moved back to the front of the group, and Tank handed him another magazine.

Entering the gym was a little creepy. It was old and had been in disrepair for some time. The boards on the floor had been ripped up and salvaged by nearby neighbors. The row of second-story windows had been broken out, letting flocks of birds in to nest on the tall rafters and shit all over the tired interior.

A man, woman, and two young girls stood in front of what had been the bleachers for a basketball or volley ball court. The man had his hands on the shoulders of the two girls who appeared to be about six and maybe ten years old. They were pretty and wore purple hijabs.

Rick spoke to the man. "Askari—give up. We will see that your wife and daughters will be well cared for. They don't need to be a part of this."

The group had stayed out of the gym per Rick's instruction, and he and Lester stood in the doorway. The walls were concrete blocks, painted the school's colors of purple and gold.

"This feels bad, Rick." Lester said.

"Be prepared. Something is about to happen. I don't feel good about it," Rick said, as he and Lester started taking steps backward. The entire group moved to the protection of the concrete wall.

Askari walked a few steps with his wife and daughters. He said nothing—but kept his hands on his daughters' shoulders.

"I will not give up my family! Praise Allah! Allah is the greatest! Allahu Akbar!"

Askari then pulled the hijab from the girls' heads and upper torsos, revealing suicide vests strapped around their young bodies. The girls smiled and then yelled shrill, well-practiced ululations and tongue trills. Then, with detonators in their young hands, they began to run towards Lester and Rick.

As Lester dove behind the nearest wall, he pointed the heavy BAR towards the two speeding girls and pulled the trigger. It was the most horrific thing he had ever had to do, but it had to be done. The explosions blew away much of the concrete walls, but mostly the upper portions. The ceiling collapsed inward and fell to the gym floor. The entire fire team had busted concrete blocks on their bodies. Some had to be dug out of the rubble, but miraculously no one was seriously wounded. Rick ordered a couple of SEALs to find Askari's remains. They found his shoes with his feet still in them and his battered skull outside in the road.

He was gone. The threat was over.

Rick ordered the Cobra and Comanche to level the school building after he returned to the comfort of the Blackhawks. It was finally over. A small war in the scheme of things, but the right people stepped up and won it. The world would be a little safer now. But, as usual, not for long. Now, it was a race for the six passengers of the *Tropic Queen* to catch their flight to Aruba. If the helicopters would wait for them to grab their luggage at the hotel, then drop them at the airport, they could make the flight. Rick made sure it happened.

Epilogue

Debi walked very slowly down the ramp leading to American Airlines 767, leaving Panama City. Lester slowed down and waited for her to catch up.

"You okay, babe?" Lester asked.

"Just so damn tired. I've never been like this."

Maria was just a few feet behind Debi. "Sweetie. You've never been pregnant before either. Let me fill you in on the horrors of having a kid," she said, as she draped her arm around Debi's waist and helped her onto the plane.

"But I'm just barely pregnant," Debi protested.

"Honey, your body knows what's going on. I promise that's what's happening to you. Been there. Want to know what other wonderful things you have to go through to have children? What do you know about hemorrhoids?" Maria asked, not expecting an answer.

Lester placed her luggage in an overhead bin and helped her to an aisle seat in case she had to run to the restroom. She acted as though she appreciated so many people willing to help her. For part of the flight, she tried to sleep, borrowed some antacid pills, and turned down an offer for a rum and coke, even though she really wanted one. She ran to the restroom once to throw up, and then avoided any snacks or soft drinks.

"Lester, I so don't want to be one of those ladies that stays bed-bound for their entire pregnancy. Please tell me I won't be like that."

"I know you won't put up with that. I know you well. We've been together for, what, three years now? Isn't that longer than you and Brad were together? Can't remember, but I hope we've beat that record," Lester said, and then wondered why he would bring up a touchy subject.

"You can be such an asshole at times, Lester."

"Sorry. Forgive me?"

"Maybe in a year or two," Debi chuckled.

The plane landed in Aruba late at night, and they learned through Monte that the *Tropic Queen* was already there. Three stretch limos were parked on the tarmac, one for each couple. Drivers picked up their luggage, which wasn't much. They all asked what was going on but got no definitive answers. As they neared the ship terminal, they could see festive lights strung on both sides of the gangway.

"There's a party going on, I do believe," said Debi, who loved parties. She inherited that from her mother.

The three limos pulled up side by side, and Captain Polycron opened the limo door for Debi and took her arm. He had his formal dress uniform on and looked very handsome. Admiral Hearnsberger was there in his glory wearing his dress whites. He opened Simone's door and let her slide her arm in his. Maria was surprised to find that Jim Webb, the Washington, DC director of Interpol now, was there to take her up the gangway. He was wearing a first-class tuxedo.

Lester, Monte, and Jordan fell in behind the procession. Once on board, they were led into waiting elevators and taken to the main ballroom on Deck Eight. As they arrived, they found a reception line that must have had a hundred dignitaries.

It was quite an honor that the President of Panama was first to greet them, the Chairman Joint Chiefs of Staff shook their hands, and the vice president of the United States and many more officials were present. It was a huge surprise to see Rick Summers at the end of the line in his Naval dress whites. They would ask him later how he pulled off getting there before them.

Once they were seated, after a very long cocktail period where a million questions were asked, there were speeches. The first was the president of Panama, who gave the Panamanian Medal of Freedom to the six people from the ship and to Rick Summers, who was in charge of the defense of the canal.

The last to speak was Rick, who had fought with the group, starting with the scud missile engagement. He knew about the fight Lester had with the two jihadists on the ship, his attack in Nicaragua, and the infamous peeing in the helicopter gas tank in Costa Rica. He talked about all their fire fights, including the final one in Guatemala.

"There are many people who fight in world wars and never see the action this group of people has seen in the last few days," Rick said. "It should have been over at the canal, but they all knew it had to be finished or a very bad man would have recruited people to do it all over again. All of them risked their lives, but one man has to be honored above all others. Would Lester McFarlin please come to the stage?" The entire audience stood and applauded.

Lester was embarrassed by the attention but knew what he was going to say, even if he didn't know the award that was being given to him. He was met by the vice president of the United States, Roger Clifford.

"Lester, this is the quickest in the history of our great nation that we have given this award. It was the president's idea, and he's so sorry he can't be here, but you and all your team have an invitation to a state dinner. It gives me great pleasure to award you the Presidential Medal of Freedom with Distinction," Clifford said and pinned it on a palm tree above his right pocket on Lester's tropical shirt.

He then handed him the box that contained a sash, lapel pin, and other versions of the award. "Normally, this award is given to senators, movie stars, or civil rights leaders. If you were a soldier, you would have a combat medal, but hopefully you will accept this as a small token of appreciation for all you have done."

"Thank you so much, Mr. Vice President. I did vote for you by the way, and it looks like I made a great choice," Lester said and got a laugh from the crowd.

"I only accept this for all the people who fought some very determined Al Qaeda jihadists who were determined to give Islam a bad rap. We know there are good Muslims. While we shot at people wearing suicide vests at the Panama Canal Visitors Center—these same people blew it up while I was lying on the roof. Next to me was a Muslim—also a Navy SEAL—who explained the yells and chants being performed by the militants. He escaped the collapsing roof with me and my friends. He was risking his life to fight Muslims who had taken the wrong path.

"I want to thank all the people who fought alongside me. Some people provided valuable information behind the scenes. I wish to thank Holton Matthews and Lance Gordon for their help." Lester had talked to them during the cocktail hour and waved to them at their table where they were sitting with Debi and Simone. Both blew kisses at Lester. He smiled at their antics. "None of us will ever be the same, but hopefully, the evil we stopped will overcome the horror we absorbed in our minds.

"I'll leave you with a little war humor. Rick had made a comment trying to prepare our troops for battle. He asked us to pay attention, or we might get shot and find ourselves carrying on a conversation with our guts while we held them in our hands. Well, before the battle and the destruction of three scud missiles, things were quiet as we all walked along a dirt road that night toward our objective. Suddenly, out of nowhere, Simone said to herself, but we all heard her, 'I don't know what I would say to my guts.' Well, naturally, we all cracked up. It certainly got us a little relaxed before the shooting started. So, we were all very lucky to not have had a conversation with our guts. I don't know what I would say to mine either. Thank you so much for this honor."

The End

Charles L. (Chap) Harper

Chap Harper is the author of five published books. His most recent, Shortcut, is a thriller which begins with investigations by Interpol agents into strange satellite phone chatter in Lyon, France. At the same time, a former law enforcement officer, Lester McFarlin, questions strange occurrences on a cruise ship where he is enjoying his honeymoon. As the inquiries continue, a far-reaching and complex plot is uncovered concerning Islamic terrorists who plan to blow up the Panama Canal and all the ships in the locks.

Harper's first book Once Upon a Reef was published by Green King Publishing in 2012. He followed up that novel with Once Upon the Congo in 2015, Beer, Bait, and Ammo in 2016, Under Cuba in 2017, and Shortcut in 2018, all through Smoking Gun Publishing. Chap attended the University of Arkansas and retired as an officer with the CNA Insurance Companies. He and his wife Susan live on Lake Hamilton in Hot Springs, Arkansas.

Other Books by Chap Harper

Once Upon a Reef - 2012

Once Upon the Congo - 2015

Beer, Bait, and Ammo - 2016

Under Cuba - 2017